FarrowHaven
AdventureLand
Spring

FarrowHaven AdventureLand

Spring

1

Gigi Shoe

FarrowHaven AdventureLand

Copywrite © 2024 by Author Gigi Shoe. All rights reserved.

Poem Portions: The Fairy Well of Lagnanay
by Lord Samuel Ferguson

For rights and permissions, please contact:
Gigi Shoe
gigishoe.com

ISBN: 979-8-218-56655-5

For Lisa Malone

Freshman year, in a crowded hallway during passing period, you told an anxious, second-oldest daughter, it was okay to write *anything* she wanted

Thank you

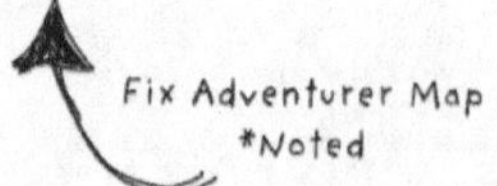

1. Dew Drop Inn
2. Kelpie Beach
3. The Forum
4. Farrowhaven Academy
5. Fairgrounds
6. Bubble 'N Brew Tea Shop
7. Wild Buds Flower Shop
8. Three-Horn Bookstore
9. The Tavern
10. Faerie & Friends Bakery
11. Prismatic Pixie Boutique
12. The Marina
FARROWHAVEN
Fix Adventurer Map
*Noted

Chapter 1

3 Maius
17 Terradium, Ogmios Residence

Meadhbh Mathers,

<u>Congratulations!</u>
You have been assigned: **<u>Provisional Overseer</u>**
at: **<u>Island (1) FarrowHaven AdventureLand</u>**

Some of the key responsibilities of your role include:
(1) The development & execution of the Adventurer Season
(2) Restoring 5-Star Adventurer Satisfaction

We are excited to offer you the starting compensation
package:
Salary: 86,000
Length: Maius–Decembius
Additional Compensation: Forum Office; Food per diem

We look forward to answering questions about your role at an
official meeting on: **<u>23 Maius.</u>**

Have an Adventurous Season!

District Council of Terradium--

"The Adventurers expect a certain *prestige* on the island that has been lacking in recent years." a sharp voice from the High Council caused Maeven to flinch, pulling her attention from the wall of windows showing the city spread below. Maeven was distracted by the dragon that flew across the horizon and landed on the hospital roof, dropping off a passenger before lifting into the air again.

The seven Councilors sat on a raised dais. Spread out in a crescent shape, each arguing from their own chair; the same plain, wooden type she occupied. Attendants stood evenly behind each one in uniform: red pants with gold stripe running down the side, red suit jacket with gold buttons, holding a golden tray with items requested—usually a specific drink, but sometimes phones or snacks were spotted by delegates in the nosebleed section of the Forum. Small pedestal tables beside each Councilor's chair were loaded with files and information about FarrowHaven AdventureLand.

The High Council had been discussing the previous season's dismal numbers, one of the least productive years in the centuries run of the park, and now reviewed her proposed solution before voting on her *probationary* placement for the year.

Maeven had only recently been given the summons; becoming the youngest junior delegate assigned an overseer position. She'd spent the previous week furiously pouring over the decades of past reports buried in storage. The former Overseer had kept very, *very*, scarce notes. She did her best to get up to speed and create a plan for the reconstruction of buildings, expanded customer service training for the villagers, and solutions for the other areas of Adventurer concern. She was exhausted and hardly slept the previous night from nerves.

"Which is why we've replaced that Naiad woman with Ms. Mathers." Councilwoman Ogmios countered and waved a hand nonchalantly toward Maeven. This drew the other Councilor's attention in her direction. Back straightening, she smiled confidently. A twinge of empathy ran through her toward *that naiad woman*, Marisol, who had successfully run the park for thirty years.

But times were changing, and the Adventurers wanted newer, flashier, more mesmerizing experiences than the current *FarrowHaven AdventureLand* offered. Maeven had fresh ideas to upgrade the ticketing system, professional aquatic choreographers to liven up the merrow routines, and maybe even add electricity to the village square!

Though, that was still nearly impossible due to the protective fog which lay over the island. In 1922 the Council attempted to install wiring, but the fog retaliated with lightning which fried the wires and caused weather disruptions for seven weeks afterwards. The villagers almost revolted when they suggested the telephone lines in 1956. Maeven thought it couldn't *hurt* to survey the island again and give it another try with new advancements.

"I do understand the concerns of the Council," Maeven's voice squeaked, and she cleared it before she continued in her steady, low tone. "And I can assure you that I am perfectly capable of handling the various areas of apprehension—"

"I remain unconvinced that she is the best delegate for the position," Councilman Tander grouchy voice protested. He dramatically leaned backward in his seat to peer down over his large nose. He was older than her great-grandmother and clung to his steady traditions, fighting change with whatever teeth and dull-claws he had left. "We need someone with *experience* to get the park back into tip-top shape."

"The conditions of the buildings alone will garner many geomancers and several metalmancers to complete." Councilwoman Rhodes added. The Councilwoman often agreed with her elder colleague. Maeven's fiancée, Urian, suspected Rhodes wanted to hold a bit of persuasion over the other council members when the time came to fill Tander's seat. He was old and would probably retire –or die—in the next decade.

Maeven wasn't interested in the politics of the High Council. Urian had constantly complained that she was wasting her potential by becoming an Island Overseer. He claimed her aeromancer skills, as well as her attention-to-detail, were needed in the city more than the adventure park wastelands.

"What makes you think delegate Mathers is unable to command a group of druid *mancers*?" huffed the younger Councilman Chandler with a smirk toward his fellow colleague. Maeven had been the top delegate in her class and recently led multiple historical excursions for Adventurer artifacts. Surely, she had proven her abilities enough to warrant a bit of confidence. "A witch of her pedigree should find that an easy task."

Maeven tried not to beam with pride at the Councilman's words. The Councilor led the senior delegate class, most of whom filled the open seating of the stone amphitheater around them, and they chuckled with their professor.

They loved him.

Urian's shifting body caught the corner of her eye. She glanced over at where he sat in the front row; eyes locked on the High Council as they deliberated amongst themselves. His dark hair and cinnamon skin stood out against the starkness of his crisp white shirt. Urian shifted and straightened the arms of his navy suit jacket before he crossed them over his chest in deep concentration. A peer leaned over to whisper in his ear, and he responded without removing his eyes from the dais.

"She may command *mancers*, but what of the villager's behavior toward the tourists?" Councilwoman Rhodes listed the various species: merrow, naiads, giants, who had been rude or intolerable on-island lately. Maeven narrowed her eyes toward the proposal she'd put together which was lying closed at the bottom of the Councilor's stack—ignored.

"Not just their behavior but we have thousands of complaints from Adventurers about the costumes and appearances. Apparently, they looked tattered and weak last year, not majestic and steadfast!" Continued Tander, as if he hadn't heard the interlude from Councilman Cromwell, and instead picked up the *FarrowHaven AdventureLand Handbook* which he waved halfheartedly at the room. The handbook talked about the specific requirements for costuming, among other rules. Villagers were required to adhere to a strict dress code while the AdventureLand was open to Adventurers during the months of Junius-Octobius. Uniforms maintained a cohesive appearance across the seven islands for branding purposes.

"All situations any experienced delegate could handle. Miss Mather's has proven herself capable in many areas of hospitality, historical accuracy, and customer service."

Councilwoman Danu spoke up, also in Maeven's defense, as she handed a piece of paper to her second attendant.

The attendant read the page number aloud to the room and the sound of shuffling papers filled the forum as the delegates and High Council scrambled to find the same number amongst their own stack.

Maeven had memorized the files and knew which page the Councilwoman referenced.

It was her acceptance application from the *Historical Archives* that formerly granted her additional funding for the restoration of the adventurer artifacts brought back by a team of druids, recently returned from her previously approved proposal for an archeological dig on the fifth island.

It had been a huge accomplishment to write the grant for the dig. Even more so to receive additional funding for the restoration of the artifacts they found—and the accolades for doing so.

"It will be her first solo-assignment, the giants alone will be difficult for any experienced delegate to undertake," Protested Councilwoman agreeing with Tander. Maeven felt her heartbeat quicken at the thought of two high ranking council members voting against her placement.

Councilman Cromwell sighed loudly and waved forward a junior apprentice; one of several he appointed to follow him around and take diligent notes. The apprentice opened a large binder and began reading from it.

"Ms. Mather's has a plethora of experience within her portfolio because of her aeromancer *intent* which allows her to transport bubbles full of messages across short distances, thus keeping herself physically safe and ensuring the proper language translations. These interactions have been operated peacefully and successfully with various species, most of whom inhabit FarrowHaven island, including, but not limited to: giants, trolls, faeries, satyrs, fauns, merfolk and other relatives such as, merrow—

"Yes, yes, alright, we don't need the entire historical glossary read aloud." Tander waved off the apprentice with a scowl. Maeven glanced down and rubbed her lips together to conceal a smile from spreading across her face. Councilman Cromwell had been an advisor in her undergrad, and she was thankful for that previous mentorship and loyalty.

"There *is* a concern about the lack of communication between the worlds." Councilman Danu spoke up from beside Cromwell.

"An easy fix, wouldn't you say?" Cromwell continued with a shrug.

"Perhaps a weekly update?" suggested Ogmios which garnered a nod from several delegates around the room.

"Delivered in person?" added Tander just to make his voice heard and the task difficult.

Returning to the city every week in person would be time-consuming and costly. Since the protective fog prevented electricity from being used on-island the long-distance portals didn't work. The closest location to the islands where electricity *would* work was a lone mountain range, previously reachable by a seven-hour drive through semi-dangerous, windy, mountain roads.

After several complaints—seventeen driver deaths occurred during the previous decade and the lawsuits were becoming expensive—the Council hired geomancers to carve out a flat section along the base of the mountain where portals were erected. The long-range portals connected to the Adventurer's world, while the short-range portals were for staff and deliveries to the city. They also relied on the merrow driving the ferry back and forth through the fog to FarrowHaven island, a time-consuming trip on top of the seasonal tourist demands.

"Would you like her to read them aloud to you as well, Tander?" Councilman Cromwell teased and led another round of roaring laughter from the delegates.

The High Councilwoman leaned forward and banged her gavel once against the round wooden block. "Order, there will be order in the forum." The laughter died instantaneously and only a rare cough could be heard.

"A weekly report of the island, sealed, and delivered by *intent* shall be adequate from the delegate." The High Councilwoman decided.

"Should we expect rebellious behavior from the naiads?" Hesitated Councilwoman Rhodes.

"No ill will against the new Overseer has been reported." Councilor Cromwell confirmed, and Maeven was thankful for that. The last thing she needed were villagers, naiads or otherwise, upset over her appointment.

"Are there any other concerns to note?" High Councilwoman Morgan hovered the gavel over the block as the amphitheater waited in silence. Several heads turned to Councilman Tander who barked a sigh and held his hands up in protest as if he had *no choice* but to vote affirmative.

Maeven watched the gavel drop, in slow motion, down against the wood, confirming she was officially the new *probationary* Overseer of FarrowHaven AdventureLand!

There is limited time on-island to make an impression, Maeven Mathers.

You can do this!

Chapter 2

<u>**Welcoming Port Assignments:**</u>

Objective: Repave & resettle stone structures, including parkway road, castle walls, spire towers, arched windows, lover's balcony
Assignment: Geomancer

Objective: Resettle & sand wood structures, including bridge, support beams, stairway, balcony railing,
Assignment: Sylvamancer

Objective: Replant flowers, vines need to trail along outside of castle, maybe add trellis – see sylvamancers. Bring trees back to life!
Assignment: Naturamancer

Objective: more iron benches & trash cans, polish lampposts, fix stained glass window
Assignment: Metalmancer

Objective: Weave new flags/tapestries for hanging in castle foyer, new banners for advertising – colors must align to Council branding!
Assignment: Pixie

Objective: Repaint signs for ticket sales, double check accounting books!
Assignment: Faun

Objective: Set up "fishing village" scenery at Welcoming Port, sanitize all cooking items for food preparation & create mock tasting menu
Assignment: Merrow

Objective: Clean out and prepare miniature menagerie for winged creatures at Welcoming Port, make sure enough feed is stocked to supply all dragonlings, hawks and phoenix's weekly during the season
Assignment: Animancer

"You're confident you want to do this?" Urian asked her one last time as they stood in front of *FarrowHaven AdventureLand* entrance with shock and dismay.

Maeven's heart sunk after stepping through the long-distance portal and laying eyes on the dilapidated condition of the welcoming port. It looked worse than the reports described. Urian had followed moments after with the rest of her luggage and instantly barked a laugh at the scene.

The stone buildings were crumbling, and the castle facade was lackluster to the eye. Weeds sprang up from the cracks in the ground and vines ran along the walls. The portal lot hadn't been repainted for several decades, the arrows and lines directing Adventurers to the ticketing booths were barely visible. No breeze waved in off the shore to their right which left the flags and banners, diluted in color, lying limp and lifeless in their places.

"It, uh—it does need a bit of work." Maeven muttered as her eyes scanned the horizon again in search of something, anything, positive to comment on.

"At least I know where you'll be for the next...forever." Urian's lips pressed together as his eyebrows rose in disbelief, a small shake of his head. She wasn't sure if he meant to direct it at the terrible scene in front of her or her terrible decision to become an Overseer.

"That's not funny." she replied but was more preoccupied with the growing mental list of tasks. The collapsing castle in front of her was top priority. Adventurers could not be blamed for demanding a refund if *this* was their first encounter after walking through the portal.

"Nowhere to go but up, right?" her fiancée dryly shrugged with another shake of his head.

"I supposed so, thank you." She shook her head to try and rid the negativity from it. This was her first challenge, the *reason* she was appointed. The island needed change which started with repaving and repainting the welcoming port.

"Write soon?" Urian commented but she couldn't tell if he was asking or instructing. He leaned in, wrapping his arms sideways around her shoulders for an awkward hug. Urian caught her off guard and she could only tap his forearms with her hand as they wobbled. He kissed her temple quickly then let go and walked back through the portal.

Maeven bent over her luggage so Urian couldn't see her eyes roll. She shouldered her office bag with a bit of her aeromancer *intent*, her hands free to grab both suitcase handles.

When the season began in three weeks, each portal would have several attendants helping direct traffic and carry luggage. They'd point guests through the twisting lines, keep them entertained while they waited, and answer the same question over and over, with a *continuous* smile on their face.

For now, Maeven lugged her oversized suitcases across the brick pathway, over the wooden drawbridge—the wheels catching on every. single. bump. —under the archways and into the center of the empty castle square.

Just like the outside, the inside was a crumbling remnant of the once glorious building that she remembered from her youth. The ticket booth colors were dull; cobwebs lined the iron bars that served as barriers between the staff and Adventurers. Old posters and tattered tapestries hung haphazardly off the stone walls and trash from the previous season still sat inside metal barrels. Wooden picnic tables, weathered and unsightly, spread around the empty square.

Noted.

The exit led to the North of the square where the path turned east and zigzagged downward to the ferries docked below. There were four on rotation that moved slowly back and forth between the Welcoming Port and the island. She spotted one below and breathed a sigh of ease.

You can do this.

It was FarrowHaven for *Brighid's* sake. She'd spent her previous childhood summers growing up on-island and knew it like the back of her hand.

It hadn't been *that* long since she'd been back.

Maeven took a deep breath of the ocean air. It filled her lungs, and she smiled. She'd forgotten how clean it was up North. She'd forgotten how cool the mornings were in Spring and how warm the days grew.

How did you forget that?

The downward slope of the path leading toward the docks angled enough that Maeven's luggage pulled her downward faster than she was comfortable walking. She didn't want to expend any *intent* which might make her clumsier.

Like a boomerang, when *intent* was used, it went out into the world and eventually, some of that made its way back to its user. There was only so much change one person could commit to the world before something was demanded back from them.

Unfortunately, for Maeven, she tended to become clumsier when her missing *intent* came back to bite her.

Digging her heels into the path, her shoes slid against the small gravel.

She glanced out across the untamed bushes and flowers that lined the walkway and saw the ferryman scurry across the deck of the boat. He pulled at the ropes and prepared to depart.

Prepared to depart!

"Hellooo!" Maeven called toward the ferryman, unable to wave her arms.

She picked up speed and started to trot down the walkway, her luggage picking up speed as well and pulling her further and further along. Maeven leaned back to slow herself down as the final zig came closer, her heels digging into the pebbled gravel but not stopping.

Her suitcases had a mind of their own at that point. A wheel on the larger suitcase caught against a rock. The sudden stop threw her body forward over the rectangular fabric of her stalled luggage. With her hands occupied by the handles, Maeven was unable to throw her *intent* in time to catch herself and she went down in a hard tumble against the gravel.

Bright bursts of fiery pain spread down her left arm and leg which had taken most of the fall. She was getting too old—and was slightly out of shape—to take serious tumbles.

"Everything alright?" A deep, accented, voice caused a shiver to run down Maeven's spine. She looked at the webbed hand offered to her then glanced upwards. A mix of dark skin and navy scales covered the man's forearm. Colorful fins erupted from his elbows—past the broad shoulders and muscled chest to a bright, white, grin that blazed at her behind the deepest blue eyes she'd ever seen.

She gently placed her hand in his and let herself be drawn to her feet. The merrow guided her to sit upon an iron bench, his arm wrapped protectively around her shoulders.

"Typbeoua," he still held her hand and lifted it to his lips, pressing a deep kiss along the back. "You can call me Ty, if you like." his accent, undeniably familiar, slightly melodic, and rhythmic; an attribute to his seemingly easy-going lifestyle.

She felt transfixed by him.

The pain in her knees became a distant memory.

He retreated to grab her luggage, and she found herself staring after him; mouth hanging agape and eyes softening. She wanted to go with him wherever life was that easy.

What a fool you are making of yourself, Maeven.

"Yes, I'm alright," she squeaked, finally answering his previous question. Maeven closed her eyes, clearing her throat. She stared at the ocean before her and tried not to peek at the merrow. Lustrous gills lined his neck flapping open with each breath. In his human form, his vitiligo skin and scaled legs stuck out beneath khaki shorts. His ankle fins shined blue against his dark, thickly soled, webbed feet. Her light hazel eyes met his deep blue, and she smiled, too wide.

"You don't happen to be from 'ze Council, do you?" His pronunciation of *'ze Councill* reminded her of a memory that itched the back of her mind. She knew this merrow from somewhere, his mannerisms were familiar, but she found herself nodding like a schoolgirl at his words. He placed her luggage beside the bench and crouched down in front of her, so she looked upon him with awe.

"That's me!" She raised her arm, ever the perfect student.

You are a mess!

She giggled, "Yes, that's me. I'm here for the season."

Oh, witches before me, a giggle!

At your age!

He grinned toward her; his eyes giving a twinkle as she gazed serenely into them. "We did not think to be expecting you for a few days at least."

"I like to be prepared—overly prepared." She blushed and coughed to clear her throat from its girlish tone.

"Ty!" the sharp snap of a female voice broke Maeven from the trance she was being pulled into. "Do *not* be compelling her!" Maeven blinked as the fog around her thoughts lifted and her reasoning returned. She yanked her hand to her chest, rubbing away the residual compelling charm left there before glancing at her rescue.

A tall female merrow, with a strong jaw and determined, voluptuous march, headed their direction from the ferry gangplank. She wore a long, colorful, crocheted dress that wrapped around her waist and tied as a strap around her neck. Her hips swayed with each step. Her dark hair was natural, tied up in matching fabric. Decorative chains draped around her wrists and waist, clinking louder the closer she walked.

Behind her followed three children of various ages and sizes with matching attitudes and varying degrees of colorful scales, skin and fins.

"Bennie! Sis!" Ty turned toward the woman and held his arms out in a joking protest. Bennie stopped in front of him, arms crossed over her chest; her purple fins displayed. A single webbed finger tapped against her forearm, and she gave a pointed look.

"Do not be compelling her with your charms," the female merrow raised a single finger and pointed it toward her brother.

Clear your head and get it together!

Maeven should have known better than to let him kiss her hand. Merrow were known to have compelling powers in their saliva.

"Ah, I was just teasing her!" Ty playfully replied and swatted the finger she wagged away. The children reached the group and jumped from all sides onto "Uncle Ty" amongst laughter.

Bennie pointed toward Maeven's luggage and gave a knowing look of instructions toward the children. "Help our new Overseer onto the ferry."

Ty pulled himself free with a nod of apologies toward Maeven. He grabbed her luggage and headed toward the ferry. The two women watched the children trail after him like ducks, quacking toward his back.

"Benthesikyme?" Maeven swallowed to help coat her dry throat.

"Ach, please, call me Bennie, you know this!" a bright smile spread across Bennie's face and her arms pulled Maeven's short frame in a tight embrace.

Maeven hadn't seen Bennie in over ten years. She was no longer the gangly kid Maeven used to hang out with on-island. Maeven would visit her mother during the summer months but as adults they hadn't kept in touch after Maeven attended University on-island four. Bennie's face filled out, she was plump and healthy, perhaps a little grayer, with crow lines along her eyes from smiling. Her skin and scales blended in like a dark winter sunrise around her profile.

Bennie was a merrow, distant cousin of the mermaids of the southern islands. Her family ran the ferries between FarrowHaven and the Welcoming Port along with owning Kelpie Beach, a popular destination where Adventurers could take pictures with the merrow, swim with them in the coral bay, and take rides in custom-made submarines to the underwater kingdom.

"You have children?" Maeven asked, stunned to say the least.

"I do, five." Bennie nodded toward the children who followed Ty up the gangplank onto the ferry. Typbeoua! He had been a scrawny, thirteen-year-old when Maeven last saw him. Now, a full-fledged merrow and driving the ferries!

Maeven looked between her former friend and the children before she erupted into uncontrollable laughter. The heat of the rising afternoon sun made the new information, combined with the alarming state of the welcoming port, seem like a joke.

Bennie wrapped her arm around Maeven's shoulders and steered her down the pier, toward the gangplank. "Let's get you on the boat," Maeven's laughter continued between deep gasps of air to fill her lungs, tears falling down her cheeks.

Goodness, get a hold of yourself!

"Breathe, *mon cheri*," Bennie's voice soothed like gentle ripples of water down her spine. The merrows hand caressed Maeven's arm as they walked. Bennie lightly stroked her *intent* of soothing, calm, waters into the witch's skin, Maeven's anxiety easing with each wave. Eyes closed, Maeven focused on slowing her breaths—inhaling for several seconds, hold, hold, hold, and exhaling—which flowed with the lyrics of Bennie's melodic hum.

Bennie led her up the gangplank and into the covered portion of the ferry. They sat on a wooden bench along the row of windows and the tallest child pressed a cold cup of water into her hands. Maeven nodded thanks and gulped the water a bit too fast, spilling droplets down her chin.

"Tell your uncle to get us moving to the island!" Bennie shooed her children with a tut-tut of her hands as she took a seat beside Maeven.

Maeven shook her hands and arms out and felt more like herself with each moment.

"We didn't expect you on your first day," Bennie turned toward her, arm draped loosely across the back of the seats. Maeven heard the engine roar to life beneath them and the ferry slowly backed away from the dock. "We thought you'd assess from the city for a while before coming over to the island."

"I wanted to get a head start on the reconstruction," Maeven replied with a sigh as she leaned her head back against the window frame. She felt the churn of the ferry paddle wheels below the water, slowly moving them across the sea toward the island. Suddenly tired, the adrenaline from the morning already spent, she could easily take a nap.

"Does our sleepy island need that much help?" Bennie joked—FarrowHaven AdventureLand was anything but tired.

"There's so much to get completed before we open for the season in three weeks." Maeven's eyes widened and she turned to Bennie with renewed energy and enthusiasm for her role. "I'm quite shocked the Council didn't replace Marisol earlier because this puts us in a *real* bind."

"Will the Adventurers not have enough to occupy themselves?" Bennie crossed her arms over her chest and shifted her legs ever-so-slightly away from Maeven's.

"More like, not enough desire to return." Maeven shrugged and shook her head.

"Glad of that," Bennie muttered.

Maeven met her former friend's glance. She wasn't sure she'd heard her correctly. "Hmm?"

"I'm glad you're back." Bennie's smile widened and she clasped Maeven's free hand.

Maeven looked down at their hands and wondered if they were still friends or merely acquaintances. It had been so long since they had spoken or seen each other. Bennie moved to the southern islands during the winter months so she was never there during the off season whenever Maeven would visit her mother these past ten years.

Bennie's arms reached out and pulled Maeven into a heavy hug—the kind that makes you tighten your grip and hold on a little longer.

Maeven inhaled a deep breath, filled her lungs with the scent of salt water and lemon, and melted into the embrace.

"Feel better?" Bennie rubbed her hands up and down Maeven's back and she nodded in return. She did, in fact, feel better. Her mind felt calm and at ease instead of frantic and scattered.

"Come on, you'll want to see her as we pull in." Bennie stood and nodded toward the outer deck as the ferry approached the island.

Maeven followed Bennie out and leaned her arms against the railing. It was hard to see the island at first; a thick fog hung in the air even though it was the middle of the afternoon. It shielded their sight with an ominous giant wall.

They headed straight for the dark clouds. Only inhabitants from the island could sail a vessel through the barrier. To others, the clouds would become a storm and redirect their navigation away from FarrowHaven.

The ferry's engine was cut off and they began to coast, waiting for the moment *she* allowed them to enter. They didn't wait long. Tendrils of water reached out to wrap around the hull of the boat, latching on like squid tentacles and navigating their direction. Slowly, they moved through the fog, and *she* appeared. The island shimmered like a mirage beyond a veiled curtain. The current shifted and pulled them forward.

When they passed through, Maeven held her arm out and let her fingers dance in the fog. As a child, she tried to grab onto a piece of the magic it inhibited. It felt familiar to her own power; she was adamant it was meant for her alone. According to her grandmother, children hardly realize that their gift, especially an aeromancer, was common and rarely special. But her mother, Eliza, had always gasped and exclaimed in glee whenever Maeven showed her a trick—bubbles or objects that floated. Eliza made Maeven's power feel rare.

Maeven's fingers fell away from the memory. The weight of the fog pressed around her then—

—Popped!

The curtain lifted like a sheet in the wind, and they emerged from the darkness to see blue sky and bright white clouds, clear green water below and the mountainous atoll of FarrowHaven rising above. The ferry engine started up again, aiming right, their destination the eastern docks.

The island was hundreds of feet wide and narrow. The central mountain rose high, its ridge expanding east-to-west along the length and partially cutting off the back of the island. It blocked the Northern, rocky, land from being occupied and loomed over the village below. The coniferous trees blended into bright, tan beaches. Kept clean, they stretched for miles in either direction then curved inward around the reef, creating the crescent shape of the island.

She could see the buildings that dotted the town square behind the beach with benches and gas light poles lining the cobblestone sidewalks. The town disappeared as they rounded the curve of the island, blocked behind the tall spruce and pines.

The ferry positioned itself away from the waterway that led into the protected reef. Most adventurers expected to be dropped directly on the beach, some wanted even closer, but there was strong discourse against the environmental factors this caused. The coral offered guests an opportunity to swim with a mixture of sea creatures: turtles, manatees, and an assortment of fish, and the ferries could damage the ecosystem if they entered, especially during low tide.

Instead, the docks were built on the east side and the island offered unicorn-drawn carriage rides into town. For those who chose to walk the path themselves, there was live entertainment spaced evenly, to not overshadow one another, between the hours of eight a.m. and four p.m.. Fauns playing the lute would encourage adventurers to dance, faeries offered baked goods and pixies enticed the sale of princess hats, dresses and accessories while metalmancers waved swords and shields, wands and crowns to enthusiastic children—*custom swords available at the metalmancers guild in town!*

"Bye mom!" a child's laughter distracted Maeven as the ferry started to slow for docking. She turned in time to see Bennie's boys strip off their clothes and jump into the water. Their fins blended in with the colorful fish and coral beneath as their tails transfigured. They started to play, splashing and jumping through the surface to show off with flips and rolls. Bennie laughed and clapped in encouragement at their antics.

"Training for the aquatic performances, I see." Maeven smiled toward their acrobatic tricks. Bennie's smile faltered, her eyebrows narrowed briefly, and she quickly cleared her throat to cover it.

Maeven continued to stare forward without acknowledging the merrows' change. "They're gorgeous children," she continued, her eyes watching every movement as they swam between the fish and sea creatures—did merrow children need to be monitored in the water?

"Thank you," Bennie replied with a proud nod at her brood. "Aodhan, my oldest, just turned nine. Behind him is Ioannis with the deep orange and green—and the one with the dark green there is Tadhg. The others are home with my husband, Brarios."

"You married Brarios, huh?" Maeven smirked. Her friend harbored a long-time crush on the merrow in their youth. Maeven remembered when Bennie first laid eyes on the dark orange and green colors of Brarios' fins and announced, on the spot, that she was going to marry him.

"More like *he* married me." Bennie winked in response and Maeven laughed with her as the ferry eased into its numbered slip.

"Where are you staying while in town?" Bennie continued and nudged Maeven with her elbow.

"I've got a reservation at the Dew Drop." Maeven confirmed as Ty walked past them and grabbed the rope connected to the end of the ferry. He jumped onto the pier and began to tie off on the dock.

"I thought you'd stay with your mom instead of in town." Bennie responded and a quick frown passed over her face.

"She's in the East, studying at the University on-island four." Maeven shrugged since that was all the information her mother had put in her letter a few weeks past.

"Well, you might not be enjoying the Dew Drop," Bennie shook her head and tsked a few times as she began to lead the way down the gangplank.

"What do you mean?"

Chapter 3

Affiliate Code of Conduct Violation Form
Date of Report: 25 Maius
Name of Reporter: Maeven Mathers

Affiliate Name: Dew Drop Inn
Affiliate Owner/Manager: Scottland Carmichael/Aldrick Barringham
Affiliate Location: 4 FarrowHaven, Dew Drop Inn
Length of Violation: 17+ days

Type of Violation:
Health and Safety Violation – Limited/No water prevents performing basic hygiene routines and creates unsanitary conditions for Adventurers.
Unsafe Structural Conditions – Deterioration of outdoor appearance. Lack of upkeep of interior appearance.
Public Nuisance – No restrooms available to Adventurers.
Environmental Violations – Waste backing up into the attached river, spreading toward the coral reef.

Additional Comments or Information: Tensions with the Naiad Union led to the release of a temporary drought curse which dried up the taps and plumbing throughout the Town Square– other Affiliates can remain open due to private Waterway systems and approved living conditions for Adventurers.

Action Taken:
Affiliate informed of violation and charged a fee of .4% per day.
Local Overseer contacted.

By submitting this form, you are helping to maintain the safety and integrity of The Council.
Thank you for your cooperation!

x *Maeven Mathers*

Maeven sighed and ran her hands over her face then rubbed her eyes before she asked again. "What do you mean, there's no water?"

"There's no water," Aldrick pointed to the pipes and sinks around the kitchen and shrugged.

"Can you elaborate as to *why* there isn't any water?"

"Naiads." He muttered with a smirk as if his short, one- or two-word responses were purposeful.

"The naiads?" Maeven's eyebrow rose and she rolled her wrist to urge him to continue.

"Yep," Aldrick shrugged and crossed her arms over his chest.

Aldrick was a druid with sylvamancer *intent* who preferred cooking in the kitchen of the Dew Drop Inn instead of carving wooden swords for the Adventurers.

His red hair and bushy beard had grown long, and Maeven hated how handsome he looked. Aldrick had been an acquaintance of hers in her youth—around because they had mutual friends but never friends themselves.

"Alright, thank you." She shut her notepad and collected her office bag to leave. He obviously wasn't going to elaborate, and she was tired of trying to pull answers.

"Before you leave, can I interest you in a bulk purchase of my hand-crafted mugs?" Aldrick stepped forward and placed his hands out like a true salesman.

"All bulk purchase orders must go through the official channels; you can submit your application at the forum offices during normal business hours." Maeven responded in her nicest customer service voice.

"Have an adventurous day," Aldrick's tone was less than enthusiastic when he said it. She decided to deliver a copy of the latest handbook with highlighted portions about customer greetings and farewells at a later time.

Outside the Dew Drop, Maeven noted the peeling, tacky, patio paint which needed to be sanded and refinished. The furniture looked old and worn down—Maeven guessed if she ran her hand along the edge, she would get a splinter or two. The balcony above had a hole through the floor and the corner hung off at an odd angle.

The Grand Prophecy Hotel looked majestic. It was the largest attraction on the island, besides the Academy just Northwest of the village. The outside appearance looked well enough when they'd briefly passed. Vines covered the beige plaster and dark wooden beams—recently stained. She didn't think the Hotel would need as much attention as the Council had noted in their itinerary. The Dew Drop, on the other hand, where most of the staff on-island spent their evenings, needed more upkeep than allocated.

Maeven pulled out her clipboard and map of the town. She would be strategic in what she tackled first.

The Forum stood to the West, farthest to the left of the square. It was designed to look like a Temple, devoted to the Island God, Grannus, with tall, imposing columns and marble floors throughout. The first floor was used as a large gathering area for village occasions or town hall meetings. Below, in the basement, were the Council offices where she would be spending most of her days once the AdventureLand opened. She hoped the offices were in decent condition because she fully intended to settled into her assigned desk as soon as possible.

Moving counterclockwise around the outline of the square was the Bubble & Brew Tea Shop run by the island faeries who also ran the Faerie & Friends Bakery across the street.

Beside the tea shop was the Wild Bud Flower Shop that sold packaged groups of flowers, herbs and shrubs which the gnomes grew on-island.

The fauns ran the Three-Horned News and Novelty Bookstore that printed the daily activities offered to the Adventurers.

The Tavern rounded out the Northeastern side. It was one of only three locations, beside the Inn and Tea Shop to get a proper meal on-island since the Hotel and Mansion Bed & Breakfast were reserved strictly for guests staying in the house. A single dining room with a connected kitchen, above which lived the owner and chef, Carwyn. He occupied the building at the tip of the town square for centuries, half a minotaurs lifetime. It was cozy, dark and had been the perfect place for Maeven to retreat to and sort out her problems as a teen.

Lastly, the Prismatic Pixie Boutique took up the entire northern side where the pixies created custom tailored outfits for the Adventurers. Their workshop was on the upper floor, divided into stations for the pixies to work and the bottom consisted of a large store. It was always crowded with tourists waiting to be fitted with the delicate fabric custom woven from wisteria flowers. Large windows separated the Adventurers from the line of Pixies that sat at spinning wheels fabricating spools and spools of thread from the blooms.

Maeven thought watching the pixies work was more exciting than anything else the island offered.

She spotted a trio of elderly female fauns sitting outside the boutique. They occupied a bench in-between their appointments, hair in curlers and foil among their short goatish horns. Maeven jaunted over to the boutique and asked if they knew what caused the water drought.

"It was a bunch of kids!" the women explained, taking turns to be heard over one another.

"They misaimed and the curse hit the fountain." The second cried in dismay and pointed at the center of the square. Her legs were crossed, and her hooves bounced up and down. Maeven turned to look and saw that the circular fountain figurines had indeed come to life and were spitting water on villagers who passed.

"It took out water to the entire square!"

"No one within one hundred feet of the fountain can get water, all the pipes are blocked."

"They weren't supposed to be aiming at the fountain in the first place!" the less than happy voice of the middle faun grumbled. She snapped open a handheld fan and slowly swayed it up and down.

"Where else would they have aimed?"

"No where in town, those shenanigans are for the forests!"

"Who?" The third faun's high-pitched voice piped up and her shoulders briefly straightened before they slumped down again. She pulled a wooden ear trumpet from her carpet bag and stuck it in her lobe.

"The fountain." Repeated the middle faun as she turned toward her friend. She tsked and snapped her fan closed before helping her friend aim the hearing aid properly in her ear canal, then repeated herself.

"We know it hit the fountain!" The third faun removed the trumpet and replaced it in her bag. She gave her friends a confused glance and waved them off as crazy. The middle faun rolled her eyes and snapped her fan back open in a flurry of flutters.

"And no one knows the counter-curse?" Maeven asked to bring the women's focus back.

"Counter-curse? Bah!" The first faun scowled and fluffed the foil colors setting in her hair. "Damn kid made the curse up off the top of his head."

"They've tried just about everything they could think of to reverse the spell."

"Well, it would help if they knew the words they used because those naiads can't even remember properly!" She nodded toward the fountain again and Maeven looked to see the naiads were chained around the base.

"When did this happen?" Maeven interrupted the two fauns who continued to jabber back and forth with each other; the third had promptly fallen asleep on her friend's shoulder.

"Oh, a month or two ago, wasn't it?" The two friends consulted with each other and agreed it had been two months ago.

"Why wasn't it reported to the Council?" Maeven questioned, as if the fauns were privy to the Councils correspondences.

The fauns returned to their squabble as an uncomfortable breeze swept through the square and caused a shiver down Maeven's spine. She followed the wind which drew her attention South toward Kelpie Beach and the afternoon sun, covering her eyes with her hand and looking out across the sand, its vibrant tan color sparkling with shells and seaweed, seeing nothing amiss.

Several logs and sticks washed ashore and lay scattered along the stretch. The villagers usually left those for Adventurers to play with and explore. Some used them as walking sticks, but the larger ones would be climbed upon by children, arms held out for balance. She spotted a particularly large log, the perfect cylinder shape, lying on its side that would be excellent for the young Adventurers to explore.

Her attention was pulled instead to the moving fountain and the four naiads locked around the base. She bid adieu to the fauns and walked toward the fountain—examining the "lock" job that consisted of a simple chain looped around the base then threaded between the metal portion of their lawn chairs. They faced the ocean and passed drinks and smoking substances back and forth.

The fountain itself shouted insults toward the four, who ducked beneath umbrellas to avoid the water that was sprayed. Maeven almost felt sorry for them. Remembering the summer about a decade ago when the villagers voted on the new fountain design and many friendships went to blow over the choices.

She distinctly voted for the jousting griffins—even though the dragons fighting was also an excellent choice—but the winning design featured a merrow, faun, and druid atop a rearing unicorn—each facing a different direction, so water covered all areas of the round base.

"Salutations!" The cheerier she made her voice, the nicer reception she received.

"Good afternoon! My name is Maeven Mathers and I'm a representative of the Council. I've been assigned as Overseer for the season and wondered if you might have a moment of your time to discuss matters of concern on-island?"

Maeven was shocked that she was able to complete her entire greeting for the first time!

"What does thy foul beast of walking nature want with us immobile gods?" called the Unicorn from the top of the double layered fountain. Maeven craned her neck up to look at it but could only see its hooves and nostrils. She moved to the left until she was in view of its eyes, apparently it couldn't move its head.

She wasn't quite sure how to phrase her request: Please refrain from speaking and spitting on villagers until we find the counter-curse?

"The gods had cursed my kind to servitude!" The Unicorn continued to plead.

"What's that?" Maeven didn't hear everything as the stone faun began to recite poetry in the middle of the Unicorn's plea.

> *"Is there no help at all for me,*
> *But only ceaseless sigh and tear?*
> *Why did not he who left me here,*
> *With stolen hope steal memory?"*

"Ugh, *pleeeease* get him to stop!" whined a female voice. Maeven continued around the fountain and saw a stone merrow draped dramatically across the bottom of the rock.

> *"I'll go away to Sleamish hill,*
> *I'll pluck the fairy hawthorn-three,*
> *And let the spirits work their will;*
> *I care not if for good or ill,"*

"Is he reciting a curse?" Maeven questioned and looked around though nobody seemed to be listening.

"Worse, poetry." The merrow groaned from her position.

"The great Lord Samuel Fergu—" the faun began to defend the poet before the other fountain creatures and naiads groaned in protest.

"Ma'am, no disrespect," the laid-back voice of the speaker couldn't have been older than twenty and was calling her *ma'am*. Maeven turned to the naiads sitting in their lawn chairs, sunglasses on their eyes to block against the bright sun. The speaker's shirt was opened to reveal his chest, and he wore long board shorts for surfing.

Maeven wanted to smack him across the head or whack him with the elderly faun's fan. Her grandmother would have told him to sit up when he addressed her. She glanced between the faces of the teens and wondered if they had a sliver of awareness about their surroundings.

"Ryes, shh." the boy beside him whispered and shook his head but his friend, Ryes, was already on a roll.

"But you might want to keep on steppin', the fountain is mad typhoon crazy, and you might get your threads all twisted in a tornado." Ryes nodded and held his hand up then wiggled it like a merrow swimming in the bay—indication that she should swim away.

Maeven decided the young naiad was most assuredly high on faerie-dust for speaking to her that way and wondered if *he* even knew what his words meant. The new slang going around the city wasn't what she expected to hear on-island.

She looked back and forth between the fountain and the four naiads strung out in front of her. "Do any of you have the slightest memory of what curse was thrown?"

"Can I be reef ma'am?" the only female naiad with long stringy blonde hair, some pieces in braids, some with beads threaded throughout and a few in the first stages of dreading, replied.

"Jay, no—shh—" the first naiad who had warned Ryes shook his head again.

"It's fine Pacey, it's fine," Jay shook away her friend who was only trying to help. Maeven wished Jay had listened.

"I don't think you should," Maeven shook her head with the realization she might have to report this to the Council.

"We were all up on faerie-dust and we don't even know which one of us threw that curse." Jay giggled like she'd just announced the funniest sentence in the world.

Maeven groaned inwardly when her suspicions were correct that, not only would the curse remain unknown, but she was going to have paperwork to fill out about the illegal substance. She would have to think of other ways of solving this. But she needed to find her partner, and the person who should *really* be solving this problem.

"Do you know where I can find the Protector?" Maeven asked before saying farewell to the group.

"Of the island?" Ryes asked, confused. Pacey nudged him hard, with his elbow and Ryes cried out in pain then fell off his chair clutching his side.

"Yes, of the AdventureLand Island." Maeven confirmed, suspicious as to why the Protector wasn't more known and purposely ignoring the dramatic behavior.

"Uh, I think he's in the Forum?" Jay said and pointed toward the building with her head, beads clinking. It absolutely sounded like a guess. Maeven knew checking the Forum herself would be faster than trying to get more information out of the four.

Turning east, she headed toward the Forum, the Unicorn beginning another round of poetry as she departed. Maeven looked to her left at the waves. The crash against the shore was peaceful as she jaunted to the Forum, lightly skipped up the three steps, and entered the open doors beneath the tall columns. The parlor was rectangular in shape with a high, glass dome ceiling where natural light shone down on a pile of stacked boxes of various sizes and heights.

Those were not supposed to be there.

Chapter 4

FarrowHaven Islands has the #1 Worlds Top-Rated Kelpie Beach
spanning hundreds of beautiful shorelines around her coastal bay.
Her central mountain, Avontane, soars with an elevation of 6,500ft
from base to summit, stretching across the eastern-western range.
FarrowHaven Village is only a small portion of the island's landmass but
nearly all is unreachable due to her mountainous terrain.

She crossed the parlor floor, ignoring the bathroom door on her right and stamping up the three steps to the open forum floor. She pulled open the top of the first box, reached and saw that it was packed with cornhusk dolls. The dolls were wearing dresses and had decorated hair braided with beads made on-island by elderly fauns to keep busy. Maeven realized these were stock for the gift shops. The dolls would be sold along with other items to Adventurers throughout the upcoming weeks but should already have been shipped over to the welcoming port.

Refusing to dwell on the current problem but instead, adding it to her list, she turned back to the parlor floor. This time she headed to her right, where a hidden door blended in with the paneled wall—exactly where the manual said it would be. She opened it to reveal a set of stone steps that lead to the basement levels. Oil sconces, already lit, lined the stairway down, where a labyrinth of offices and holding cells resided.

During the season, the basement floor was used to keep over-intoxicated Adventurers and the casual thief from main view. The labyrinth that lay below the village spread for miles and miles of twists and turns, a mixture of cells, offices and storage.

Maeven slowly descended, two- three- four- floors. At the bottom, she headed straight down the hallway to the main office. She followed the lit scones but paused at the first crossing when she heard a noise. Her *intent* was immediately balled in her fists, ready to disarm the intruder. Who else would be here?

Maybe the Protector? Whom you're looking for, relax Maeven.

Easing her tense hands, she relaxed her *intent* back into her body and continued toward the sound. The offices were built like a labyrinth on purpose, to confuse Adventurers who wandered in the wrong area. Even though she memorized the map, she still wasn't comfortable with the reality of being in a maze without *officially* knowing if someone was there with her or not.

Light shone from behind the archway on her left. She saw the shadow of a bulking shape, much larger than the Protector, and brought her *intent* back to her hands, a small ball of wind she'd shoot toward the figure if needed.

"Hello?" she called out, continuing toward the rustling sound, the gas scones flickering under her aeromancer *intent*. The only sound in response was a low growl and the crash of wooden boxes on the other side.

Gaining whatever confidence she had, Maeven leapt through the archway to confront the possible trespasser within. Calling upon the patroness for protection, "Brighid above!", she sent a ball of controlled *intent* toward the intruder across from her.

The creature's reflexes allowed them to duck sideways as the ball hit the wall. They crouched to her left and held their hands up in surrender, then looked over their shoulder to meet her eyes.

"What in Grannus name—?" the creature exclaimed in anger. A pleasant chill ran down her spine and swirled in her stomach.

Maeven flexed her fingers several times to release the power she'd built up as he stood to his full height and turned to face her. She recognized the voice immediately.

His ominous shadow unrolled to show the detailed crown of antlers, surrounded by curls of golden-brown hair, broad shoulders and slim torso. His bulk filled out in the years they'd been apart and stood chiseled instead of the scrawny guy she remembered.

The man before her emanated his role as a descendent of the Stag God, Cernunnos, from which he hailed. In her youth she teased that he was too lanky to be destined as the future *King of Creatures*.

Well, he certainly proved her wrong.

"Beckwell?" Perhaps she imagined his form. The day had been long, the heat and excitement could be playing tricks on her mind, causing a hallucination.

"Hey Mae," Beckwell replied, his voice huskier, *sexier*, than she remembered when they were engaged.

The wind was knocked out of her even as she stood still. A god-like essence consumed her senses. Maeven widened her stance to steady herself while soaking in his presence.

Beckwell looked more gorgeous than she remembered —ten years added muscle to his tall form and girth to his legs. He crossed his arms over his chest, the bulge of his biceps apparent beneath his linen shirt. He flipped his hair to move the bangs from his eyes, a moment of boyish charm still shining.

"Mae?" He used that nickname when they were engaged in their youth. No one else called her that.

"Mae?" his hand waved in front of her face, and she blinked away the shock. This was *Beckwell* after all. Not an actual god—even if he was descended from one and had an unnatural amount of godlike essence.

"Stop that," she flicked a small ball of air at his hand. It hit the dead center of his palm, and he jerked back forcing a chuckle and a wince.

"Nice shot." Beckwell's eyebrows narrowed in surprise. This was the first time they were face to face in over ten years. The last time she'd seen him, he slammed the door behind his own back and walked out of her life for, she thought, ever.

"Appreciate it," Maeven dropped her office bag from her shoulder, the weight of the files she'd brought from the Council had started to become unbearable. She needed to remember to grab her luggage from the Inn when she left.

"How have you been?" he walked forward before she could say anything and wrapped his arms around her, enveloping her in a hug. Her reflexes betrayed her, and she folded her arms up, under his own, to return the embrace. She resisted the urge to lean her head against his chest and tuck it neatly into the crook beneath his chin as if the last missing piece in a puzzle. Beckwell still smelled like the forest, pine, musk, and her childhood memories all wrapped into one.

Maeven pulled away from him and tugged her blouse down. She cleared her throat while smoothing her vest and neatening her tie to give her nervous hands something to occupy themselves. She felt the urge to touch him, to run her hands through his curls and hold herself against him. She wanted to feel his arms holding her protectively like he did just now when they were together. She didn't realize this moment of reuniting would be this striking. Her mind grappled for something to distract itself.

"What's all this?" Maeven circled her pointer finger toward his face and squinted. When she last saw him, at the age of twenty-two, he could barely grow a few whiskers on his chin but now sported a full-grown beard. It was trimmed neatly to surround his lips with a few gray or white hairs peeking out.

"My face?" He swatted her hand away and backed up, ducking from her advance. He cocked his head to the side and looked at her with playful confusion.

"A beard?" Raising her eyebrows, the awkwardness of the moment seemed to slip away. The ease and comfort that had once been between them returned instantaneously. A wide smile spread across both of their faces. "Since when?"

"I've always sported a beard, thank you very much." Beck replied and caught her hand in his. Her body stilled, the comfortable weight of his hand, the burning of his touch against her own, made her want to leap out of her skin.

Why are you so nervous?

Why did she want to jump into his arms and hold him forever while also fighting the urge to punch him in the gut? The comfort of his touch scared her, she had a fiancée after all, and she slowly pulled her hand away, stepping out of his arm proximity and turning away from him to gather herself. She walked back to her office bag and rummaged inside as a distraction.

She wasn't feeling quite herself at that moment. Her heart was beating wildly against her chest and her face felt flushed. She fanned her hand in front to try and get air then conjured up a bit of her *aeromancer* intent. Moments later a breeze lifted her hair from the back of her neck, cooling her rising body temperature. A second after that, her ankle buckled underneath, and she grabbed the top of the desk to catch herself.

Beckwell chuckled from behind her. "How is city life?" he continued nonchalantly which caused her to roll her eyes and brought her back to reality.

You're here for a job, Maeven.

With renewed determination, she turned back to Beckwell, a clear focus on how to steer the conversation. "It's fine, how has island life been? According to the reports submitted to the Council, which appear to be few and far between, not swell at all."

"Well, you know how the Council can be about keeping secrets, protecting their records, and whatnot." Beckwell shrugged as if the island conditions were nothing to shake a fairy-godmother wand at.

"Would you like to tell me about the drought in town?" Maeven's teeth ground against each other as she reminded herself to remain diplomatic.

"A couple of kids were messing around," he shrugged, *shrugged*.

"Why has there been no mention of this curse to the Council? The Dew Drop Inn has no running water for the kitchen or bathrooms—I'm assuming the other businesses might look similar—and those teenage naiads, you remember the kids *chained* around the base of the town fountain; they don't even *remember* what curse they threw because they *made it up*!"

"Well, I meant to tell the new Overseer about that in person when I met them—and—here you are!" he threw his arms out as if he were a game-show host presenting her the weekly prize to be won. Maeven wanted to be more upset at the answer, but the fuzz around his ears still held a bit of the fawn-like innocence from their youth. She crossed her arms over her chest and gave a pointed look in return.

"It should have been in your weekly reports, which is another thing we need to discuss! Why isn't anyone sending in updates to the Council? They're supposed to be kept apprised of the island conditions and from what I've read, the reports are lacking *decades* worth of improvements— improvements which apparently were never even applied for!" the words bubbled up in her throat and vomited over her tongue. The more she talked, the more details and context were needed to properly chide him.

"Marisol was never keen on keeping detailed records." Beckwell muttered as he took a wide stance as she continued lecturing him.

"The last report was filed a month ago and the one before that was Decembius—right after Yule. Beckwell, your secretary is not being prudent enough with their duties," she met his green eyes which flashed with humor.

"As soon as I hire a secretary, I'll let them know to be more prudent." He held his fisted hand over his heart and bowed toward her in a mock show of allegiance. Maeven's eyes narrowed with a sigh.

Always a jokester.

Maeven shrugged and turned away from Beck. She grabbed her office bag and walked toward one of the four desks that stood in the middle of the room. The desks were pushed together in the center, each pointed at a different wall but all facing each other. There, she dumped the contents of her bag on the desk and directed the files into stacks with *intent*. She made sure to lean backwards against the desk and cross her ankles just in case her *intent* decided to snap back at her again.

"Jumping straight into work, are we?" Beckwell continued to tease, attempting to drag her off topic again. He'd spent their entire relationship avoiding conversations and using humor as a shield. Her eyes had always been covered in stars when she met his glassy green orbs. It was no wonder she didn't see through the dreams he promised her.

"*We* have a lot to go over, Beckwell." Maeven looked around the sparse office for some water to drink. Her throat was growing dry, and they had a long night ahead of them if they were going to get through the paperwork. The room had dull furniture, bare walls and low light from the gas lamps hanging from the ceiling.

"You look exhausted, you should get settled in and then we can pick this up tomorrow. Are you staying at your mom's house?" Beck asked and tried to shoo her away from the files.

"I suppose I'll have to open Eliza's cabin up if there isn't any water in town. Her well has always been abundant." Maeven waved him off again and tried to sound nonchalant about mentioning the lack of water. She shrugged and began to flip through the files, pulling out the top priorities and dividing the others into piles based on urgency.

"The cabin is open," Beckwell walked around to stand beside her at the desks. He read over the file names and his body started to lean forward. She took a step to her left to give another foot of space.

"What do you mean the cabin is open?" Maeven looked over at him. Her mother's cabin had been in the family for generations and was guarded by the deep matriarchy bloodline. It couldn't be opened by just anyone and certainly not for a male.

"Well, Eliza has been off-island for a while—" he continued turning to lean backwards against the desk while crossing his arms over his chest, his ankles over each other. Maeven fought the urge to slowly look him over in his relaxed position, hair tussled, and an easy smile aimed at her. "And I've been taking care of the animals."

The animals.

Maeven had forgotten about her mother's menagerie of species found lost in the woods and rehabilitated over the years. She would have to deal with the sheep and dogs and dragonlings when she got to the cabin later.

"Thank you for doing that," she nodded and turned back to the files, though she sensed he had more to say. She didn't want to get distracted by personal conversations about her mother. They needed to start focusing on surveying how many geomancers could repair the cracking stone in the entrance walls and what metalmancers could be spared to steady the stairwells; not to mention the sylvamancers that could be sanding the splinters off the Dew Drop railing or patching the wooden hole in the floor.

"We've got to get these figures settled before moving forward. Otherwise, we'll be wasting resources, and we don't have enough time to tackle everything at once. I think we need to prioritize upgrading the welcoming port and then—"

"Whoa, whoa, slow down." Beckwell stopped her with a wave of his hand, completely dismissing the work that she'd been preparing. "The welcoming port is the least of our worries." He walked around to a filing cabinet that stood against the wall across from her chosen desk. He opened the double wooden doors and removed a very large stack of files which he brought over and dropped in front of her.

"Let's talk about the island."

Chapter 5

"You cannot be accurate with these numbers!" Maeven insisted as she threw down the sheet of figures which didn't add up correctly. She found it impossible that the island was bleeding coins in flour for the bakery. They were losing crops *despite* the enormous sum spent on fertilizer. Not to mention the dramatically large amount of feed purchased for Friedman's herd of Frisian cows—Blessed by the Gods to produce milk for the entire island.

Maeven and Beck had been scouring the files for hours and arguing with each other back and forth. For every question Maeven asked, Beck had a snappy answer that he tried to brush off as nonchalant. This would provoke Maeven to dig for more details and Beck would grow irritated that he didn't have the answers—*Marisol was in charge of that!*—and they'd go around once more.

"The bakery stocks up during the winter to off-set the Adventurer season." Beck explained, again—no matter which way she posed the question—whether leading or open-ended—he had an off-the-cuff retort and would deflect to another residence in the village. Maeven's list of follow-up interviews grew to include almost every resident on-island.

"We need to call a town meeting." Maeven insisted and ran her hands over her face. She was tired. The morning had stretched into the afternoon, and she was hungry. Beck ran across to the Tavern and got sandwiches about an hour before, but her stomach was still unsatisfied.

"It'll have to wait for tomorrow, there's no way to round everyone up at this hour." Beck shook his head like he, too, was disappointed by that fact.

Maeven expected that kind of response. With a tight smile, she pulled *intent* and began to move her arms in a circling formation. Gathering the wind, she held it up to her face and whispered instructions into it before she aimed at the door and pushed. The whisper-wind leapt from her arms and flew off. It swirled once around the room, echoing her instructions for them to hear, before it swept through the open archway, back down the hallway, up the stairs and off into the village.

It would roam through the streets blaring her call for a meeting that evening. She doubted many of the villagers would fail to show up after hearing it fly overhead.

Maeven glanced back at Beck who was frowning. "What?" she asked.

"That seems like cheating." He pouted.

"That is how we get items accomplished and checked off our growing list." She shook the clipboard in front of her for emphasis.

"The list can wait; the villagers barely have time to themselves when the tours run. They're constantly bombarded with *humans* walking into their businesses, their homes, their land—" Beck began to complain which Maeven distinctly remembered from their time engaged.

"There are curfew hours for a reason," Maeven reminded him, pointing to the brochures handed to every Adventurer about the rules and restrictions while on-island. They clearly stated that all Adventurers were to retire for curfew between the hours of midnight and sunrise.

Beck rolled his eyes and leaned back in his chair, balancing on the back two legs. "The Adventurers don't respect the curfew hours,"

"Isn't that your job as Protector? You're supposed to *protect* the island by keeping the ruckus down." Maeven continued to point out. "Aren't you supposed to act as sheriff and enforce the rules?"

"We've assigned more guards on patrol during the off hours which cost us more in salary and supplies," Beck dropped the legs of his chair back onto the floor and leaned forward to shuffle through the papers. He pulled out various files from underneath, completely messing up the order she had arranged which irritated her. It was bad enough that half the files Beckwell produced were covered in old food stains, ink blotches and unfinished sentences—like the writer had begun to put down a thought then never finished it—but now he was messing up her piles!

"There's another problem beyond numbers." Beck continued as he pulled out a new file from his bag. "I haven't had the opportunity to make a Council report, as we were still gathering facts, so they're unaware—"

"*Brighid*, Beck—what have you kept from them this time?" Maeven hissed, already annoyed that he spent the past hours trying to convince her to let Aldrick create a "surprise" condiment every day depending on what ingredients the island had in surplus. Maeven shot the idea down immediately.

"There's a girl missing, an imp." He stared at the file in his hand, his mouth open, as if he wanted to say more but then closed his lips.

"What does 'missing' mean?" Maeven straightened in her chair, eyebrows narrowed, and turned to face him, her knees bumping into his, stopping her rotation.

"She hasn't been seen in a few months. Her friends and family thought she was off island studying at the University in the East. Except now, no one can confirm her whereabouts."

"Did you write to Eliza," Maeven thought immediately of her mother who was an adjunct professor obtaining research there. Maeven had no idea what *kind* of research, her mother deigned to explain or elaborate.

"That's why I'm bringing this up." Beck pulled more pieces of paper out from his pile, handing them over and ignoring Maeven's antsy fingers that tapped along her knees. "Tempest earned an early admission scholarship to the University and was supposed to start in Januarius. I reached out to your mom and asked her to check up on the girl. Eliza's return letter arrived two days ago letting me know Tempest had not been seen in any of her classes and never showed up to her dorm—her roommate thought she dropped out."

She continued to review the file of the missing imp beside a photo: Tempest Rhosewood. Over-sized, bright eyes, sparkling with mischief. A wide smile that exuberated youth against tan skin tinted with a shimmer of glitter from her Impian bloodline. The girl's dark hair, braided with jewels, hung long. The same as the strings of shells and shark teeth draping her neck. She couldn't have been older than seventeen or eighteen.

So beautiful, in a care-free manner.

Underneath the profile of Tempest, were witness interviews. First there was her boyfriend, Emrys Rainmeadow—a geomancer druid. He just graduated from the Academy, still worked there part-time as a griffin wrangler, and spent his other time in the kitchen of the Dew Drop Inn.

Beck also spoke with her older sister, Ribbon—an exotic dancer who performed acrobatic high-rise stunts during the nightly adult shows. The Big Top Tent Shows were a large coin earner on-island as the imp's seduction *intent* was highly entertaining.

Tempest's other sister, Sebille, a *former* exotic dancer, now worked in the carnival booths at the Big Top, but mostly spent her time taking care of their ailing grandmother and her own three girls.

The ailing grandmother piqued Maeven's curiosity.

Elva, matriarch of the Rhosewood family, was anything but ailing or frail. Maeven had read her file several times during her prep work. Most islanders, Maeven's family included, descended from the gods of the Tuatha de Danann, the first settlers on-island. The Rhosewood family, however, were pure Impians: born from the seeds of the very island and inhabiting it long before the new gods arrived. They still held a grudge against the so-called Tuatha invasion.

Flipping through more pages of incoherent scrawling, Maeven put together that Tempest had been on-island during the Yule celebration—six months prior. Her boyfriend, Emrys, fought with her at the annual sacrificial bonfire held on Kelpie beach every year—but from there, accounts vary about when, where, and how long the fight lasted. One friend claimed they were near the town square arguing, while another claimed they were closer to the beach side of the Dew Drop, and a third claimed they were closer North near the Academy.

Everyone claimed they were doing faerie dust.

"And we *confirmed* she didn't go off-island?" Maeven tried to comprehend Beck's handwriting; his sloppy, slanted scribbles were barely legible. She may have to re-interview some, if not all, of these connections.

Beck explained, "I think her family and friends assumed, after the fight, that she took off before the waters froze for the winter and Tempest chose to ignore everyone after that."

"They thought Tempest was sitting in her dorm at University, ignoring them?" Maeven clarified to make sure she understood the thinking. It wouldn't be the first time an islander had left and never spoke to their family again. There was no room for judgment on Maeven's part either, since her own relationship with her mother was currently tepid at best. They often went for long stretches or weeks without checking in with each other. Her mother was flighty and had premonitions that would often leave her tiresome and deranged. It was best Maeven avoided Eliza, so she wasn't angered by her mother's absenteeism—both mentally and physically.

"Sometimes it's typical for the teens to go off— hitchhike the islands for a year or two and then return acting like a hero who'd never left to begin with." Beck shrugged and Maeven wondered if he was projecting his own irritation at essentially doing the same thing in that statement.

"And now the family is worried?" Maeven continued to pull answers out of Beck since he wasn't offering them freely.

"Well, with the island opening in a few weeks, they expected her to be back to help work the summer crowds, but no one has heard from her. Alarms were finally raised." He sighed as if this information was exhausting to repeat.

"Have we checked with the Northern Port to see if they have a log of her leaving?" Maeven suggested throwing out the little-known second dock. The trading harbor was used by the islanders for import and export purposes.

Adventurers could only use it when paying enormous fees to hike that part of the island. A three day hike up the southern side, repeated on the northern, then another week through the Lemling forest, where they would catch a private ferry to the next island in the chain. More affluent tourists hired private escorts, or members of the island guard, to accompany them for protection against wildlife.

"I sent word to the guards. They searched the mountain range, and the air patrol helped comb the forest and waterways just to be safe." Beck eased back into his chair again, only its back two feet balanced on the floor, and flexed his arms over his head to settle them behind his antlers.

Maeven was drawn to his arms; he knew they attracted her, and he showed them off in his slightly-too-tight shirt which strained against his muscles each time he moved.

Maeven looked down at the file and cleared her throat. Something itched in her brain about the timeline. "The Dew Drop was the last place she was seen?"

"I interviewed everyone there, Leif, Deidra, Shoney, Rand, Olfra, Aldrick—"

"Where are those interviews?" She shuffled through the papers but didn't see a single interview from those named.

"Uh, I might've forgotten to write them down." Beck gave a sheepish smile and dropped his chair down on all fours again.

"How do you forget to write down an official interview?"

"It might not have been *that* official..." his voice trailed off and he looked anywhere but at her.

"Did it take place at the Dew Drop *bar*, by chance?" she asked, already knowing the answer was 'yes'. Well, *she* would absolutely be properly interviewing the entire staff at the Inn.

"Just like old times, huh?" Beck reached out with his foot and nudged her knee.

Maeven did *not* think it was just like old times. In her brazen youth, Maeven had spent nights occupying the top of a picnic table on the deck of the Dew Drop. Beckwell standing in between her legs, his arm wrapped around her waist and a cold mead in his other hand. Live music would play in the background, and they'd sway together, her arms loosely draped over his shoulders, their friends drinking and dancing away the summer eve together.

Beckwell and Aldrick were best friends at one point. Maeven hated to think the old times were still relevant. Maeven remembered how every evening would end in a drunken fight between Aldrick and whomever he chose to harass. The red head liked to cause trouble, betting on the good nature of his friends to get him out of it. Beck would chase him drunkenly through the woods, usually while he stripped off his clothes, then drag Aldrick back home to sleep off hid drink or faerie-dust.

"Sure, Beck." She rolled her eyes and pointedly ignored his attempt to talk about their childhood. She didn't need to bring up an old relationship to do her job. She just needed to focus on fixing one of the many, many items that plagued the island. "You have no idea where Tempest could be?"

"None, Mae." Beck reached out with his pinkie finger and looped it through her own, as if making a childhood promise. She *really* hated that nickname but softened.

She leaned forward and let her elbows rest lightly on her knees, hands held loosely in Becks.

"Why didn't you send this to the Council sooner?" she lowered her voice and tried to appear calm but inside she was *not* calm.

"It's nice to see you too, Mae." His voice turned slightly sarcastic, and he chuckled deeply. His presence was enough to make her heartbeat faster and her thoughts spin in circles.

Why is he touching you?

What is he doing?

Did he think they would pick their relationship back up?

Did he think she came back for him?

Did you come back for him?

Are you running away from your fiancée?

Your fiancée!

Standing abruptly, she dropped Beck's finger, her hands burning. She couldn't concentrate with Beck this close.

The loss of his skin meant the return of cold air to her lungs. She stirred a light breeze throughout the room and pushed her hair away from the clamminess of her neck.

Maeven took steps away from him, hands on hips and deep, steady breaths.

"I'm sorry, Mae, I didn't mean—" she held up a hand to silence Beck.

"You don't need to apologize. I shouldn't—" thankfully she didn't have to finish her sentence because the sound of footsteps and hoofbeats could be heard from the floor above.

The villagers were beginning to arrive.

Chapter 6

*Please be aware that all Adventurers are required to adhere to curfew
between the hours 12am–6am. Adventurers must be in their rented
dwellings and must **not** be in the woods or untamed shoreline.
In the event of an after–hours attack, call for a FarrowHaven Guard.*

"Good eve," Benthesikyme surprised Maeven by popping up in front of her. Maeven emerged seconds before from the basement of the Forum, arms laden with files and her office bag. Maeven smiled at seeing a familiar face, she was half worried that Bennie wouldn't show, and she would have to speak to the villagers alone.

"Bennie! Thank you for coming!" Maeven chuckled as Bennie wrapped her arms around her, files and all, and gave a welcoming hug.

"I would not miss this for the world, or any of the other worlds, for that matter." The merrow smiled in return, eyebrows raised in surprise. "That announcement was very loud."

"Ah, too loud?" Maeven would have to adjust the volume next time.

"Just a bit," Bennie teased in return. "You must come to dinner, at my house."

"Oh Benthesikyme—"

"Bennie," her friend corrected.

"I appreciate the offer, but I am so tired this evening,"

"Not this evening, tomorrow." Bennie urged with a warm smile.

A commotion in the middle of the Forum caught their attention before Maeven could respond. They turned to see several fauns and satyrs complaining about the stacked boxes. Maeven led the way toward the gathering and began to instruct villagers to move the boxes against the far wall.

They retrieved the folding chairs that had been put in basement storage and started a line passing them upstairs where they placed them in circular rows, tiered to give each species an equal advantage, around the center dais. The meeting area was much smaller than the Forum in the city, but it would suffice for the size of the village.

When everyone was seated, Maeven, followed by Beck, walked to the center dais and stepped onto it.

The villagers quieted themselves and took their seats to watch. In the front row sat most of the gnomes and dwarves whose statures stood between two and five feet high. Behind them sat the druids, satyrs, imps, faeries, faun and merrow.

The pixies, averaging a foot in height, floated in woven baskets around the domed, glass ceiling, while the giants, nine-foot-tall beings, sat along the back row, only two representatives present.

Maeven did not see Marisol amongst the naiads whom she was really hoping to speak with that evening.

Maeven moved a few steps away from Beck, before she clapped her hands and gave a broad smile. She pulled a bit of *intent* and flattened it into a cone shape to amplify her voice around the room. "Welcome, thank you all for attending on such short notice. Some of you may know me, but for those who don't, my name is Maeven Mathers, and I will be the new Overseer for the season." She paused to clear her throat and picked up her notepad where she had listed the most critical items they needed to start fixing.

"We don't need no Overseer!" a voice called from the back of the room. Claps in agreement erupted and Maeven hesitated. Maybe she was in for more of a challenge than she assumed.

"Aye, where be Marisela?"

"There be no *Marisela*, her name was Marisol!"

"Bring the other gal back and have this yungin shipped off-island!"

"You be quiet and listen to our gal!" Bennie shouted toward the protesting voices. She stood from her seat, an imposing height. Maeven returned her customer service smile to her face and silently thanked her friend. "We all know the *Council* makes these decisions so we may as well remain cordial about it all."

"No need to eat the messenger, eh?" Carwyn, the minotaur that owned and operated the Tavern, joked. His two large boar hooves stepped loudly down the rows until he found a seat. His cousin, Nore, another minotaur, followed. Nore helped at the Tavern.

"It's, 'shoot' the messenger," Beck corrected from his stance, hips wide and arms crossed over his chest, beside Maeven.

"Why would we shoot her but not eat her?" Nore asked loudly for the room to hear. He was a bit slower than the typical Minotaur and needed extra patience and understanding because his brain was underdeveloped.

"Are we going to talk about the hair I found in my biscuits this morning?" shouted a small, female gnome.

"There was no hair in your biscuits this morning, Tierna!" Carwyn replied toward the woman with a narrowed scowl.

"Aye, there was, Carwyn! But it ain't for you to be commentin' on!" Tierna turned from the Minotaur and glared toward the group of faeries that ran the bakery.

Maeven recognized Lux, a former acquaintance from her teen years, amongst them. Six, long, iridescent wings beat quickly like a hummingbird from the faeries back showing her irritation toward the gnomes' remarks. Lux was the head baker at the *Faeries & Friends Bakery* and would have made the biscuits in question. Her hair was in natural curls and bounced with the vibration of her wings. Her dark skin glowed with irate regarding Tierna. Beside Lux, another faerie, one that Maeven didn't recognize, placed a hand on her forearm and leaned close to whisper.

"Can we discuss the Beltane bonfire?" a high-pitched voice spoke up from across the forum floor.

"We've got another two New Moon's before we've yet to discuss Beltane," a particularly grumpy faun yelled from the back.

"No, no, it's *one* new moon, not two!" another responded.

"I'd like to know what is being done about the fountain?"

"What are we supposed to do with all the G.I.N. coins? The season hasn't even started and they're backing up the waterways!"

"Not to mention the *name*, are we sure we should be encouraging *children* to collect these?"

"I think adults would be a better target audience."

"Friends!" Maeven used a bit of *intent* to send a shock of cold air throughout the room, blasting everyone in the face and silencing their complaints. "We are happy to address any concerns during our question time at the end of the meeting."

Her answer satisfied the murmurs momentarily and the villagers settled around the room to listen.

"Now, we have divided the island into categories of importance based on level of urgency. First of which, are the accommodations and their lack of water which includes the Dew Drop Inn, The Tea Shop, and Bedstone—"

"Bloodstone—" Beck corrected her.

"—Bloodstone Bed & Breakfast." Maeven rolled the correct name off her tongue attempting to avoid attention. She gave the villagers her best smile and most confident sounding voice as she continued.

"Thankfully the Grand Prophecy Hotel, the Bakery and the Tavern, have a private waterway system which was not effected by the curse. We have the V.I.P. Adventurers arriving on the 12th of Junius, and a week later three hundred additional Adventurers will be arriving and remaining on-island in booked dwellings. Remember, Adventurers *must* have a colored wrist band to remain on-island after hours. We will have one midnight ferry to take stragglers back to the mainland."

"Who will be in charge of rounding up Adventurers?" a voice called.

"Will we be expected to hunt them down every night?"

"I thought we weren't allowed to hunt the Adventurers?" That was Nore and Maeven drew the villager's attention back with a clap of wind.

"Again, please hold all your questions for the appropriate time. Now, primary projections predict a possible five-to-ten thousand *additional* Adventurers arriving on-island daily, but not remaining overnight—,"

"What measures are you using to decide which level of urgency we're assigned?" interrupted a female druid toward the middle of the room.

"She hasn't given us our assignments yet!" someone else barked.

"Did you get your assignment? I don't know what level I am," the same elderly faun with the ear trumpet mis-heard and leaned toward her gossipy friends for clarification.

"No assignments, yet Pigeon." Her friend spoke extra loudly and enunciated each word.

"If you'd hush up, she'd tell us!" a dwarf sitting down front cried toward the back. At least, Maeven though it was a dwarf. There were several new species living on island that hadn't been accounted for in the last census.

"Who is this '*we* you keep speaking of?" Aldrick yelled with a smirk as he raised his hand. He pointed between Maeven and Beck to indicate the duo. Maeven fought the urge to snap in response. Aldrick's wife, Shoney, nudged his side with her elbow and rolled her eyes at his behavior which made him stop.

"The overseer and the protec—" Maeven began before she was interrupted.

"Well, she has as much right as anyone to ask the question and be sure." Pigeon's friend snapped in response to the male dwarf.

"As I was saying," Maeven projected her voice again and regained the room's attention. "I have extensively gone through the town and identified areas of immediate need. The water being restored to all properties is first, if anyone has a new idea that hasn't been attempted or is aware of the curse that was spoken, please come forward at any time.

"Now our top safety concern is the rising level of kelpie sightings along the beach and the southern coast which, although not unusual during the deep of winter, is slightly above normal for this time of year. Dr. Naidu, do you have any insight on the patterns of our coastal pods?"

Dr. Naidu sat in the second row and looked surprised when Maeven addressed her. She was too slow to respond, though and was overtaken by Kitty Vex, lead tailor at the pixie boutique.

"The kelpie are not the problem!" Kitty flew down from her basket, iridescent wings fluttering gently behind her and enlarged head bobbing slightly. She stood twelve inches tall bearing the features of a child with oversized eyes.

"The wisteria trees have yet to blossom. Our stored silk is running low, and we won't make it through one month of Adventurers without the new crop. Is there nobody concerned about this?" Kitty's voice was high-pitched and sounded like a chipmunk which did not help her case.

Maeven was concerned about this new information. The pixie boutique was one of the highest selling businesses on the island. There, Adventurers could become engrossed in island life by getting custom woven clothes that were tailored perfectly to their style and taste. The pixies could weave a robe, cloak or dress in under an hour. A blouse or pair of trousers in about thirty minutes and accessories in about fifteen. While the Adventurers waited, they'd be fitted for shoes by the cobbler elves and get fitted out with hats, jewelry and additional accessories around town. It was a favorite location where some Adventurers spent an entire day on-island.

"Oh, the bloody wisteria again!" a satyr threw up his arms with a cry.

"Instead of worrying about ye flowers, let's talk about—"

"That's not as important as the number of coins we've been fishing out of—"

"Absolutely, no creature asked for your opinion on—"

"Apologies!" Maeven tried to contain the voices again, unable to prevent her mouth from interrupting. "Are there any insights or suggestions as to what could be the case for this change in behavior with the kelpies? Perhaps the coast?" She turned toward the naiads who often communicated with the weather patterns and seasons.

"No—don't get them started!" Beck interrupted moving toward her. She hated when he interrupted her because he was usually wrong and made matters worse.

He was, however, correct in this instance. Maeven was too blind to see that. The naiads were all in cahoots and once they got started about the environmental impact sightseeing boats had along the shoreline, and the submarines which disturbed the mythical waterfowl nesting sites, they added more demands to their growing list.

And she *still* didn't see Marisol amongst them!

Maeven made a mental note to hike out to the waterfalls the next day and hunt down Marisol since the former overseer wasn't in the village. She made another note to check the condition of the sightseeing boats, submarines, and ferries. They needed to make sure everything was kept in prime shape. There wasn't additional time allotted for closing and repairing the fleet once the island *officially* opened for Adventurers.

The naiads continued their plea by having members stand and chant: "Save the Salmon" and "Seven Swans Need to Keep Swimming", while they, loudly, announced their additional demands: no swimming in the lakes—*too much urine*, no feeding the fish—*they were getting very fat*, and no bare feet—*feet are gross*.

Maeven was more concerned that no one was on-beat or on the same demand sounding very unconfident but very enthusiastic.

"Oh, shut ye bloody mouth already, ya pee sippin fish!" a middle-aged merrow bellowed toward the naiads with a round of hurrahs from his buddies.

"Ye've caused enough trouble with the water in town as it is!"

"Aye, no one has had a decent shower in weeks!"

"Aye!" The forum erupted in villagers' voices vying for loudest declaration of who suffered worse.

The present naiads argued they weren't the culprits behind the curse and *those* naiads were indeed locked to the talking fountain in the town square. They insisted it was the pixies who were responsible for consuming more water than regularly needed, always watering their trees, which weren't even blooming.

In response, the pixies blamed the gnomes who took care of the gardens at the Bloodstone Manor—the grandest attraction on-island which distanced itself greatly from the village, literally as it was located ten miles north-east in the woods—for their overuse of water to keep their lawns manicured.

The gnomes pointed fingers toward the centaurs— folk with the head and torso of a human but the lower body of a horse, who kept to themselves in the mountainous regions—for tearing up the countryside with their hoofs on nightly runs. And the centaurs weren't even there to argue back because they rarely came down from the mountains!

Around and around the villagers went; never admitting their own fault but pointing fingers at their neighbor.

Maeven's head swam.

A low-pitched tone rang in her ear and overwhelmed her mind. She backed up, found the chair that had been placed for her and sat, eyes closed. She took steady breaths as the shouts and cries of the village grew even louder. She felt a hand touch the back of her neck, jumping in surprise. Bennie whispered softly in her ear and rubbed her hand in small circles against Maeven's back. Her body melted under her friend's *intent* but the knot that formed in her stomach tightened instead of unwinding like she'd expected.

When she opened her eyes, her aeromancer *intent* was already there, a small ball of air held between her hands sparking an angry burst at its confinement. She released her fingers, expecting the *intent* to dissipate without her hold over it, but instead the *intent* rolled forward, dropping to the floor, spinning and rising into a funnel.

It grew to fill the room, the whisps solidified into a thick wall reaching from floor to ceiling silencing the villagers. The tornado wobbled in the center of the room, pulling at the leftover *intent* used by those present.

Islanders often used their *intent* during a conversation or argument; added a bit of flash, bang, or needed confidence boost to their speech. But the leftover *intent* dripped and collected in the electrified environment.

The mass swirled and tore at the people and stacked boxes that flung items around the room. Maeven ducked as a chair flew at the head table and smashed into the wall.

Realizing her ridiculous mistake, she turned to Beck, her exhaustion from releasing so much power at once leaving her depleted to call it back. He stepped up behind her holding his hands out, palms up.

Maeven hesitated; they would be rusty; far too long since she'd drawn from his *intent* to boost her own. It took them years of practice, very *close* physical practice, to be able to share their power in such an intimate way.

The was no guarantee it would work—

Maeven entwined her fingers with Beck's and extended her free hand toward the tornado. Focusing on the feel of Beck's heartbeat through his wrist, she began to pull his *intent* and mix it with her own, imagining an unbroken line that flowed between their arms and fingers for the *intent* to follow.

The exhaustion she felt moments before left; her body filled with energy, with Beck's stamina. Her body became engulfed and convulsed forward from the force. Beck didn't flinch as Bennie caught Maeven's shoulders and held her steady.

Maeven released the *intent* she built up from Beck toward the tornado and began to step forward, pushing the wind tunnel down the center aisle. It pulled from the room as it left and the villagers were forced to grab onto the walls, floor, each other—anything that was bolted down to keep them from being sucked into the vortex.

It wobbled as it drove at the exit, growing smaller and smaller the further away from Maeven it traveled. Once it passed the threshold, it rose off into the night, taking part of the ceiling with it. Finally, the double doors of the Forum slammed shut.

The room burst into cheers and applause as Maeven fell back into Bennie's arms. She wasn't tired, on the contrary, she was energized but unsteady on her feet. Beck's strength flowed through her veins. She flexed her fingers open and closed at the *intent* pulsing beneath her skin.

It wanted to be used.

It was a moment she would contemplate days later when she was able to remember it again. How the *intent* seemed to be part of her but also seemed to be its own *thing*. Almost like its own life, own entity.

But she didn't have time to think about that for a while because seconds later a teenage merrow burst through the hall doors, bringing the room to silence once more.

"A body! There's a dead body on the beach!"

Chapter 7

It was Tempest.

Her body lay sprawled along a broken tree trunk, still half-encased inside the impermeable wood. The tornado ripped through the center and left her torso exposed. Maeven recognized the tree immediately from where it lay on the beach. She'd been ruminating earlier on how fun it would be to walk along the various limbs.

How many times had she walked past it that day?

How did no one sense a body there?

"Beck, get everyone back," Maeven threw a bubble of *intent* with her voice as they raced toward the shoreline from the town square. A group of teen merrows surrounded the trunk, whispering as they pointed toward the broken pieces. The villagers surged forward on the sand, pushing and tripping as Maeven struggled to guide her way through the throng.

Ashamed for losing control of herself, Maeven didn't want to risk using more *intent* creating a path. Beck appeared before her and grabbed her hand, pulling her along behind him.

"Step aside, please, step aside!" Beck yelled as the group shifted to make an aisle that filled behind them as they passed.

Beck strode toward the tree trunk, an arm out to keep the others back and crouched to examine the body. If Maeven could see that it was Tempest, a likeness to the photo she saw in the file, she knew the onlookers could as well. She was Overseer now and needed to act her position.

Take control of the situation before somebody else does!

"Eanna," she called to the animacer, brown spotted hair that was slicked back in long points, spotted amongst the crowd. "Inform the acolytes." Maeven whispered the order and watched the woman nod once. The brunette turned and disappeared into the crowd, emerging moments later from the back, in the form of a hawk that flew off into the night.

The acolytes lived at the Grannus Wellness Center, miles atop the mountain. They maintained the hot springs and infused them with their own healing *intent.* The most esteemed healers on-island were there, and it was the only building that could house a body due to the freezing temperatures within the mountain caves.

"Attention," Maeven turned to the crowd and clapped her hands a few times to draw their sight. Her hands instinctively moved apart as if preparing a ball of air and the crowd took a noticeable step backwards. Embarrassed, Maeven dropped her hands and continued, "Please return to your dwellings for the evening—"

"We are *not* returning to our houses!" Aldrick responded with indignation. An angry voice amongst the crowd that earned a roaring cheer.

"No *witch* is going to order us around!"

"We've as much right to be here!"

"It's the missing girl, isn't it?"

"What's happened then?"

"With respect to the *deceased*—" the villagers grew quiet and murmured amongst themselves as Maeven tried to rationalize with them. "—please return to your dwellings for the evening and we will update everyone as soon as we know what exactly has transpired."

"We know what *transpired*." Aldrick continued, mocking her vocabulary then turning to face the crowd and pointing toward the scene. "What happened is that Tempest was killed, and the naturamancer druids conspired to cover it up with the naiads!"

The accusation was immediately damning. Several naturamancer druids, known to carve items from living trees and plants, shouted a protest. The groups' voices on the beach turned to angry accusations. Maeven's mother had been a naturamancer, she supposed it was *possible* that one had grown a tree around the poor imp.

"You can't blame us for this! You sylvamancers work with trees as well!" one man pointed at Aldrick in response. It was true that most sylvamancers could also work with wood, but typically only dead material.

"We only work with slabs of wood!" Aldrick countered. Arguments and finger pointing started up amongst the villagers.

"Don't be pointin' fingers at us!"

"These imps are caught up in their own mess—"

"No imp would be harmin' one of their own—"

"The faeries *clearly*—"

"You know as well as I that it's the pixies with the problems—"

The arguments grew louder, and Maeven did her best to calm them. This was her fault for allowing her emotions to overwhelm her when she created the tornado. She should have known to be extra cautious her first night back on-island. There was more raw magic here than in the city with its metal buildings. And raw *intent* was easily usable, which meant she'd not only utilize it more naturally, but it would also be more powerful. Like training a muscle, her body wasn't used to having an endless supply available to amp her up whenever needed. It was easy to overuse without proper moderation.

And yet, Maeven was stupid enough to create a miniature tornado that not only destroyed the ceiling of the Forum—a nice, straight line now broke the front façade in half—but also broke open the dead tree, exposing Tempest's body.

The roaring of the villagers merged into a cloudy buzz.

Maeven created list after list in her mind, trying to focus on what she *could* control and ignore the cries around her. She didn't know what to do. She couldn't control the anger of the people around her. She couldn't control the panic of the creatures who pointed fingers and claws and hissed behind sharpened teeth.

She could only control her own thoughts and actions. Thoughts that didn't need a list of building repairs or import/export from the bakery at that moment. Her eyes squeezed shut as she fought to maintain her composure. Placing a hand on her chest, she slowed her breathing to match the *thump-thump-thump-thump* of her heart.

Again.

And again.

Until she heard the hoof-beats against the cobblestone that matched the thump.

The acolytes had arrived.

Maeven opened her eyes to watch the centaurs stamped through the square; she'd never been so happy to see them! They galloped through the street, aiming for the semi-circle of onlookers that parted for the majestic creatures. Above them flew Eanna in her hawk form. She glided down and transfigured as her feet touched down.

Maeven watched the villager's step back to let the small herd enter the crescent shape they formed. Most of the acolytes fanned out to put themselves between the body and the rest of the town—blocking the view as much as possible. Maeven and Bennie stood nearby as Beck walked forward to greet the leading centaur. Several acolytes walked in the opposite direction past him. They carried brown leather satchels and began to examine the surroundings. They knelt and unloaded tools and a white sheet once they reached the body.

"We need to get the villagers to go home," Maeven grabbed Bennie's arm and whispered furiously. If anyone could compel the villagers to go home, it was her. "There are too many eyes right now."

"I'll speak to Epona." Bennie nodded toward the acolyte murmuring in low tones with Beck. The centaur was female, in her later years, her hair already turned silver and her coat showing the first signs of white. When she became pure as snow, she would retire to the stables of her god for reincarnation.

Epona must have sensed Maeven's concern, because she turned to address the crowd.

"My friends," Epona held her arms out in greeting. Most of the villagers murmured and nodded their heads in response. "This is an unfortunate circumstance for us all. We ask that you allow us privacy to see proper care of the body. Please return home for the evening and you will all be updated tomorrow. Pray and make sacrifices to Grannus, that her soul may find peace." The crowd began dispersing without any continued whispers or angry words thrown at each other. Maeven was a bit jealous of Epona's ability to soothe them.

Looking down, Maeven noticed a piece from the tree trunk. She bent and picked it up. Examining the outside which appeared rough and raw as bark but when she turned it over, the underside was smooth, almost polished.

Tempest hardly looked injured. Maeven glanced over at the girl, her body preserved over the months she'd been missing in the petrified trunk., She had few imperfections, her skin paler without any of the tan color left. A dark smudge caught Maeven's eye, and she reached forward, moving Tempest's shirt collar with a small bit of *intent*, to reveal lines, singe marks?

Her body looked electrocuted.

"Please, don't touch anything," a female acolyte, red hair braided backwards away from her face, snapped toward Maeven.

"Here, look—" Maeven pointed toward the bruises that ringed Tempest's neck. "It looks like she was singed, possibly suffocated in the tree?"

"We'll be able to do a full examination of the body once we return to the wellness center. Please don't disturb the body." The woman continued with an irritated tone, like she had to deal with Adventurers disturbing scenes all the time. But Maeven was not an Adventurer, and she would need to maintain a kind relationship with the acolytes.

"Yes, of course." Maeven nodded and backed away several steps. She turned and found herself face-to-face with Epona.

"You should look away," Epona's voice was gentle but firm. Maeven hadn't sensed the head acolyte behind her. "A death in this way, this evil—" the centaur shook her head, a shiver shot down Maeven's spine.

A chill swept through the beach and those still there clutched their hats and coats. They shuffled off the sand as the acolytes herded them away.

"Who would do such a thing?" Maeven muttered to herself.

"Evil grows in all." Epona replied though she was looking at the sun as it began setting across the ocean horizon. Maeven turned to watch but hated how serene and beautiful the moment appeared. As long as she avoided glancing downwards.

"The Council will want to investigate." Maeven felt stupid even as she stuttered the words. It was not the proper time to speak about a council investigation. Or perhaps it was, but it felt wrong to discuss in front of the body.

Either way, it was apparent that Beck—and Marisol—had dropped a lot of responsibilities when it came to the island.

"Perhaps you should investigate yourself." Epona responded. The centaur turned toward Maeven, and her eyes gently roamed down Maeven's form, studying her. Maeven knew the acolyte was seeing more than just her outward appearance. Epona was reading her lifelines and seeing where the planets were on the day of Maeven's birth; using that knowledge to grasp why Maeven spoke and acted the way she did and how best she reacted. The acolytes were specialists at reading the stars and understanding your character based on it. Sometimes the acolytes could even tell you what your future had in store for you.

"Perhaps," Maeven was remiss to agree but knew that centaurs often spoke truth in rhymes you might have to dissect to understand. Maeven decided she was absolutely going to see Marisol tomorrow and get as much information as she could. Then she would begin solving the islands problems, *all* her problems—including Tempest's death.

Several druids and satyrs passed by at that moment, distracting Maeven. They were called upon to discuss the best way of breaking the remaining tree trunks without disturbing the scene. Maeven hated to see Aldrick walking amongst the others, his head bent toward Beck.

"Please let me know as soon as you have your reports finished." Maeven bowed her head toward Epona and backed away, so she didn't spook her. Dismissing herself, she paused when the woman spoke.

"We will see you again soon, Maeven Mathers." Epona nodded her own head toward the witch in a stationary bow.

Maeven's cheeks warmed with a blush. Another prediction that could have many nuances. Being in their presence always felt like a heavy weight was on her shoulders; expectations of a future laid out on a path she couldn't change. To hazy to see in front of her and hard to keep her feet upon.

Maeven made her way over to Beck. Aldrick met her eyes and ended their conversation, shaking hands and walking away just as she reached them.

"What did he say?" Maeven asked with a nod toward Aldrick's back.

"Quite impertinent of you to demand information." Beck responded with a tease.

"I'm a representative of the council, who will want to investigate, which means *I* am tasked with investigating and will be involved in every step and privy to all information. Now, what did Aldrick say?" Maeven ground her back teeth to keep herself from lashing out at him even more.

"The sylvamancers are going to crack open the rest of the trunk and the acolytes will remove the body then transport it to the wellness center for an autopsy." He informed her, staring over her head toward the work that had already begun. She briefly glanced toward the workers.

"Did we get photos of the scene?"

"We did." He nodded his head toward a quintet of druids. Maeven recognized the tall female standing in the center as a tràighmancer, a druid who worked with sand. Her left hand sat in a wooden box, being held by a second druid, while a third druid shoveled sand inside. The sand was quickly depleted by the tràighmancer. Her second hand waved in the air and produced glass imprints of the scene she surveyed. The imprints were being caught by the last two druids, wearing thick leather gloves extending the length of their arms. This helped ward off the heat of the freshly pressed glass, sizzling against the ground when dropped. All the attendants followed the tràighmancer as she walked around, capturing the important images. They worked at a fast speed like a practiced dance.

Maeven was impressed. She had never seen a tràighmancer working in person before. She read they'd only been hired in the past few years and were still on trial period. It was fascinating to watch how the sand was painted like a sketch then superheated into glass.

"Impressive," Maeven said with a head nod and a large yawn. She hadn't realized how late in the day it had grown. Her back ached from carrying her office bag. They would still need to clean up the Forum building and appraise what damage the ceiling took. They'd need to stabilize it for the evenings and survey repairs; start to re-interview the villagers that had a relationship with Tempest before her disappearance—

"Head home," Beckwell said, nudging Maeven with his elbow, she didn't resist and let her legs slowly shift away from him.

"I'll deal with sleep later," Maeven tried to cover up a second yawn but only managed to screw up her face by squishing her eyes and lips together.

"You'll be worthless later if you don't go home and get some sleep. I'll handle this and get some of the guys to start cleaning up the forum, I'm sure that's on your list this evening." He knew her mind enough—and obviously she meant to do her best to help in any way she could.

"Thanks, I could use some extra rest." Maeven realized he was right and threw in the towel early—there would plenty of opportunities later to argue with Beck over trivial matters. She may as well enjoy the luxury of sleep in this instance.

Chapter 8

You may encounter a bean-tighe at your rented dwelling.
These house spirits prefer rooms kept tidy
and treated respectfully for ease of visit.
Please do not slam the doors and upset the house spirit!

An hour later, Maeven found herself on a winding, bumpy road, clutching the handlebars of an old moped. Bennie was gracious enough to lend it to her while on-island. In theory it would cut down on the short trek back and forth from her mother's cabin in the woods. In practice, however, Maeven remembered how terrible her balance remained.

Her luggage, retrieved from the Dew Drop and left at the forum, was much too large and would be brought over the next day by gig. Her trusty office bag, strapped tightly over her shoulder, held a few days' worth of clothes beside her files.

Maeven's irritation and exhaustion grew further when she hit a hole and the oversized helmet slid down her eyes, rattling her head.

A crossroad of wooden signs approached and pointed visitors to various regions in the forest. She turned the wheel and clutched the brake handle, willing the bike to turn smoothly. The small tire barely held onto the gravel as she skidded onto the dirt road that led to the *Witches Cottage*.

The clearing ahead had a mock hut constructed for the Adventurers. It was designed to look like a beehive. The druid that played the witch would sit inside, stirring a steaming pot—usually herbs and fruit, and wait for the Adventurers to figure out her riddle and receive their prize.

Her mother's actual house lay just beyond the clearing, down a hidden road. A glimmer she usually saw out of the corner of her eye once walking past, shielded it from prying eyes. Maeven would need to be sure and touch up the illusion over the entrance before the Adventurers descended. She never mastered those, but her mother's illusions were impeccable. Maeven had always preferred the spells that revealed secrets, not hid them.

The scooter suddenly slowed, the whine of its motorized engine began to drift off and it rolled to a stop. Maeven attempted to stick her legs out on either side to balance. She was *really* bad at this part because her hips were thick, and her legs were short. They struggled to touch the ground on either side of the floorboard unless she lifted her bottom off the seat. Once she did that though, she completely lost balance, and her feet slipped in the wet earth. Her arms were too weak to hold up the moped which fell on her as she tumbled into a puddle.

She lay in the mud and contemplated her death. It was only fitting that she would die under the weight of a crappy, very old, bike. At least she wouldn't see when Death came to claim her soul.

But she wasn't *dead*.

She heaved herself up and pushed the moped off her leg. It would be bruised and sore but wasn't broken. Maeven rolled onto her knees, her skirt thoroughly stained and pushed herself to her feet. Walking toward the illusioned path, she took slow, struggling steps forward pushing herself into the boundaries that guarded her mother's house from the Adventurers.

With a slight pinch, she was through, and her stride became lighter, easier. But she was exhausted. The day was long and full of adrenaline. So much happened that she barely remembered to write it all down in her reports.

Screw it.

I'm too tired for this!

She paused to mutter a string of *intent*, gathered and aimed downward. The ground began to roll into small mounds underneath her feet. They lifted beneath her and allowed her to slide effortlessly over the uneven forest floor. She shifted her weight back and forth and began to move as if skiing. The mounds did all the work and carried her weight forward.

Maeven closed her eyes as she sped through the trees. The smell of spruce and pine overtook her senses as she slipped along the Windstream carrying her home.

Home.

Her home was a one-bedroom condo, thousands of miles away, overlooking the busiest city in the modern world—with Urian. She wasn't sure what she moved toward but she knew it hadn't been home in a few decades.

After the death of her father, Maeven was sent to live with her maternal grandmother. Her mother, Eliza—wasn't quite up to the task of raising Maeven after becoming lost in her own grief. Maeven's grandmother deemed the island too wild for her granddaughter and saw to it she attended a *proper* school and was given a *proper* routine to keep her mind and magic busy. Maeven hated it and threw several tantrums until her grandmother agreed to her return every summer.

For three precious months from Junius to Augustius, she got to wander the island. Walking the paths or running barefoot if she wanted. Singing at the top of her lungs without being told to be quiet. Wearing her hair loose and carefree down her back with clothing that wasn't tight and restrictive around her limbs. She would be free to roam for hours instead of sitting in a classroom.

With her eyes shut, Maeven held her face to the sky, the warm spring sun creeping through the thick canopy. In the stillness, the trees spilled newly formed leaves that floated to the ground in circles. The birds cawed from their roosts and creatures fled from their dens and hovels to prance around her.

The forest was alive as it whispered about her return. The closer she got to her childhood home, the louder it grew. She felt a bit like Eliza to them. They sensed her mother within her blood and her ancestors before.

A cacophony of insects. A shrill of birds, the thump of sticks and rocks against the ground. Then, all went silent.

The house stood before her and ground froze in place. Maeven she paused, foot stretched out, hovering briefly before the next step.

The moment was more glaring than she realized.

What if things changed?

Or worse, what if things are the same?

She opened her eyes and stepped forward.

Her mother's house was solemn; an old friend exacerbated by the sight of Maeven's return. A loud, low groan began to emit from the shaking home.

A friendly face at last!

The A-frame sank into the ground, merging into the earth. It was covered in moss growing along the ground, continuing along top of the triangle roof. The mass moved ever-so-slightly, humming in anticipation of her approach.

The wooden siding on the face, darkened with cobwebs, and large circular window that hung in the center, were dirty from lack of upkeep and would need time and attention.

Two twisted chimneys emerged from overgrowth: limbs trying to escape their grave. A noticeable lack of smoke rose from either and Maeven felt a very noticeable drop in her stomach.

Glancing to her left, she saw the old well, with a small stack of haphazardly thrown wood beside it. Maeven fought the urge to walk over and glance down the dark hole, to see if anything hid inside. The thought of lugging buckets of cold water again didn't thrill her and she hoped her mother still had the well water system hooked up to the washroom.

A breeze picked up around her and brought a distinct smell. The hairs on the back of her neck rose and her eyes searched the tree line. She began to walk around to the back of the house, following the smell.

Brighid bring her patience.

It brought the scent of wet animals.

Her ears twitched and her head turned at the sound of a snap—several snaps.

Squinting down the path in the leftover light of the setting sun, she saw her mother's *madrai* and dragonling barreling toward her at top speed.

Roscoe, the *madrai* was an enormous, fat, hound about sixteen hands tall. He looked like a basset hound but was the size of a rhinoceros. Giant, white-and-brown speckled ears flopped against his head with each bound. A long, pink tongue rolled out the side of his snout and a trail of slobbers hung off the end. Annoyingly stubborn, he was a prize rescue valued as a rare collectible by breeders.

Behind Roscoe, flew the black dragonling, Rickashay. Flapping her one-and-a-half good wings—an accident as a newborn left her left-side permanently crippled—she wailed at the *madrai* for leaving her behind.

Rickashay was only able to fly in slow, awkward tilts. The creature bounced like a drunk gnome, its path routinely changing when she rolled or turned in midair. An uncoordinated, off-balance, mess that was now Maeven's to care for. Roscoe faltered and turned around to race back and allow Rickashay to land on her back. The dragonling clutched the thick rolls of the hound and cawed.

Maeven cursed her mother's idiotic pets. She shrieked in annoyance as the two finished their race, knocking Maeven to the ground and descending upon her with tongue licks and talon scratches.

"Roscoe! Stop!" Maeven shoved the *madrai's* cold nose and slobber off her neck. Rickashay clawed at her head, trying to perch and preen her hair. She happened to be the smaller breed of dragonling—cousin of a dragon, averaging twice the size of a typical house cat, but more like a large iguana with the personality of a tiny ferret.

"That's enough!" Maeven pushed *intent* toward Roscoe and Rickashay. It swept them backwards off her body. The dragonling gently soared against the drift and Roscoe rolled sideways onto his back—giving a whine for belly rubs. Maeven stood and dusted her clothes. She balanced herself on one foot and with the other, rubbed Roscoe's belly a few times—a decent amount of love but not too much that he would become annoyingly persistent for more.

Turning back to the house, Maeven walked up the three front steps of the porch and ran her hand along the thick vines burying the door beneath. The two ancient slabs that formed the front door were carved from an oak tree her grand-, grand-, grand-, ancestor had planted centuries before. When it eventually fell, every piece was reused to build the house, and the door, carved with protective sigils, was her favorite piece.

The magic of the house *bean-tighe* stemmed from this tree. A single taproot stretched through the base of the doorframe, reaching upwards into the attic from deep in the earth. It tied the house across her family's land, to the trees that filled the forest. The door would not unwrap itself for anyone but her lineage due to the generations of *intent pressed* into the wood grains.

She was one of the few remaining Morrigan women.

Placing her hand upon the knotted vines locking the handle, she pulsed *intent* in three quick bursts to unlock them. The house gently hummed and vibrated as the vines slithered to untangle themselves and retreat. She pushed the door open once freed and heard its hinges creak from sitting for so long. Eliza was certainly enjoying her time on the fourth island if she hadn't bothered returning home to check up.

The house was dark, the last tendrils of sunlight seeped in from the center window above and Maeven bumped her way to the couch. She fell atop it and was asleep before she could kick off her shoes.

Maeven stood on the private beach, her favorite secluded spot, watching the gentle waves caress the shore. The water stretched forward with the sand surrounding her ankles. With each pull of the tide, her toes sank a little deeper and the suction became stronger.

Two warm arms wrapped around her waist, and she felt Beck's presence press against her back. Leaning into him, a smile spread, and she giggled against the feel of his lips trailing kisses down her neck.

"This was always my favorite part," Beck cooed into her ear, his face nudging hers in a teasing way. Goosebumps appeared along her arm as his fingers began to dance along the hemline of her shorts.

"What was?" her words were a whisper, throat tightening in excited anticipation.

"Mae," his antlers stole her glance. She tilted back to look at him, a coy smile on her lips.

Beck leaned down to kiss her. She closed her eyes to greet his lips, but moments passed and they never touched.

Maeven opened them to see Beck watching. He smiled and his head bobbed as he stuck out his tongue. She was confused. He leaned down again and ran his tongue along her cheek. It scratched her skin with soft painful pricks causing pain.

Maeven snorted awake as Rickashay's tongue grated against her cheek. She shrieked; the rough sandpaper texture leaving small scratches along her skin. A blast of *intent* launched the dragonling from the bed. She flapped her wings to catch air and hissed in return. Light filtered in from above and Maeven sat up, looking around to get her bearings.

The house was alarmingly cold that morning. She'd forgotten to add a log to the hearth which warmed the rooms below and lofted bedroom. Maeven shivered in her muddy clothes from the day before, her cheek stinging.

She'd need to get fresh wood from outside and start a new fire. Not that there was great wood to use. It was wet and soggy from sitting on the ground all year *not* stacked nicely in the rick. This made the wood smoke excessively instead of lighting and heating the room.

"Rickashay!" Maeven cried again as the dragonling landed on her head. She felt the talons dig into her skull and pull at her hair, already frizzing from the added humidity of the island.

Maeven flicked a ball of air toward her and the dragonling took off in a lazy crooked circle, wailing at the door. Roscoe barked in enthusiasm from the other side and Maeven stomped across the room to let them reunite. She boosted Rickashay out the door with a small burst of *intent* then closed and leaned against it.

The house hummed and shivered slowly. From the ceiling, burst forth small, blue flowers. They rained down in slow, lazy spirals. Maeven lifted her hand and caught one as it glided past.

Round with small notches, five petals, bright blue with a yellow center—Forget-Me-Nots.

She smiled at the gift; her face turned upward.

Maeven surveyed the house that needed a *lot* of sprucing up. The floors were roots of surrounding forest trees; intertwined over and under until they formed a hard, flat surface. Maeven remembered her mother singing and dancing around as she cared for the roots.

In the winter Eliza sanded down the rough areas to prevent splinters, then rubbed lemon juice and orange oil into the grooves for polish. In the summer she soaked them in orange oil and imbued her own naturamancer *intent* into the dilution.

The sitting area where Maeven had fallen asleep last night was dark. A thick layer of dust ran along the top of the coffee table. Her eyes scanned the bookshelves standing floor-to-ceiling around the hearth. They narrowed and curved as they followed the shape of the walls. Full of leather-bound books, knick-knacks, pictures of Maeven in various stages of aging; a few small tonic bottles and tinctures throughout.

The hearth was in the center of the house, a grand carving out of the original tree trunk. A flat top cast-iron skillet swum back and forth over the fire and could be swapped out with a cauldron. Maeven remembered Eliza, serving large bowls of hot root stew to herself, Beck, and Bennie as a kid. Her mom would recall the group with tales of her own teen years on-island then drift off into sadness when she thought of Maeven's father. Those episodes of happiness were few and far between after his death.

The kitchen nook was behind her. An icebox sat under the butcher-block island and counters spread out with jars of various sizes and colors. A few candles, half melted down to the stub, and copper pots hung from vines on the ceiling. All appeared in order though covered in dust.

To Maeven's front was a carved, L-shaped, wooden stairway to the second-floor loft, her mother's bedroom. The debarked banister, sanded and oiled, was the focal point of the small house. Carved with the intricate history of her family, it ran the length of the second-floor wall and curved to floor level. Her mother used to hang strings of herbs year-round, stockings during Yule, and flowers during Ostara.

She jumped when Rickashay howled from outside. Maeven rolled her eyes but turned to see the ruckus.

When Maeven opened the door, the wind stopped its howl. The birds halted their song, and the crickets paused their tune, waiting in anticipation. Even Roscoe and Rickashay quietly lifted their heads from where they tussled to wait and watch.

The air was cold that morning and she grabbed her cardigan from her bag. Maeven stepped out onto the porch, a deep inhale as she lifted her arms above her head to stretch.

Rickashay shrieked and flew at Maeven's head. Maeven ducked and swatted the dragonling away again. Roscoe took it upon himself to bark toward Rickashay and run away, back to the path that ran behind the house, through the woods, leading to a large clearing where Maeven and her parents had built the barn.

The barn, *Brighid*.

Maeven completely forgot to check the sheep last night amidst the disturbance in town. She sighed in exhaustion at the thought of making the trip to feed and water bovine.

The sooner she started, the sooner she would be done.

Grumbling to herself, she pulled her cardigan tight around her torso and began to march toward the animals.

As a child, Maeven loved to wander these paths, her bare feet tripping over the roots that stuck up from the ground, snaking and ambling through the trees. Her soles would become stained by moss and mud when she jumped from pile to pile. Her mother would follow aimlessly behind while her father sang—strumming a lute and making up songs to bring her mother's mind back.

Sometimes it was the premonitions, sometimes it was just her own thoughts, and sometimes it was the trees—their ability to speak with her could overwhelm the senses at times and took Eliza mentally away from Maeven and her father.

Maeven would present her father with the simplest rock or bug, her hair flowing unbound down her back and bouncing in her face when she stopped. Her father would accept the gift every time, showing her mother each item and describing them. They would continue this pattern, Maeven bringing items and her father showing them to Eliza, until her mother's eyes cleared, and she returned to them again.

Now, as Maeven walked the same path, Roscoe and Rickashay racing ahead, her shoes tripped over those same damn roots. Her arms scrambled to find balance and she jerked backwards. Her flat shoes, now absolutely ruined, slipped out from underneath. She caught the nearest tree branch and righted her body. The last thing she needed was to be covered in *more* filth. Regaining her balance, Maeven continued down the path, a few soft curses under her breath.

As the barn neared, Maeven was thankful that spring was on the way. A few sheep dotted the fenced field and Roscoe ran off, straight through the fence—his body becoming transparent as he did—to round them up. His deep bark made the animals run into a frightened huddle.

As Maeven approached the barn, her pace slowed. The top portion of the double dutch-door was opened, the lock of vines that should have been there, gone. Muted noises came from inside. She sent out a breeze and swung the door completely open.

"Hello?" Maeven called out but heard no response. She reached the door and peeked inside, the central aisle was clear, but a noise came from the loft above. She watched as the figure shifted and his antlers showed against the window light.

"Beck?" Maeven shook her head, confused, and screeched toward him, slightly too intense.

"Good morning to you as well," He called back with a chuckle.

"What are you doing here?"

"I'm training a griffin, what does it look like?" he dropped the pitchfork and stomped to the ladder. Descending to the barn floor, he advanced upon her—shirtless, skin glowing from exertion.

Maeven bit her lip to stop from gawking at his form and backed away as he approached. His grin was mischievous and distracted her from the reason she was in the barn. Beck's face quickly fell as he looked behind her.

"Samson, no!" Beckwell called and pulled her attention to the movement. Maeven turned just as a large head of horns collided with her chest, taking the breath from her lungs. Her body flew backwards and slammed into the barn wall, where she promptly blacked out.

Chapter 9

"This was always my favorite part," Beck cooed as he turned toward her. His hands caressed her cheek and trailed down the open skin of her neck and collarbone. Goosebumps appeared where his fingers touched and she shivered against his arm, wrapped tightly around her waist.

She pressed herself against him and a small moan escaped her lips. "What was?" her words were a husky whisper which she hoped looked cute—er—sexy.

"Mae," His antlers, an imposing form on top of his head, always stole her glance. He tilted his head to the side and watched her with curiosity, ears alert.

Beck opened his lips to speak but made no sound.

Mae, his voice echoed but his mouth only smiled.

Mae.

Mae.

She *really* hated that nickname and decided to keep her eyes closed.

"Mae?" Beck spoke softly like a frightened animal, cautious about spooking her on accident. Maeven wasn't going to lash out, but she was *absolutely* going to roast that gods-forsaken goat for dinner.

"Beck?" Her body felt warm in his arms, cradled in his lap. She fought the urge to snuggle closer against his chest. His scent burying itself back into her memory.

"Are you alright?" he whispered. She practically heard the withheld chuckle he desperately wanted to release. He better not laugh.

Beck's fingers ran through her hair. He stroked the side of her face, along her cheek and lightly grazed down her jaw and neck.

"Do I look alright?" she sighed, her body aching, head throbbing; she would probably have a bruise on her sternum.

The scent of manure overwhelmed her nose.

"Should I give you an honest answer?"

"Not really, Beck." Maeven swatted away his fingers, but he caught her hand. His skin, familiar in hers.

Maeven's heart thumped wildly against her chest. Beck acted like no time had passed. Like they hadn't spent ten years apart from each other. No harm done when they last parted.

Before she could pull away, he bent down, his musky scent filling her nostrils and sending a wave of warmth through her body.

Even with her eyes closed, she could sense him hovering over her, waiting for *her* to make the final press against his lips.

Her stomach dropped and Urian's face flashed in her mind.

She couldn't kiss him.

Opening her eyes, she met Beck's, mere inches from her face. Seeing her hesitation and the catch in her throat, he leaned down, shifting at the last second to press their foreheads together instead.

Beck buried his fingers in her hair and closed his eyes. His nose dipped into her hair and took a deep inhale of her scent. He released her and moved back—a cold chill immediately filling the void.

Moments later he stood and offered his hand. She rolled away from him onto her knees to stand by herself. It wasn't her sweaty palms that caused her to avoid Beckwell. It was the racing of her heart and the desire to wrap herself around him and never let go.

"Need help?" Beckwell's hand appeared in front of her face again, and she took it this time. He pulled her up in a quick motion that sent her head spinning.

She wavered backwards and Beck caught his arm around her waist.

"Woah, there." His hand felt warm against the small of her back and her breath hiccupped.

Heart hammering faster, she knew this was *too* familiar. Their bodies were *too* comfortable with *too* little space between them.

Maeven stepped away and whimpered when she looked down at herself. The wetness on her back legs was a clue. She was lucky enough to land in the dirty hay Beck changed from the pens.

Stripping off her cardigan, Beck was gentlemanly enough to take the collar and help pull it from her arms. "I'll walk you back to the house so you can clean up, if you want." He offered holding her sweater out with one finger and a disgusted grimace.

Maeven grumbled and glanced around the barn before they left. The large stall on her left was where the sheep and chickens entered from the field. At night Roscoe took over as guardian of the barn to keep the flock safe.

Across the aisle, the mother ewes were settled down with their kids—three new ones between two mothers, and another three ewes left to give birth. Eliza's buck, Samson, had certainly been busy.

"I want a good ram stew," Maeven murmured, resisting the urge to cook the male over an open spit. Samson stood pleasantly next to the females outside, chewing on fresh grass. He bleated deeply toward Maeven, and she stuck her tongue out before following after Beck.

Leaving, she sent a blast of *intent* toward the barn doors and watched them shut with a loud bang. The vines moved on their own accord and re-formed a tight knot around the handle.

"Did you bring my suitcases?" She tried to keep her voice nonchalant, but her nerves were rattled. She wasn't feeling quite herself around him. Her heart was beating too quickly, and her face felt flushed.

"I left them on your porch this morning, did you not see them?" Beck asked his own question in return. Obviously, she hadn't seen them.

"I didn't see them but thank you." Maeven responded and lengthened her stride to reach the house faster so she could get clean.

"What are your plans for the day?" Beck asked, easily matching her pace with his long legs and unending stamina.

"My plans are to prop myself up in the forum office— no!" Maeven stopped herself and remembered the more important task. "No, actually I need to head up to the waterfalls and see Marisol."

The hike shouldn't take longer than a day, the trail was only a few hours up the Western Mountain side and back.

"I'll go with you," Beck nodded his head agreeing to accompany her on her travels even though she hadn't asked.

"I don't need you to go with me, Beck. I'll be perfectly fine hiking by myself." Maeven shook her head at the idea.

"I'm not going for your benefit," he responded, catching up in a single stride and falling in beside her steps. "I need to check the trails and clear any debris from the winter snows."

"Okay, but I'm not helping you clear *anything*." She remarked as they reached the house.

"Yes, why put your *aeromancer* magic to good use when you can watch me tire myself out hauling trees." Beck rolled his eyes.

"Well, if you didn't leave the task to the last minute, you wouldn't be pressed for time or have as much to move."

"I would still have the same amount to move."

"So, you wouldn't have needed me either way."

"Again, why would you not use your *intent* to help?"

"Because I'll end up falling flat on my face when it comes back to bite me!" she insisted on giving his arm a whack for good measure. Beck knew perfectly well how her *intent* worked.

"Small price to pay for hours saved, right?" he grinned but she ignored him.

Maeven skipped up the steps and looked to her right where, sure enough, Beck had tucked her luggage against the railing. He also put a bag of food from town which smelled delicious. Grabbing them both, she retreated toward the door.

"I'm going to take a shower and eat this food. Do you want to wait for me?"

"I've got a few things in town to do, I'll be back in about an hour with Caius."

"Oh perfect!" Maeven smiled at the name of Beck's pet moose that would pull his gig. This would cut down on the travel time to the trailhead.

"I missed you, Maeven." Beck grinned and took a deep breath, hesitating, before he moved up the porch and stood in front of her. "And Mae?" she couldn't help but meet his glance, the flutter in her stomach matching the rhythm of her pulse.

"What?" she whispered gazing into his green eyes that lit with trouble.

"Take a shower, you smell terrible." He gave her a teasing salute and she narrowed her eyes. Closing the door behind him, she leaned against it as the vines slithered into each other and knotted themselves up.

She missed him as well.

Maeven regretted the miserable cold shower she took in the washroom. The pressure barely built up enough to give her more than a bucket dump's worth at a time and she was now covered in grime *again*. The hike toward the waterfalls was *not* what she was expecting.

Beck had returned *without* Caius which meant they did have to walk the extra thirty minutes to the Western Trailhead. The waterfalls lie north of the village, a few hours up one of the shorter mountain trails. It was moderate enough to appease Adventurers who couldn't commit to the full Seven-Isle Hike, but easy enough that any skill level could traverse in a day.

The waterfall was where the naiads chose to build their headquarters. Their log cabin was big enough for the running of the eco-educational walks and river-boat tours.

The biggest draw to the waterfalls was the tiny vial of healing water, barely ten drops, that the naiads sold in their gift shop. They'd negotiated their own terms back in the initial opening of the park—a genius decision from their former matriarch.

Both Maeven and Beck broke off from the main road into the forest when they saw the sign for the Waterfall trailhead. She'd never been big on hiking up the mountains. It had nothing to do with exercise and everything to do with her lungs and lack of breathing as the air grew thinner. Her breaths were ragged an hour into the hike, and she was extremely grateful when they came upon several downed trees.

She paused where one made an easy spot to roost while Beckwell worked to clear logs from the path. Rummaging in her office bag, she brought out one of the pastries she'd saved from that morning, taking small bites while watching Beck work.

She pulled her eyes from his form and stared into the leaves of the trees, looking for anything to distract her from his arms and how they grasped the limbs, dragging them backward with ease—the entire trunk thick enough for two to wrap their arms around. Maeven bit her lip, the thoughts in her mind turning indecent as she looked away flustered.

Absolutely not! She reminded herself while fanning her face and cramming the last of the pastry into her mouth.

"Ready?" Beck called from where he stood, hands on hips, foot lifted on the trees that now sat on the side of the path. He only needed a cape and a powerful fan to blow his hair back and he'd look like her favorite childhood hero Dashing Rob Roy.

"Yes, ready," Maeven called and shook the thoughts from her mind. She thought of Urian, her fiancée, and wondered what political mess he was getting caught up in. He loved a good conspiracy theory about the Council. It helped to calm her racing heart and bore her mind.

They continued without speaking; walking and stopping for Beck clear debris from the forest paths. His back muscles strained beneath his light shirt, dragging the logs individually out of the road so the Adventurers wouldn't complain later. His forearms rippled with tension when he effortlessly tossed down the logs. While Maeven was thankful for the clear path, it exhausted Beck, and cost them time.

Maeven was true to her promise and did *not* help Beck. At one point they had to clear a pesky Clurichaun nest that had taken over the trash can at a resting spot. Maeven did lend her *intent* and helped push the swarm away from their faces as Beck cleaned it out.

The reached the waterfall an hour later, much further and longer a hike than she remembered, and stood before an unlocked iron gate about four feet high. It separated them from the naiad's land.

The waterfall was heard in front of them. Hundreds of feet high, tumbling down the side of the mountain from three different points, into a wide pool spreading out in front of Maeven and Beck. It appeared a cool, welcoming reprieve after the sweaty hiking—except Adventurers were not allowed to swim in the sacred waters.

They *could* have their photo taken in front of it as a memento!

Further down the lagoon, the pool split into two rivers; one that wound its way slowly down the mountain and provided rafts for the Adventurers to ride—lifeguards were stationed along the route—while the other falls was a river boat tour that circled back around to the lagoon pool and asked for hefty donations.

Maeven let herself through the gate—more for show than to keep anyone out—and continued into the waterfall area in search of Marisol. She ignored the wooden bridge on her left which led toward the rivers and continued around the bend where the two-story log cabin stood. The bottom floor had been renovated as a gift shop which the naiads stocked with vials, less than ten drops each, of healing water and jewelry made from island river rocks—also with healing properties!

The second floor was where Marisol and the other female naiads lived. They were a sisterhood devoted to the protection of the waters on-island and preferred to live apart from men.

Maeven aimed for the log cabin, instructing Beck to check the rides while he waited. She headed for the porch grateful to finally collapse on the front steps. She puffed a few deep breaths and stretched her limbs preventing a cramp. Maeven hadn't hiked in quite a while.

Composure regained, she pulled a bit of *intent* and flung it over herself to fluff her hair. She straightened her hiking shorts and blouse, re-tied the scarf around her neck, then entered the gift shop.

It was quiet inside; the overwhelming rush of the waterfall no longer pierced her ears. The sunlight filtered into the shop and lit the various items for sale. She walked through the short aisles and found the back door with a sign: Park Employees Only. The door opened into a hallway where a set of stairs led to the second floor. Maeven listening to the muffled voices and footsteps above.

"I'm here to speak with Marisol," Maeven called up the landing, hoping someone would hear and come out to greet. She weighed her options. After fidgeting at the bottom of the stairs for several minutes, she began the ascent of the wooden stairs then rapped loudly on the door.

Chapter 10

The door flew open seconds later. Marisol appeared to float before her like a regal goddess. Maeven brushed her hair back from the sweat that again clung to her neck.

"Meadhbh Mathers," Marisol's voice was low like a deep well. She stood taller than most women with long graying hair, skin that glowed like the river dirt with wide eyes behind a wrinkly smile.

Marisol had been a friend of Maeven's grandmother, almost an aunt to Maeven in her younger years, and got along especially well with Eliza. For a while, before the death of Maeven's father, Marisol had been a staple in her household. Afterwards—well nothing was the same after her father died.

"Hello Marisol, do you have a moment to speak?" Maeven put on her brightest smile, a sense of ease washing over her from the room.

"For you, I have several." Marisol stepped back and opened the door wide. She held her arm out and gestured for Maeven to join her inside the home. Maeven nodded a thanks and stepped through the door, tea immediately pressed in her hands by an adopted daughter.

The adopted daughters were the orphan naiads of the rivers and lakes. Usually left on the riverbed for Marisol to claim. No one on the island really knows where they come from, but they all love Marisol as their mother and are happy to remain with her by the waterfall until they are grown.

Maeven thanked the daughter and sniffed the tea. The heat was rising and easing her tired bones. She was happy to sit on one of the couches in the large open living room. The area encompassed the kitchen and dining table, enough seating for upwards of twenty daughters. The numbers had always stayed between seven and thirteen in the house. A closed door in the far wall led to the private sleeping quarters where a faint baby's cry was heard.

"A new daughter?" Maeven asked as a teen daughter emerged holding a girl, no older than two years old.

"Hmm," was Marisol's reply as she turned to welcome the child who reached her arms out yearning for the older woman's warm touch. Maeven almost felt the urge to climb into Marisol's lap beside the toddler and snuggle into her embrace. The little girl pressed her head against Marisol's chest, listening to the waves in place of a heartbeat. Maeven knew from experience how comforting and soothing it was. Marisol stroked the girl's golden hair softly, eyes closed, then kissed the top of her head. "Our newest daughter from the Goddess,"

Naiad children were gifted by Nantosuelta, the winding-river goddess. Her depiction was shown on a tapestry hanging on the wall behind Marisol. The Goddess stood in the middle of a river, holding a cornucopia of eggs, a naiad daughter hatching from one in the middle. Fertility and abundance of nature were prevalent in everything the Goddess touched. The tapestry went on to show how the daughters hatched from eggs in the lagoon of the waterfall, toddlers, swimming and diving amongst the waves created by the falls. Older daughters plucked them from the waters to dry them off for Marisol to name.

"Beautiful," Maeven murmured admiring how natural child rearing was for Marisol. Something the women in her family lacked.

"You look so much like her—" Marisol reached out and stroked Maeven's cheek, moving her hair to the side for a better view.

Maeven's body froze. Her mind grew fuzzy and ears filled with white noise as she blanked out Marisol's words. Her mother, Eliza, Maeven *did* look like her. All the women in her family looked the same—one generation after the next. They were cursed in that way: forever destined to be the only female of their generation, passed down through a line of women who didn't have a motherly bone in their body.

"Spitting image, still?" Maeven joked and lifted her face to Marisol's, a smile plastered there against the ache in her chest. She hated talking about her mother; hated the way everyone smiled and praised Eliza for her naturamancer powers and ability to create healing ointments. Eliza loved and cared for the villagers on-island but had been rather absent from most of Maeven's life.

"In every way," Marisol continued to study Maeven's face, lost in her own contemplation as she stroked the little girl's hair.

"Have you spoken to her recently?" Maeven tried to sound nonchalant about asking.

"We spoke just this morning," Marisol confirmed. The answer alarmed Maeven and hurt a little to hear that her mother had reached out to others on-island.

"Did she send a message?" She was rather embarrassed that she even needed to question if Eliza had reached out, indicating that she hadn't heard from her either.

"She sends her love and wishes you *an adventurous season*." The thin smile stretched tighter on Marisol's face and the adopted daughter began to fuss and push against the arms wrapped around her. The girl started to cry, and Marisol soothed her once more, but the little one would not be tamed again.

"As she would," Maeven tsked.

"You Morrigan women will fight against each other until the very end." Marisol shook her head without acknowledging the hurt that was behind Maeven's eyes. Marisol had always coveted her neutral stance on the stubbornness and pride that Maeven's family possessed.

"Daughter," Marisol called the older sister over and handed the squirming child back. Maeven took the moment to acknowledge the griffin in the room.

"Thank you, Marisol, for seeing me under the circumstances of my—job appointment—for replacing you." Maeven didn't want to look the woman who had been like family to her in the face when she thanked her, but knew it was the *right* thing to do.

Marisol met her eyesight and softened again, her eyes glistening with tears that she sniffled backwards.

"Oh Meadhbh," Marisol came forward and hugged the young witch. "I always knew you would take over from me one day," pulling back and she glanced Maeven over like a pecking hen, "I just didn't think it would be so soon!"

Maeven laughed and a few tears slipped down her cheeks. "I'm thirty-three, how old did you want me to be when I took over?"

"Oh at least live your first one hundred years of life before settling down," Marisol chuckled at her own naturally long lifespan. Whereas Maeven's ancestor, the original Morrigan, was an immortal goddess, each generation saw a shorter lifespan than the last. Maeven would only live to be a few centuries old.

They moved through the open kitchen and sitting area to an office with two glass doors.

"What questions do you have, Meadhbh?" Marisol was one of the few who called Maeven by her full name.

A walnut desk stood in the center of the small square room, the walls lined with bookshelves that gave just enough space for Marisol to move around to sit. The trinkets along the shelves were selectively chosen to represent important items in Marisol's life, river rocks, framed original nametags from the first adopted daughters, a basket of apples, and several shells from the beach. A square window against the right wall had its shutters thrown outward, opened to the cool breeze and the sounds and scent of the waterfall.

"A few, actually." Maeven seated herself on the settee; hurriedly setting her bag on her lap and beginning to ruffle through the files for the one on giants.

"Something easy to start?" Marisol joked and placed a pair of square glasses on her face then held her hand out to accept the file from Maeven.

"Well, do you know about the G.I.N. coins?" Maeven handed over the file that Bennie had given her the night before. It went unnoticed by Marisol who simply set it on the desk unopened.

"The coins are not good for the springs, especially with the young daughters wondering about." Marisol folded her hands on top of the desk and leaned forward intently.

"I completely understand," Maeven nodded and looked at the carefully prepared file. "Can we find a solution, though?"

"Absolutely, you should probably take that up with the Giants." Marisol nodded and urged Maeven to continue. Maeven was confused by Marisol's words. She seemed to give answers that invited more questions.

"Um, yes, okay, about that—where do I find the Giants?" Maeven asked since she had never sought them out before. Even her wildest summer nights didn't involve the Giants who were a solitary species and not to be messed with. Their size alone was enough to warn Maeven off and she never agreed to Aldrick or Beck's begging to hunt for their homes.

"Aye, you've probably never been to the Fomorians camp." She looked down at the file, opened it, scanned the first page, and closed it again within seconds.

"Of course, I would never want to become involved or overstep my position—"

"That's exactly what your job is, Maeven." Marisol gently put a hand on her knee to stop Maeven from speaking. "You're in charge of the island, everything that happens is now your business and it's your business to know the answers. Do you understand?"

"My business?" Maeven wasn't sure how that connected to the giants but remained silent to listen and placed her hand delicately upon Marisols to hold.

"Of course, your position as Overseer is to make sure there are *no questions* about the AdventureLand, so you should never have any questions of your own. Everything is yours to know, and you should always seek answers when needed." Marisol cradled Maeven's hand in hers and squeezed tightly.

"But how do I seek answers if I'm never supposed to have questions?"

"You need to solve the questions before you need the answers." Marisol nodded but Maeven was still very confused.

"How—do I know, which questions need to be answered?"

"That is your job to understand."

Maeven could tell the naiad was trying to impart serious information to her, in a puzzle-ish way that only made her irritated. She liked facts and files, and specificities spread out in a spreadsheet. She liked to know exactly which items were needed to complete what project and when it needed to be completed and how it was supposed to be completed to satisfaction.

The unknown was terrifying.

"Know questions—about, *what* exactly?" Maeven was very confused and not following Marisol's train of thought at all. "Marisol, I don't understand—why would there be questions about AdventureLand? What does that have to do with the Giants?"

"The Giants are only trying to bring awareness to their species, and I signed an unbending agreement. You'll have to seek Arron out and speak with him," Marisol shrugged and let go of Maeven's hands, leaning away to relax against the tall chair-back.

"Where might I find Arron?" Maeven asked to write down the information as Marisol listed the location of the nearest bridge. The Giants liked to group together up stream in the mountain crevices where the melting snow became river heads.

Maeven didn't have the proper clothing to hike into the snowy terrain, her last pair of shoes were absolutely ruined now, and she would have to make a separate trip later with better equipment—or just send Beck.

Marisol nodded and made her own list of notes. Maeven noticed how diligent she was about taking careful notes...not at all in-line with what the Council referred to as "sloppy" and "inadequate" work.

"You haven't noticed anything strange, have you?" Maeven asked, successfully catching Marisol off guard, which had been her intention.

"In what regard?" The older woman blinked several times but kept a neutral face.

"Oh—" Maeven bit her lip and scanned her brain for the right words, "Has anything unusual happened? Or *not*, happened, I suppose? Perhaps the waterfall or the eggs? Anything out of the ordinary?"

"Our fells are healthy, and the waters flow free." Marisol responded in her eloquent way of phrasing. "Why do you ask?"

"The wisteria hasn't bloomed yet," Maeven murmured and hesitated to say more. She got a sense there was something amiss, a tingle down the back of her spine. Maeven thought back on the small, odd moments she had noticed around town and shook them from her mind.

"The wisteria often blooms late every few years." Marisol shrugged nonchalantly, "Just like the pecan trees give an abundance every other year, wisteria often need to pull back to regenerate their flowers for the next season."

"Have they always done this?" Maeven asked. She hadn't studied such a phenomenon in her biological classes at the University. She studied almost every plant and flower variety on-island and wasn't familiar with this breed of wisteria.

"As long as I've lived." The naiad was several millennium old which reassured Maeven. Perhaps the pixies hadn't rationed their adequately. She would need to order supplies from the mainland to get them through the Adventurer season if that were the case.

"The curse upon the fountain, Marisol, what can be done about that?" Maeven didn't want to sound like she was begging, but she was certainly about to start begging.

"I believe we have Dr. Naidu; she may be willing to speak with the teens and see if she can work the memory from them." That was new information to Maeven. She was becoming used to the lack of communication on-island.

"Dr. Naidu? From the University," Maeven was surprised but remembering the professor from the night before. Dr. Naidu sat on the University's board as top bard in the nation and wrote the book they studied about oral storytelling and recanting memories. If anyone could coax the story of the curse out of the over-baked teenage naiad memories, it would be her.

"The same, she's studying memory loss, specifically in relations to mis-aimed curses and is very interested in this topic. She'll be here for the summer and has agreed to help."

"Wonderful." Maeven repeated as she wrote the notes down on her pad. She remembered seeing Dr. Naidu the night before and wanted to bend her ear on the histories of the kelpie.

"Any additional questions?" Marisol confirmed nodding.

"Did you know Tempest was missing?" Maeven didn't know why she asked the question. She knew Marisol had nothing to do with the imp's death, but she was confused at the silence of the islanders. "Why didn't you tell the Council about the disappearance of Tempest? We could have been searching—"

A clap of lightning and a loud roar of thunder broke across the sky outside, causing Maeven to jump in her seat. Dark clouds had gathered above them and the afternoon quickly turned dark. It would be a long, cold walk back to the village if it rained.

Chapter 11

"Her family didn't want to alert the Council," Marisol shrugged as if the answer weas obvious. Maeven might have eventually guessed that, knowing the Rhosewoods preferred to keep to themselves.

Another boom of thunder sounded from outside followed by a bright flash of lightning. It was going to rain, and she was going to dread the hike home.

"Thank you, Marisol, for your time and...advice," Maeven finished with a smile. She still had questions, but she wasn't sure what those questions were. The nagging feeling that something was missing clung to her thoughts and caused unease in her stomach.

"You're always welcome, Meadhbh Mathers," Marisol stood and embraced Maeven in a deep hug, one she hadn't received since she was a child, leaving the island for the first time and saying goodbye.

"Would we be able to stay the night? With the rain about to start..." Maeven asked, nodding out the window.

Marisol was more interested in raising a knowing eyebrow toward Maeven, "We?"

"Beckwell is downstairs," Maeven murmured looking out at the droplets that started to fall.

"If you'd like to stay, the boathouse is open. Men, of course, are not allowed upstairs." Marisol indicated the house they sat in and how it was reserved for the adopted daughters alone. Maeven knew about their rules and wondered if they might bend them for her. Not that she didn't appreciate the boathouse, she just didn't appreciate a night alone with Beck.

"Thank you, that's very generous." Maeven stood and allowed Marisol to lead the way outdoors. They'd need to get settled before the rain really began to come down. At that height in the mountains, storms came on fast and could wipe out trails within hours. They would have no way of making it safely back to the village and she would miss dinner with Bennie's family that night.

Beckwell stood on the porch outside, waiting for Maeven, as the first drops of rain fell. "Marisol said we could stay in the boathouse," Maeven nodded.

The boathouse stored the innertubes during the winter season and had a one-room sublet on the top floor; used sparingly. With a nod, Beck grabbed her hand and ran off into the rain, the other shielding his eyes from pellets.

Maeven followed beside Beck toward the boathouse, her office bag tucked underneath her sweater though barely covered. She did her best to hang onto the strap; her head ducked against the rain, eyes staring at the ground with complete trust in Beck to lead the way, hoping not to fall. They reached the boathouse and ran up the outside steps to the second floor where the door was thankfully unlocked.

The boathouse, like most places on the island, hadn't changed since she'd been gone. It was still dark, the only natural light streaming in from the small window above the door. Beck lit the gas lamp beside the entrance and went to the far side to light a second. The room began to give a soft glow, illuminating the sloped roof and short four-foot walls covered in wood paneling.

Beck could hardly stand up straight, his head hit the low attic ceiling. He ended up scooting on his knees over to the single, full-sized bed. The room was sparse of any decorations and the only other furniture was a dusty rug, two wooden chairs, and a few boxes filled with mementos.

Maeven stripped off her sweater and stepped out of her shoes. She laid them out on the back of the chair and plucked at the wet fabric against her skin.

"Please, feel free to continue." Beck joked, watching her move the most soaked layers.

"Very funny," Maeven replied with a scoff. "My clothes aren't that wet. I'll surely survive the night."

"But will you survive sharing a bed with me?" he wiggled his eyebrows and tucked his hands behind his head, relaxing against the headboard.

"I've survived worse things, so I think I can handle it." She joked and sat on the empty side of the bed.

Beck lowered his hands, his arm going around her shoulder and she shrugged him off immediately.

"Don't get any ideas, Beck." She grabbed his hand and pulled his arm back over her head, letting it fall into his own lap. He nudged her with his elbow.

"Do you remember the last time we stayed the night here?" he questioned, bringing up the summer of her nineteenth year, when they finally gave in to their teenage desire. She flicked a bit of *intent* and pushed his body a few inches away, giving her more space on the bed.

"*That* will not be happening again." She moved the pillow from behind her back and smashed it between their two bodies as a layer.

"Oh sure, that'll stop you this evening,"

"Me!" she shrieked turning toward him, as if *she* were the one who couldn't control herself when they'd been dating.

"Absolutely, you were unrestrained!" he teased and tossed the pillow back at her. She caught it and hit him with it when he wasn't looking. She hugged the pillow to her chest and turned her body around to face Beck directly.

"What did Marisol have to say?" he continued, and she recounted most of the conversation. She didn't feel the need to bring up her mother or Marisol's weird warning—*was it a warning?*—toward the end. Some things needed to be kept to herself until she figured out what was itching in the back of her mind.

"I need you to go visit the Giants and sort this out, within the next two days." Maeven told him, impressed with herself and how assertive she sounded. "Someone named Arron?"

"Why within the next two days?"

"It seems like a feasible time allowance."

"But why do I need an allowance of time?"

"Because we have a list of places to fix and items to take care of and we have limited days available; Beck, are you serious at the moment or are you joking with me?" Maeven couldn't tell if he was kidding, and it was starting to frustrate her. She needed him to work *with* her to get the island prepared not drag tasks out longer. It was infuriating how he procrastinated!

"I'll get it done, ease up." Beck teased and reached out toward her as if she needed a steady hand. She rolled her eyes and flicked, for real this time, his hand away.

"I *am* eased up." She shifted and rolled her shoulders like that proved how at ease she could make herself. Really, she popped her back and rolled her neck for good measure.

When she looked back up, Beck was watching her; his eyes bright and mischievous, teeth biting his bottom lip.

"You're as beautiful as the last day I saw you." He murmured and chuckled low. Maeven didn't see anything humorous about his words.

"Why did you leave?" She was serious and direct. They were trapped in the boathouse with the rain pounding on the roof. This was the perfect time to ask him the question she had been wondering for the last ten years:

Why did he leave?

When she graduated from University, Beck was happy for her, he was encouraging, he was beside her the entire time—for five years of university on island four he visited her every weekend. Then he moved with Maeven to the Capital for her two years of residency before she earned a spot as a junior delegate.

The day after they celebrated, he packed his belongings and left for FarrowHaven. It was the last time she'd seen him. He sent one letter, a single line, '*I don't want this, I'm sorry*', and that was all she'd known for ten years.

"Do you really want to do this now?"

"Absolutely," she insisted and waited.

She would wait in silence for several minutes as Beck hemmed and hawed with himself. He avoided answering and sputtered nonsense before he was finally able to process what words wanted to be said.

"I didn't want—I couldn't stay in the city; I couldn't do it." His shoulders dropped in a defeated manner, but he clenched his jaw. "FarrowHaven has to have a Cromwell; the island doesn't prosper without one and it's been my family's responsibility for centuries."

"You never told me you didn't want to stay in the city." Maeven wasn't sure what she hated more: the fact that he never mentioned this *once* during their years of dating or that she knew he was telling the truth.

Beck was a Cromwell and ten years ago his father had been appointed to the High Council—Beck would have naturally been forced to step in as Protector at some point. Binding him for eternity to the island as its King of Creatures.

"I didn't know how to tell you. I'm so sorry, Maeven." Beck leaned forward and grabbed her hands, giving them a comforting squeeze and cradling them on his own.

"You couldn't explain in a letter?" she asked, realizing that it didn't make sense to be questioning what could-have been, but somehow her mind was still grasping for a better explanation. They'd wanted different things, had duties that didn't align with each other, and he *had* sacrificed a few years to be with her in the city after graduation.

Why hadn't she ever asked if he was happy?

"Mae, if anything would have taken me from the island, it would have been you."

"What is that supposed to mean?" Maeven's eyes narrowed in question. What an annoyingly idiotic thing to say.

"It was either you or the island," he dropped her hands and leaned away from her, trying to find something to look at other than her face. "And I tried to make it work with you, I thought I could do it long term, once you settled in the city."

"But you picked the island." She knew that Beckwell hated to talk things out in this way. A small part of her admitted that she liked to watch him squirm, however unnecessarily childish he was being. Maeven needed the answers more than he deserved to be comfortable in that moment.

"I didn't have a choice," he stared at his hands, his jaw clenching, his fingers picking at his nails.

"We all have choices, Beck." Maeven looked down at her own hand, where her engagement ring sat on her finger. It wasn't anything like she wanted; it didn't fit her taste or style, but she had accepted it because...because Urian was a good catch, a good fit.

Urian was well liked, loved even—by lots of people, and yet...he didn't light a fire in her stomach the way Beckwell did, even now. Sitting across from him, angry to hear that he'd chosen this stupid island instead of her.

Aren't you picking the island now, too?

"Not everyone's *intent* comes back around and causes them to stumble and fall. Sometimes there are far greater damages that affect more than just oneself."

"Spoken like a true King," Maeven bitterly muttered, upset at herself for bringing up the subject in the first place.

Chapter 12

The next morning, she'd woke in the boathouse, wrapped in Beckwell's arms, his legs entangled around her own, the blanket thrown haphazardly over them both. Maeven blasted him with icy *intent* and began the silent march home. It was barely dawn when they neared Eliza's cottage and Rickashay met them by the well, shrieking and holding a half-charred envelope.

"Tempest's family has asked us to visit." Beck read from the letter once he'd retrieved it from Rickashay's claws.

"At the imp mounds?" Maeven clarified and turned back to face him from halfway up the front steps; it was quite an honor to be invited to visit the Rhosewood mounds.

"Where else would we visit them?" Beck questioned her sarcastically since the mounds were where all the imps lived and most importantly, where Tempest's grandmother lived.

"I need to get something to eat first." Her stomach rumbled in complaint.

They agreed to meet at the Forum around noon. Maeven wanted to get a hot meal at the Tavern in town and speak with Carwyn.

Maeven grumbled to herself as she ambled into town after a cold shower. She tried, once, to get the moped started but didn't want to risk the mud splatter so chose to walk instead.

Rickashay followed her when she'd first left the house. After several shrieks, Maeven finally acquiesced to let her ride by shoulder. Now, she quite regretted that decision as Rickashay's talons snagged the fabric of her sleeve. She groaned and stamped her feet for a few minutes, causing Rickashay to shriek and tighten her grip.

With a deep breath and a blessing of prosperity, she pulled open the door of the Tavern. The bell rang from above her and she paused on the threshold for a hush to fall upon the patrons. She waited to see if they might ambush her with questions.

There wasn't.

They didn't.

The patrons ignored her and continued with their meals and conversations with naught a glance at the door.

The Tavern had certainly changed in the time she'd been gone. She must have missed the report on the upgrades and renovations made. Where before the restaurant had been dark and closed off, it was now bright and open. Where there was once a wall of photos showing generations of patrons on the island, there were now new floor to ceiling windows that looked out onto the square where more tables had been set up for patrons to eat outside.

The light they brought in showed off the colors on the walls, peach and yellow and turquoise in blobs and splotches. The cozy, wood booths were replaced with a long central wall wrapped in oak tambour where a dozen tables and chairs filled with patrons breaking their morning fast. It was so much brighter than she remembered and lacked the previous warmth.

Now, it felt rather gaudy and loud.

Behind the half-wall was a counter that ran parallel with stools for individual patrons. A mirrored wall reflected a chalkboard with fancy writing describing the different meals offered.

She found a seat at the counter and smiled when the Minotaur, Carwyn, placed a clay mug in front of her and poured hot tea into it. From his other hand, he produced a plate boasting toasted bread, an assortment of cooked meats, and two fried eggs. The amalgamation was exactly what her stomach craved.

"Water be damned, I can still make a good meal." Carwyn chuckled in greeting. "I've got a temporary rig set up in the back kitchen but mostly Nore has been lugging buckets every morn."

"So good to see you, Carwyn." She smiled wide and dug into the food. Many a summer she'd spent guzzling down his latest creation while sipping hot tea and complaining about her mother or friends—usually Beck. "And yes, I will need to take a look at any updates you've made recently."

"I thought I'd be seeing you earlier, miss." Carwyn chuckled and wiped down the counter. Like most minotaur, he was bull from the shoulders upward where the rest of his body was man. Two large horns emerged from his head; his nose was rounded in between two tusks that protruded from his enlarged bottom lip. His ears were pointed and scaly, which offset the hard leather of his hide. His frame stood towering above the patrons at seven feet.

Distracted by the bell ringing above the door, Maeven turned to see the druid, Chester Friedman, walk in holding a crate of fresh milk from his farm. The last dossier she read said Chester owned a herd of Friesian cows that produced daily milk for the villagers. He set the crates on the counter, in a braided circle of honeysuckle. The islanders believed the ritual kept the milk from souring by pulling sweetness from the flowers.

Before Chester could make his exit with the empty bottles, Maeven was spurred to remember the feed reports.

"Chester!" she greeted and popped off her stool to walk toward him, her hand held out in greeting. "Maeven Mathers, Council Representative and Overseer for the season, perhaps you remember me as Eliza's girl?" She tried to drop her mother's name which usually jogged memories of Maeven as a child.

Chester held the empty crate of bottles against his chest, a panicked expression in his eyes darting between Maeven and Carwyn without responding.

"Right, err—I wondered if I could have a quick word with you about the amount of food your herd eats—" Maeven continued earnestly but the door opened and the bell rang again, pulling her attention to where three more wooden crates appeared to hover by themselves.

"Hadid, 'morrow!" Carwyn greeted the newcomer behind the crates and stepped around the counter. He directed Chester to walk before him, simultaneously ending the conversation Maeven was trying to start, and opened the door a third time.

"Oh but—" she called behind the men, however Carwyn had already pushed Chester out the door and turned to help carry two of the crates from Hadid, revealing the gnome underneath.

"Poor Chester is too shy for his own good, he'd be frozen all day. Your food is getting quite cold, little Maevie." Carwyn interrupted before she could say more. She watched Chester round the building with his milk crate as Hadid stepped closer to the counter with the last crate.

Gnomes are, of course, quite prevalent on-island because of the mountainous terrain. There were two prominent groups: those that inhabited the Northern side and worked the caverns —mining gems that could be used for souvenirs—or leading the occasional tour to well-paying adventurers, and those that inhabited the Southern side and worked as gardeners—maintaining the open fields and orchards while supplying the village with fruits and vegetables.

"Good morrow!" Hadid responded as he disappeared below the counter. He appeared again along the far end and proceeded up a short set of stairs carved into the side. A section of the counter had been converted with a raised floor so shorter patrons could still sit at eye level. Hadid popped up at Maeven's side and smiled warmly, clasping her on the shoulder with a small shake. "Well now, if it isn't little Meadhbh all grown up!"

"Hello Hadid, it's wonderful to see you!" Maeven greeted the gnome who always had a story to share or an adventure to tell.

"And what have you been doing to keep yerself busy these days?" Hadid asked with a large, knowing smile.

Maeven wondered where to even begin or if Hadid was merely asking if she and Beck had started their relationship back again. She guessed the village gossipers talked for months about her breakup with Beck, leaving her in the

Capitol moving back to the island, single, to await her homecoming.

They *certainly* knew why she returned now.

And it wasn't for Beckwell.

"It's her first morning back, Hadid, leave her be." Carwyn interrupted as he set a similar meal in front of Hadid. The gnome clapped his hands together and rubbed them in excitement.

"Always appreciated, Carwyn." He murmured, digging into his plate.

"Well, I appreciate those morel's you've just brought me." Carwyn nodded toward the wooden boxes he'd set on the floor behind the counter. Carwyn picked up his kettle from the stovetop and poured a strong cup of clove tea for Hadid.

"Morels?" Maeven leaned toward the boxes in question completely forgetting her desire to question Chester about his grain or respond to Hadid.

"Aye, dug them up this morning, we did." Gnomes had small, muscled, fingers that allowed for digging into the hard ground.

Hadid was a fungus farmer who routinely gathered the largest, most flavorful mushrooms in the forest. His pigs were the best truffle hunters in the chain of islands. And Carwyn could turn everything into the most delicious creations! Maeven's favorite was his morel mushroom bisque, her mouth watered at the thought of eating it again.

"I see that glint in your eye, Meadhbh Mathers." Carwyn shook his finger in her direction.

"When was the last time you cooked your bisque though?" she pleaded leaning forward and peeking over the counter for a better look at the mushrooms. They were gorgeous in color, pale brown, with plenty of holes which meant they were extra nutty in flavor.

"I cook it for people who haven't been away for ten years." He replied, a point of calling out her absence.

"But now that I've returned it would be glorious of you to recreate your amazing bisque, a little *welcome home* dinner." She smiled enthusiastically and willed herself to believe she'd be lucky enough to convince him.

"*Welcome home dinner*," Carwyn huffed, "I shouldn't even have to throw one, you should not have been gone so long." The lightness of their exchange suddenly felt very heavy, and the wind was knocked from Maeven's sails.

She sat back on her stool and picked up her fork to scoop food into her mouth, avoiding a response. Hadid noticed the change as well. He quickly finished his meal and said his goodbyes, hustling out the door as a few merrow entered.

"Carwyn, can I get more tea?" an imp called from her table. Carwyn went off to help the mixed group of imps and faeries, leaving Maeven to her meal.

"Now, you listen to me, missy," an elderly faun stumbled up to Maeven and clasped his hand, hard, atop her shoulder. The movement caused Maeven to drop the spoonful of eggs down the front of her blouse. She closed her eyes and took a deep breath, pasting on her customer service smile.

"Salutations, Harold." The Council would expect Maeven to greet him like any other Adventurer, even if Old-Hoof Harry, err—Harold, was a tad on the loony side. She scooped up the runny eggs with her spoon and used a cloth napkin to dab at the yellow spot. She spied Carwyn smirking from where he poured a fresh cup of tea, and pointedly ignored him.

"The dragons," Harry whispered and waved his hands and fingers wildly in her face. He called attention to the dragonling. Rickashay was crawling around on the floor in search of bugs to devour.

"Yes, Harry, what about the dragons?" she was *going* to be respectful during this conversation. As a Representative of the Council, she would need to at least *attempt* to listen to his latest conspiracy theory. Harold deserved as much, even if he was an aging faun who was losing his hearing as quickly as he forgot what century he lived in.

"You know?" he exclaimed in shock. His eyes widened when she realized she said the wrong thing—although, *what* that could be was oblivious.

"I know...what?" she responded

"The dragons," he leaned in, voice lowered, giving Maeven no choice but to bend her ear as well. She smelled the stale malt on his breath, he'd probably been at the Dew Drop all night. "They've been replaced!"

"Replaced?" Maeven lowered her voice instinctively but shook her head of such nonsense.

"Replaced by mini–a–ture drones!" Harry's teeth were yellow, his breath reeked as he gave her a toothy grin—over-enunciating each syllable spoken.

Maeven gave a tight-lipped smile in return then sat straight again on her stool. Carwyn gave a chuckle and finally came to her rescue.

"Is he going on about the dragons again?" Carwyn called which caught the attention of several villagers who turned to see about the commotion.

"That's why they're so small!" Harry's hands waved above his head and his voice grew louder.

"Dragons have not been replaced by drones," Maeven said, loudly, to make sure everyone knew she didn't agree. Part of her job would involve dealing with incohesive nonsense that was less than, shall we say, ideal, but it was too early in her assignment to handle on the third day.

"They're spying on us!" His wheezing grew louder as he pressed his hands into Maeven's back and shook her in her seat; his faun hooves clanking against the wood floor of the diner.

As soon as Harry jostled Maeven, Rickashay screeched and sent a few sparks of fire toward the faun in warning. The dragonling flew onto Maeven's head and perched there, musing her hair with her talons and hissing toward Harry.

Maeven had never seen the dragonling so protective. Rickashay arrived as a stray that her mother found deep in the woods one stormy evening. Maeven and her mother nursed the dragonling back to health. Their nights and days were spent making sure she ate and drank and gently moved her wings and talons to keep dexterity viable. It was apparent that Rickashay had latched onto Eliza during her rehabilitation.

Maeven hadn't even realized the dragonling liked her.

"Hands to yerself there, Harry." Carwyn rounded the counter and pulled Harry toward the door.

"Be done with it, Harry!" called voices around the diner. A table full of sea-weary fishers, a mix of merrow and druids, a group of females faeries, sat eating their breakfast and bellowed after the faun.

"Everyone knows you're talking nonsense!"

"Crazy Old-Hoof Harry,"

"Why do you think them things is so small!" Harry continued pointing at Rickashay while being guided gently out the door.

"I'll see you in a few hours for lunch!" Carwyn called after Harry as he closed the door, the bell jingling in place.

Maeven wanted to disappear into the counter and pretend she hadn't accidentally encouraged his wild talk. On her head, Rickashay, cawed and egged the rousers on more.

"Hush you," she scolded the dragonling which went unnoticed.

"Always a fun sport in the morning," a faerie in her mid-thirties, near Maeven's age, appeared with a grin. The woman's eyes twinkled bright purple from their enlarged size and Maeven found herself smiling in return. She vaguely recognized her from the town meeting, sitting beside Lux.

"I honestly didn't think he was still around," Maeven whispered her reply and took several sips of water to clear her throat.

"He'll probably live for another century telling us his conspiracy theories," the woman laughed and shook her head.

Turning toward the faerie, Maeven held her hand outstretched to shake. "Maeven Mathers,"

"Siofra Danu-Cromwell," she met Maeven's eyes and stared directly into them, her hand tightening ever-so slightly in their prolonged handshake.

"Beckwell's wife."

Chapter 13

If you choose to wander off path, keep in mind,
Faerie rings may appear when not looking.
Do NOT step into the ring!
Do NOT follow the voices. Stop!
Find a FarrowHaven Guard or Villager!

"Siofra Danu-Cromwell?" Maeven's ears filled with a buzzing, high pitched tone. She must have misheard the woman—and yet—continued to smile and shake her hand. Maeven tightened her hold on Siofra's hand, or vice versa, but neither of the women released their grip.

Maeven couldn't pinpoint Siofra—her features distinct yet missing from Maeven's memory—but she *did* recognize the name, Danu. Councilwoman Danu sat on the High Council.

Siofra's skin glowed; its various colors of white and reddish-brown splotches covered her arms, torso, and face. Her dark purple eyes pierced Maeven with a pointed look. Her wings, two long, iridescent ovals that sprang from between her shoulder blades and four smaller wings along her lower spine, twitched in anticipation of Maeven's response.

Maeven slowly processed what she heard. It could be a dream; she'd been having some weird ones since arriving back on the island. Perhaps she was hallucinating. The ringing in her ears ceased the white noise lessened and she regained her balance.

Beckwell's wife.

Beckwell was *married*.

It felt like the air left her lungs. Maeven dropped Siofra's and turned away to sip—chug—her tea.

Her Beck—no, he wasn't *her* Beck anymore.

He was just Beck.

Worse, he was *Siofra's* Beck.

Her pulse sped up and a line of sweat formed on her brow. She felt the droplets beading under Siofra's watchful stare.

"We never expected to see you here, again." Siofra continued, softer, as if she hadn't dropped a bombshell in Maeven's lap.

"It wasn't planned." Maeven was on autopilot. She felt her jaw falling further down her neck the more she processed what Siofra was saying. She was having a hard time staying focused on the counter in front of her. Maeven shifted her body and took a steadying breath. She needed to leave immediately.

"It's a lot to process, I realize." Siofra continued beside Maeven. The pale yellow of Siofra's magic shimmered around her arms and wove itself through the hands she held in front of her. "Beck always said I could be too blunt. I prefer to rip a band-aid off instead of easing it with warm water."

"Quite the band-aid." Maeven barked a laugh and smiled wide—too wide—blinking a tear out of her eye. "The food must have some spice this morning."

Maeven reached down and gathered her bag with a shaky hand eyes away from Siofra so she wouldn't see her internal struggle. "I—uh—I must get my day started. There are so many shops to look at—unicorns and moose."

Maeven made a hasty exit out the door with Rickashay clamoring behind her. She was in such a hurry to leave, the door almost shut on the damn dragonling, except she turned back and caught the wood.

Instant regret hit her when Siofra followed her out. Maeven spun again on her heel and walked briskly toward the Forum. She was going to be sick.

Bolting for the closest overgrown hedge, she upheaved the breakfast Carwyn served. Her shoulders dropped and the tension left her back, a tingling shiver crawling down her spine. Maeven had never cursed the faerie's ability to possess *intent* more than she did in that moment.

Of all the issues she assumed would pop up that day, meeting Beckwell's *wife* wasn't on her list, nor was being sick in front of her, or being soothed by her empathic magic.

Maeven felt like an idiot to assume that, after ten years, Beck would still be single—still pining away for her in the woods, waiting for her to return. Perhaps a small part of her still dreamt of the possibility—hoped that one day they might be reunited and take another chance on each other— once they were older, more mature.

But she'd been wrong to believe in such fantasies.

"Water?" a flask appeared under her nose, her face still bent toward the hedges and dandelions. She took the cup and drank deeply, swishing a last mouthful around before spitting it out. The taste lingered in her mouth positive it would be there for days.

"I'm sorry," Siofra said.

"He should have told me." Maeven nodded her thanks and handed the flask back to Siofra.

Siofra answered, "I wanted you to hear it sooner, rather than later—since I suspect you'll be spending a lot of time together and I doubt he told you this morning when he fed the sheep—"

"The sheep—?" Maeven blinked and stood straight, forgetting what sheep were or why they were important to the conversation.

Siofra watched, her bright eyes intense and narrowed as they flitted between Maeven's dark ones. Her wings fluttered against her back which gave away the annoyance that her voice tried to leave out. Maeven could tell this was a topic of repeated argument.

"He went over yesterday, never came home last night, wasn't there this morning, which is more than he's done since Eliza went off-island."

The sheep.

Her mother's sheep that *Beck* claimed he'd been taking care of all winter. Suddenly it clicked that Siofra had been the one caring for them.

"Thank you, for feeding the sheep. I would have come earlier if I'd known." Maeven muttered dryly.

"Maybe that's why I did it." Siofra hesitated which caught Maeven off guard. It was beginning to dawn on her what kind of situation she may have inadvertently placed herself.

Siofra stood a respectful distance away so the two women could look at each other. She was tall and lightly muscled, the opposite of Maeven's short, curvy legs and extra padding around her arms and torso. Siofra's hair was dark, locks that fell in ringlets to her waist while Maeven's short, unruly, blonde never did. Of course, her haircare consisted of running a quick blast of warm *intent* through her strands every morning to straighten them out.

Maeven fought to keep her composure and remain professional. "Well, thank you, for letting me know." She nodded and turned, though she wasn't sure where she was going. If she went straight to the Forum to meet Beck, she would have some hateful words to throw his way.

Spotting the iron tables set out around the square, she chose the closest one and threw herself down in the chair. A wave of emotions coursed through her racing mind: confusion, fury, slightly insulted she hadn't figured it out sooner.

Why hadn't Beck told her?

Why hadn't he waited for her?

Why had she expected him to?

Rickashay shrieked, landing next to Maeven and reminding her of the audience of villagers roaming around the square. She glanced over at the Tavern where several patrons turned away when spotted through the bay windows. She almost sent a blast to shutter them closed.

What in Brighid's name have you gotten yourself into, Maeven?

"Are you in bits this morning?" called one of the teens, still chained to the fountain. Maeven looked over and sighed but stood up to deal with the fountain disaster. If she knew what, *in bits* meant she might answer but a smile also did the same.

Maeven walked to the edge of the fountain and pulled out nine hazelnuts from her pocket. Without hesitation or wavering from her desire to befriend the fountain, she approached with the nuts in her left hand. Walking clockwise, she dropped them one-by-one into the water, stepping around the lawn chairs of naiads, at equal distances When she finished, she stepped back and waited.

The hazelnuts bobbed in the water. Seconds passed. Then minutes.

"What uh—what did you think would happen?" asked Pacey, golden-haired naiad who looked genuinely curious. Jay peeked over the side of her umbrella to see if anything happened. The fountain statues took that moment to attack the four with more water.

Maeven *hoped* the hazelnuts would bribe the fountain into returning to its natural state, but she got her answer moments later when all nine hazelnuts were pulled simultaneously beneath the water.

They didn't turn to stone, but the River Goddess accepted her offering. Perhaps they might have some luck!

"Adventurous!" the naiad's cried. Maeven clenched her teeth against the slurred way in which they cheered.

"My man, pinch me!"

"I am winging out!" Ryes repeated a well-known chant that the Griffin Jousters of the Academy like to throw around.

"For Brighid's sake," Maeven tsked toward the four teens who laughed giddily. The fountain responded by shouting insults at their slang and spitting another round of water upon them. They held their umbrellas up against the stream which caused it to shoot in all directions.

Maeven formed a quick ball of *intent* and directed the water away from her clothes so they wouldn't be ruined. Rickashay cawed and dove at the fountain then began to pellet it with small fire blasts. The dragonling produced mostly smoke but there *were* a few flames. Missing as she dipped and dived, none of the fountain creatures could move their heads to properly aim at Rickashay.

"Any memory of the curse yet?" Maeven asked as the teens laughed while watching the scene.

"Nah, ma'am we don't even know what day we're on." Jay giggled and took a sip of her straw, clinking it around with the ice against the glass cup.

"Day?" Maeven tilted her head to the side and watched their faces for any recognition of the slip of tongue. "How many days have you been locked here?"

"Like four or five?" Jay shrugged and finished her drink with a long slurp. "Why?"

"Well, I could have sworn that someone commented they hadn't a good shower in weeks—" Now she was questioning her own memory.

"You must've heard 'em wrong," Ryes piqued up from beside Jay. "You look pretty tired, no disrespect."

"Have an adventurous day!" Maeven turned away from the fountain before she blasted them with cold *intent*. She grabbed her office bag from the table and headed toward the Forum. A quick whisper-wind toward Rickashay instructed her to go home. Dragonlings would not be welcome in the underground imp mounds.

Maeven stopped in her tracks when the bakery door opened, and a child skipped out. It wasn't, so much, that the girl looked like the spitting image of Siofra, but the other biological half.

Tall lithe limbs and child-size wings sprouted from her back, her skin the same vitiligo as her mother. She wore a pair of bell-bottom jeans and a ruffled top, her bare feet stomping in puddles made from last night's rain, splashing dark splotches across her legs. The water soaked her pant hemline, and she smiled, jumping into more. Maeven saw only the back of her head, covered in long, light brown curls that bounced with each step.

Until the little girl turned in her cheerful play and for a brief second, Maeven met her eyes. The same eyes Maeven had longingly gazed into that morning. Those piercing green watched her from the bakery next door.

And above those eyes, small antler buttons emerged from her head.

Maeven's heart iced over and her pulse sped with anger. She *certainly* had a few choice words to say to Beckwell Cromwell.

Chapter 14

It's important Adventurers only visit designated spots marked on the town map. Adventurers found in staff-only areas will be charged an upgraded package fee. Unsavory behavior results in seclusion time within the Forum Labyrinth.

"Why didn't you tell me you were married?" Maeven shouted down the hallway emerging into the basement offices. She knew he was in there; she could sense his presence even through the walls.

"Now is not the time!" Beckwell called back. She heard him coughing and clearing his throat, he was always anxious during confrontation.

Rounding the corner of the room, Maeven halted abruptly in the doorway, catching herself as she tripped. She wasn't prepared for the centaur, Epona, who stood beside Beck in a regal position, a serene smile on her face.

"Epona, so good to see you this early." Maeven immediately forced her mouth into a bright smile and clenched her teeth. Maeven held her hand toward the centaur to shake. The centaur nodded her head instead and Maeven chose to go with an awkward hand wave in return.

Great second impression.

"And you, Overseer," Epona said in return, the first to formally address Maeven by her title. A small nerve struck the back of Maeven's mind, and she wondered why the centaur was being so formal when before she had been friendly. "I had only a few minutes to stop by and drop off the center's report on our young victim."

Maeven noted the file that Beckwell had casually tossed on the top of his desk. It had probably been sitting there for several minutes, forgotten by the two who were speaking for much longer than *a few minutes*.

"That was quick," Maeven tried to cover her surprise as she dropped her office bag on her desk and looked back up.

"It's important to the islanders that we solve this efficiently." Epona said the same words Maeven would have recited if someone had asked her the Council's position on investigating the murder. She was impressed with Epona's view of urgency.

"I agree, we appreciate the centaurs' keen knowledge about—"

"Dead bodies?" Beck interrupted with raised eyebrows.

"A little tact, Beckwell." Maeven hissed toward him. "About various islander anatomy and ability to perform an autopsy, keeping the body at a controlled temperature—"

"I shall leave you to discuss amongst yourselves. Please send a message if you have any questions." Epona interrupted and quickly said farewell.

Maeven bit her lip, conscious that she might have over-stepped. But then she remembered Marisol's words, how it *was* her job to over-step. To think of the questions and figure out the answers before everyone else.

Or something along those lines.

As soon as Maeven heard the door shut behind the acolyte, she turned back to Beck, eyes narrowed, annoyance returned.

"Why didn't you tell me?"

"Maeven—I didn't—I should have—," he held his hands up defensively and backed away from her. Always the scared little deer.

"You *should* have, you absolutely should have!" she bellowed and then took three deep breaths to try and calm her anger. Maeven shook out her hands and flicked the pent-up frustration that was building in her fingers.

Her emotions had been unstable since her arrival on-island and the free flow of *intent* was beginning to create a pressure in her chest.

"It was wrong of me not to tell you, the first day you got back." Beckwell continued amidst the raging storm in her head.

"Yes, Beckwell, which would have been prudent as opposed to me learning about it from your *wife* at the Tavern this morning!" she hissed through clenched teeth.

"Brighid," Beck cursed and set his hands on his hips, leaning awkwardly from leg to leg as he shifted to stay in place. His natural instincts were to run during danger. Let him feel awkward in the situation *he* created by not being honest from the start. "I should have been the one to tell you, not Siofra. I'm sorry you found out that way."

"Thank you," Maeven huffed and the weight of being in the dark was lifted from her shoulders. She still held a tight knot in her heart. The feeling of betrayal, confusion and anger but it was settling. "What about lying about the sheep?"

"That was also very stupid of me," He nodded, slowly at first, then faster when he realized taking accountability was exactly what she wanted from him.

"In multiple ways, since your wife *actually* took care of them." Maeven began to tick his list of discrepancies from the past two days off on her fingers.

"She offered to do it! She likes being with the animals!" Beck deflected and shook his head.

"You are *literally* the future King of Creatures!"

"Is that *really* your concern, right now?"

"You lied about having a wife," a third finger raised since she counted two, one for not feeding the sheep and one for making his wife go instead.

"I just apologized for that." He whined.

"And what about your daughter?" Maeven's eyebrows rose as a pregnant pause followed.

"How did you find out about Faris?" He narrowed his eyes, and it sounded like he was accusing *her* of discovering *his* secret in a sneaky manner.

"I didn't actually, that one was a wild shot, but you just confirmed it for me," Maeven's eyebrows rose at his audacity. Her eyes were beginning to clear from the lustful mist that covered them last night.

"When would have been a good time to drop that nugget?" Beckwell started to ask. "When you were throwing outdated reports at me—"

"I was not *throwing* them!" she defended and wondered if she had thrown them or just tossed them gently his direction.

"—or when we found Tempest—or, or maybe when you were knocked out by Samson or maybe in bed this morning?"

"That, that probably would have been a good time." Maeven stopped him and pointed a hand at the desk like the options were listed in front of them.

"That is the opposite of a good time for me." He tried to distract her with another smile and inuendo.

She hated that it worked a bit to soften the anger in her chest. She was still mad, but he was incredibly charming as well.

Don't let him lure you.

She *did* need him on her side if she was going to fix the island problems, and now solve a murder. Maeven shook her head, not recognizing the man that stood before her.

Ten years is a long time, Maeven.

"Is there anything else you'd like to tell me?" The fight left her voice, and she asked, now, in a quiet manner which allowed Beck to take a calming breath.

"I did forget to tell you that I was married, but it's not as straightforward as you might think—"

"What about your daughter?" she interrupted. The mood for listening to how he fell in love with another woman and had a child with her, or even if it was a one-night stand that grew into marriage, had passed. She didn't have the stomach for it now or probably ever.

"Again, when would have been a good time?" Beck's eyes gazed at her, begging her to be reasonable. But she was reasonable, and she saw through his deflection.

"Probably sometime in-between it all!" she waved her hands wildly to dismiss his question. She wasn't interested in hypothetical answers to problems that no longer existed.

"Maybe when you were cradling me in your arms,"

"I was not cradling you!" Beck scoffed and rolled his eyes which only annoyed Maeven more. He *was* cradling her in his arms.

"Of course you were, you stroked my hair!" A snort left her nose before she could stop herself. It was so easy to fall into old, comfortable joking with him.

"You had bits of hay in it, I was doing you a favor. I have zero intentions of pursuing you in any way, to be clear." He insisted.

It was Maeven's turn to scoff at that and she uncrossed her arms over her chest. As if *she* wanted him to pursue *her* in any way. He was married and he had a daughter. She was engaged. She needed to remember that.

You need to remember that.

"To be clear," Maeven responded and held her hand out for Beckwell to see the ring that Urian had produced a few weeks after he'd proposed. It was a small diamond, princess cut that had been his great-great-grand-ancestors at a time. "I'm engaged."

Beck's mouth was already open from their argument, and he gaped, silently at first before producing a few gaw-huffs and then snapping it shut.

"Well congratulations, someone has finally decided to bind their soul to yours for eternity." His sarcasm was not lost on her and she narrowed her eyes toward him. "However, we do have more important things to discuss."

"The file about Tempest?" Maeven asked ignoring the hurt punch to her gut at his antagonistically dismissive response.

"No, Elva has asked us to visit." Beckwell rolled his wrist as if the motion would restart her memory.

Elva Rhosewood was the reigning matriarch of the Impian Kingdom. Her ancestors were the original inhabitants of the island. They'd been there thousands of centuries before the Council ever discovered the Other World and conceived an agreement to open the portals to tourism.

Elva now ran a campsite for tourists who wanted to "rough it" while on-island. They provided basic sites with amenities and were highly popular with groups of college friends or childless couples. Most of the families and newlyweds liked to book rooms at the hotel or inn to take advantage of the beach proximity.

"Do you see any offerings to trade?" Beck asked and shuffled through the opened boxes that scattered the room. Maeven rolled her eyes.

Of course, he didn't have materials ready when needed. He seemed to run the office out of boxes. Nothing was unpacked or put where it should be, organized for the staff to work quickly and efficiently. There was also a distinct lack of furniture in the building which contributed to the bad organization. The Council had set aside a decorating budget which Maeven was now determined they would use to their advantage.

It was impolite to show up to an audience with a matriarch without an offering. Maeven headed back upstairs to the boxes that had been moved for the town meeting. They stood against the left wall of the foyer. She rummaged through, finding trinkets and toys, dreamcatchers, metal crowns with stones melted in, wooden knights and horses, tops that started with a pull of a string and spun endlessly until stopped, wands that sprinkled dusty glitter for a few seconds at a time.

Finally, she found a box of polished rocks and picked out a bar of gold topaz. Maeven returned downstairs and tossed it to Beck who also returned from—wherever he had disappeared. He looked over the topaz and pocketed it, apparently passing inspection as an acceptable offering.

They headed back upstairs. Instead of taking the front doors, Beck led the way toward the back of the building, out a single side door to the stalls. Maeven smelled fresh hay and pine needles then heard the distinct grunt of a moose.

Caius snorted from his stall and let out a long, deep bellow. Maeven's heart almost exploded with joy at hearing the giant moose welcome. Caius had been Beck's companion for decades. He was given to Beck as a foal, lost from his mother, and Beck took him on as his first ward.

As Beckwell descended from Cernunnos, and was subsequently King of Creatures, he was responsible for every living being on-island. Orphans were automatically given to Beck to raise and rehabilitate. Caius chose not to leave once he hit maturity.

Maeven greeted Caius, who lowered his head for a scratch between eyes and ears, as Beckwell gathered the tack for the moose. He hitched the creature to the gig they'd ride to the imp mounds. A two-wheeled cart with a single bench seat, just wide enough for three people to sit comfortably. Caius had been their driver for many a wild night back in the day when she, Bennie and Beck caused ruckus on-island.

When the gig was steady and Beck finished tightening the straps around Caius, Maeven climbed into the cart. She opened the seat bench which also doubled as storage and was thankful to see it still held blankets. She pulled one out then sat on the bench, spreading the blanket around herself, tucking in the sides underneath her hips and legs, until she was cozy. She crossed her ankles over each other and folded her hands in her lap then cleared her throat, waiting for them to leave.

"Comfortable?" Beckwell teased when she noticed he had stopped and watched her. Holding the reins, he pulled himself into the gig and sat beside her. The bench no longer held three people comfortably as Maeven's arm bumped into Beck's several times while they adjusted around each other.

The gig now only held two people in *almost* comfort. Maeven ended up with her shoulder and arm underneath Beck's, his overlapping hers in an annoyingly protective manner which he insisted he needed to steer properly—like Caius didn't know every location on-island. His thigh pressed against her own, burning where touched—even through the blanket.

Neither of them spoke as Caius slowly trotted his way to the imp mounds along the edge of town. The moose veered off the main road East into the forest. They drove for some time before coming to the turn off—illusioned so Adventurers wouldn't accidentally stumble upon its location.

Caius pulled the gig along the edge of a large meadow and stopped with a huff. Proving Maeven's point that he knew his way around and barely needed Beck to drive. Dropping the reins, Beck turned his body to face Maeven and leaned in to speak.

"That serious, huh?" she widened her eyes teasingly.

"Yes, there are a few things I need to remind you about." Beck cleared his throat, and Maeven produced a dramatically loud sigh.

"Such as?" she asked with a comically pointed look.

"Such as, don't say *anything* about the Council; do not even mention that you're here because of the Council."

"But I *am* here because of the Council—the entire town knows that." Maeven shook her head at him quizzingly.

"Let's not draw unneeded attention to that fact. Let them think you're here for the summer season or something of the sort." Beck waved her concern away.

"Lying does not seem like a smart way to introduce myself." Maeven retorted unsure of Beck's advice.

"Don't lie, just don't bring it up—secondly, do not, in any way, provoke or cause offense to them, especially Mama." Beck pulled the stone out of his pocket and waved it in her face. "If they offer you something, you accept it."

"I'm not a changeling Beck, I know that!" Maeven grabbed the yellow topaz away from him.

Beck tried to snatch it back from her hand. She pulled it out of his grasp and held her arm straight so he couldn't reach. He bent toward her, leaning his weight against her chest and grabbed her wrist, aiming for the topaz. Maeven gasped when she felt his hand on her cold skin and dropped the stone. Beck pulled away, triumphant in getting the topaz back.

"Actually, don't say anything—let me do the talking." He mimicked closing and locking her lips then throwing away the key. She rolled her eyes and waited for him to finish—she certainly would have pitched the key into an air bubble and flung it somewhere far, far away if the positions were reversed.

"Yes, I'll just be a silent statue." Maeven teased so he would be appeased for the moment.

"Perfect, lastly, do not, under any circumstances, look them in the eye for long periods of time." He continued and she struggled to keep her composure. She had graduated with top marks from the University, which *he* didn't even attend. Maeven probably knew the rulebook better than Beck.

And she didn't need a reminder to not look into an imp's eye.   Impians could read your thoughts if you allowed unbridled entry through your pupils. Even a glance might reveal a closely held secret, a memory you may not even recall that could be useful against you in the future.

"Beckwell, I do not need you to tell me how to do my job." Maeven reassured him but she doubted he listened.

"Excellent," he jumped from the gig and gave Caius a pat. He walked around the front and waited for Maeven.

They walked toward the field, competing for space on the rock path that was deteriorating. The two continued for five minutes, muttering softly to each other until Beck stopped short. Maeven, who was watching the ground, throwing down small balls of *intent* to smooth and flatten the pebbles, hadn't been paying attention and bumped into his back. She mumbled an apology and stepped away amidst his chuckle.

"Why did we stop?" she glanced around their position in the middle of the field. Spread out in every direction were mounds covered in green grass and small yellow flowers of varying lumpiness. Like someone squished a ball of putty and shaped it repeatedly to see what forms could be created.

"We wait," he replied.

"Wait for what?"

"We wait, patiently."

"I am being patient, I'm simply asking—"

"We wait, patiently, and quietly," Beck closed his eyes with a grin. Maeven gawked at him and bit her tongue to stop her next response from lashing back.

After a few moments in which they stood patiently and quietly, it was her first time after all so agreed to try for ten minutes, figures began to emerge from the mounds. They strolled casually like they were walking out their front doors onto a porch. Hands on hips, strands of wheat between teeth, and straw hats shielding from the sun that was just rising above the treetops.

These were the Impians who first originated on-island. They'd never built much on the land and their ancestors hadn't thought much before selling it cheaply to the Council centuries ago. The only return was a promise to never leave their home. That was something the Council was happy to accept since they also agreed to run the campsites which, in the end, benefited everyone.

The small crowd parted for a female Impian who came swaying toward them, her hips catching Maeven's attention and keeping it as she neared. The imp wore a loose, almost see-through dress that hugged her curves in all the right places. Maeven blushed and looked away from the woman's, err perkier, areas.

Tattoos covered the woman's hands, arms, shoulders and neck, intricate swirls and twirls of vines and archaic symbols. Giant flower petals spread across her stomach. A snake tail wrapped from her left ankle, circling her legs, covering and intertwining with the flowers upwards, around her shoulder and down her right arm, its head resting on the back of her palm.

Her hair was in long, thick tendrils, the color of wet sand with gems and charms entwined. Her features were sharp; lips full, nose slightly pointed and ears moderately pointed but' covered in piercings. Her jewelry lay layered in various shells, beads, and shark teeth around her neck and waist which *clink-clink-clinked* with each step.

The only sound in the meadow.

"Hello again, Beckwell." The woman purred while walking around him. She ran her hand along his back and shoulders as she moved to Maeven.

She felt rather drowsy.

"Ribbon," Beck barked which snapped Maeven out of her bleary-eyed daze. Beck took a step toward Maeven and pulled her backward. Ribbon laughed and turned to stand face-to-face with Maeven, a flirtatious smile.

"Hmm," Ribbon took Maeven's left hand and flipped it over to look at her palm, tracing the lines delicately with her fingers. Maeven fought the urge to meet her eyes and focused on the snake tattoo. It started to shift underneath Ribbon's skin. The snake slithered before her eyes and moved toward the edge of Ribbon's palm, the entire length of the tattoo gliding around her body as it did. A long red tongue flicked out between her knuckles, dark and daunting, smelling Maeven's hand.

Maeven wanted an award for her stillness. Mentally screaming and resisting the urge to yank her hand away, she waited, for Ribbon's familiar to finish its inspection. When it was satisfied, Ribbon released her hand. Maeven clutched it to her chest and shook out her fingers, a tingling sensation lingering.

"Mama will see you now," Ribbon stared intensely at Maeven before she turned to Beck, "Only her."

"No," Beck immediately snapped. "That wasn't the deal."

"The *deal* changed." Ribbon's calm voice and narrowed eyes became much, *much* less flirtatious.

"The deal doesn't change—"

"It changed when my sister's body was *finally* found." Her response was lower than the last and Maeven strained to hear. That was never a good sign.

The shift happened quickly around them; the other Impians who watched from their front porches moved a few paces closer here and there. Even Beck's ears twitched at the tension.

"Mama will see *you*." The command was apparent in Ribbon's words even though *Maeven* was the Council member.

No offering apparently necessary.

"Wait here," Maeven removed her bag from her shoulder and shoved it toward Beck. The manual stated that Impians felt more secure without bags; knowing you couldn't easily steal their posessions. Beck stumbled backwards and stammered, fumbling with the pack in his hands. "There are snacks inside if you get hungry. Start copying your files over with better handwriting."

"You're not actually going in there, are you?" Beck asked and Ribbon's eyebrows rose at Maeven's instructions.

"I was invited, Beckwell." Maeven *did* know the rules for engaging with the Impian folk; she made high marks in class. She knew not to make any deals or agreements she might have to break due to Council regulations and she wouldn't agree to anything if she couldn't think of every possible outcome.

"Wait here," she repeated, then followed Ribbon, who'd already turned around and walked away. Maeven avoided looking at the back of her curves which swayed and subtly bounced. Maeven tried not to move her hips, so Beck wasn't drawn to them as she walked away.

Let him stare at Ribbon then go home to his *wife*.

Ribbon disappeared into the earth and Maeven kept her gait steady. Fighting the urge to shut her eyes, she continued straight into the mound and was swallowed by darkness.

Chapter 15

The darkness was momentary. A small ball of light appeared in front. It bounced and flew around her eyes. Then headed toward her head and circle until it settled back in front.

The light bobbed backwards beckoning her to follow.

Maeven pursued, not interested in losing the little light, and heard Ribbon's giggles ahead. "Little Maevie is all grown up," her voice sang as the light grew larger and brighter the deeper into the mound Maeven walked. She reached out with both hands to try and touch the walls but didn't feel anything on either side. The ground felt hard beneath her feet until she stumbled, and her knees landed on planks of wood.

The light grew and became overwhelmingly large. She tripped up the stairs, her arm raised in front to shield her eyes. Ribbon's laugh guided her with no choice but to trust that the gods would protect her from whatever game might be in play.

Impians were known to play tricks on Adventurers and villagers alike. They didn't care about the circumstances surrounding a meeting, sometimes it was the perfect opportunity to play a game with someone new.

Maeven was determined to *not* be a new toy for Ribbon.

"Quite the brave little witch, isn't she?" Ribbon's husky voice whispered beside her ear. The proximity caused Maeven to jump, and Ribbon chuckled in glee.

Psycho! Be brave, do not show your fear and irritation!

Ribbon grabbed Maeven's wrists and tightly squeezed. She froze, unable to wiggle away. Her laughter rose in an echo around the ceiling, moving upwards in a cylinder vortex and growing louder with each rhythmic squeal.

The snake's head was now on Ribbon's shoulder. It rose up, out of her body, and flicked its tongue at Maeven, bobbing back and forth. Maeven felt frozen, terrified of the snake and the howling that rang in her ears.

"Enough," a deep voice snapped.

The lights that blinded Maeven settled into a low dim around the room. She stood in the corner of a circular office—no—library? It could have been either. Maeven tilted her head upwards, feeling dwarfed by floor after floor of shelving. The ceiling was made of round glass like the observatory in the city. She knew it was the top of the imp mound she had stepped inside.

How deep underground did they travel?

The sun still shone just as brightly as if it were a one-story and illuminated the cylinder walls and spiraling staircase. It wound itself around and around the seven, eight, nine, floors that she could visibly count, stopping every ten shelves where a balcony would run the circumference. Each floor had a ladder that moved around to access the items. Not a single floor had been dusted in decades.

Shoved haphazardly inside of each shelf were thousands, upon thousands of books and items of oddities in every size, shape, color and magical desire. Maeven could have spent hours reading and studying and cataloging each item.

Where had Mama Elva grown such a rare trove of stolen treasures? These were more than mere offerings from islanders. These were prized possessions that had been missing for decades.

Did the Council know she possessed them? Aging a few items Pre-Adventurer Era, Maeven wanted to gently lift them with gloved hands into hay lined crates for transportation so they could be cared for in a museum instead of deteriorating on the dusty shelves.

"Hello, my name is Maeven Mathers—" Maeven paused in her welcome because her mind blanked on what to say next. Beck had warned her not to mention she was from the Council, and she almost slipped and went with her traditional greeting.

"I see the High Council sends only their most eloquent delegates." Ribbon's light voice teased. She crossed in front of Maeven and handed a cup of tea to her grandmother.

"It would appear," Mama Elva spoke from her maroon-cushioned armchair beside the hearth. She accepted the tea and set it on a side table without a glance.

A roaring fire lit the marble fireplace ensconced in stone. Maeven's heart fluttered when she saw the six-inch *Connemara marble stone egg* molded into the center of the mantle. It was the size of an ostrich egg and the brightest color of green she had ever seen. The marble was rare, collected only from the Northwestern side of the second island. The amount embedded in the mantle would cost a fortune. The extreme rarity of the marble eggs left them a collector for the deepest of pockets.

Where had Mama gotten *those*?

"Question?" Mama flicked her cigarette ash into a chalice—it was the *Ardagh*, used during the first opening ceremony of the tours—and beckoned Maeven to the velvet couch opposite.

Mama's long, thin fingernails rapped the rounded top of her black cane and her eyes surveyed Maeven intently.

"It's a bit peculiar," Maeven continued to stare at the head of the cane as she moved to take a seat on the couch. "A crozier studded with blue and red gems, oddly similar to the one you hold there, was stolen at the turn of the 17th century and its whereabouts have never been known."

"Peculiar indeed." Mama smiled. Her face showed age; hundreds of years and a wrinkle for each one. She was a direct descendant of the Tuatha de Danann, the original gods, which extended her longevity. She wore long pieces of deeply dyed silk draped around her bald head and down her back, imbedded with the same gems in Ribbons hair. Her clothes loosely clung to her gangly body, sinking beneath large swaths of fabric. Covered in jewels: her fingers, wrists, neck, ears and even nose; a large hoop around her left nostril connected another hoop around her ear lobe by a golden chain.

Mama looked every bit like the queen she was, the price of living for centuries.

"I remember you as a little girl," Elva spoke watching Maeven intently. "Your grandmother was a real feisty one,"

Maeven couldn't agree out loud, but she silently did.

"To business, my granddaughter," Mama continued as Maeven took the seat offered. Ribbon sauntered about the room, handing a cup of tea to Maeven before flouncing to the sofa and draping herself along the free cushion.

Maeven shifted in her seat and adjusted her skirt. How could Ribbon be so unabashed about her body? How did she feel free to cavort her half-naked form over the couch like a vixen staring at her prey—and with her grandmother sitting there, honestly!

"Drink up," Ribbon smiled at the teacup, "I made it fresh,"

Maeven had the cup halfway to her lips but paused. Why was Ribbon being so friendly? Why wasn't she more concerned or upset about what happened to Tempest? Maeven assumed that imps dealt with grief in their own way and some preferred to pretend daily life was normal.

She glanced at Mama Elva and noticed she was sipping freely from her own.

"What information do you have for us?" The question was directed at Maeven, and she glanced up abruptly, meeting Mama's eyes before looking quickly at the fire.

Brighid, that was stupid!

Mama smirked as she lifted her own cup to her lips again, eyebrows raised. Maeven mimicked Mama Elva and took a sip of the tea, honeysuckle and cinnamon, then gathered her confidence to speak.

"I want to offer my deepest condolences for your loss," Maeven first responded before answering the question. Truthfully, she didn't know what information she could release, there was hardly anything to know. She hadn't a chance to look at the file Epona had given to Beck that morning, review the crime scene, or speak with any witnesses. It was dangerous territory to trespass the unknown with an imp.

"Your condolences or the Councils?" Mama asked about her condolences.

"Both, as a representative of the Council—"

"I care not for the Council's condolences." Mama waved away Maeven's words like a pesky unicorn-fly.

"My own, then." Maeven confirmed with a nod and kept her eyesight on the ground.

The carpet was expertly woven; she knew pixie skill anywhere. But this wasn't island pixie, oh no—this was Eastern pixie stitches—work that was more intricate and braided with detailed spells and protection charms. Maeven wanted to scream about the rarity of the piece and lift her dirty shoes from the spot.

"And what do your condolences mean to me?" Mama Elva responded. What *did* it mean? Were they just *words* she'd been taught to say when someone suffered a loss? Was there emptiness behind them?

Maeven took another sip of tea to try and clear her blurry mind. She blanked again on what she needed to respond about.

"Tempest," Mama said, as if reading her thoughts. "When will her body be returned?"

Who was Tempest?

Maeven felt hot. The fire beside her warmer and larger—was it growing? Her eyelids grew heavy, or she may just be tired from the heat. "The acolytes," Maeven murmured, trying to follow the conversation while her thoughts drifted, muddled together.

Was that the *Spear of Lugh* amongst a bag of golf clubs?

How long had she been here? Why was Ribbon laughing at her? Ribbon was so pretty. She was so confident and exsssssotic.

Mama Elva clapped loudly in front of Maeven's face; scaring her enough to jump from the couch and release her *intent* directly into the ground like a jet stream. Her body flew upwards, she shrieked and fell back down on the cushion. Ribbon laughed as Maeven bounced to the ground and landed on her tailbone.

She cried out in pain and cursed, while her head cleared.

The tea.

The tea was a mistake.

"Ribbon, you must stop this nonsense!" The matriarch grumbled and shuffled slowly to the shelves, muttering under her breath. Ribbon bent down to help lift Maeven from behind. Maeven tried to push her arm away except her backside gave a sharp jolt of pain. Bruised, if not broken.

"I was just playing," Ribbon replied with a teasing chuckle in Maeven's ear. Maeven narrowed her eyes at the imp and her non-humorous joke.

Maeven could smell the spice of her perfume, cloves and nutmeg, and didn't want to admit how at ease it made her feel.

Maeven had no choice but to lean into Ribbon and back onto the couch. Mama moved about the shelves, touching every item. She clinked glass and crystal and moved books and jars in complete disorder, causing quite the ruckus. Maeven winced against the sound and tried not to think of how many centuries those items sat.

Ribbon joined her grandmother, insisting that *she* would get the item. Mama brushed her granddaughter off harshly but slowly tottered her way back to her high-back velvet chair.

Ribbon reached back into the depths of the shelves, up to her armpit, and moments later, removed a small, blue tin. She twisted off the top and scooped out a large handful of white cream with a nod toward Maeven.

"Lift your shirt up."

"I beg your pardon?"

Ribbon rolled her eyes and motioned with her finger for Maeven to turn around then indicated the cream. "It will dull the pain."

"Is that *all* it will do?" Maeven asked just to be sure the cream wasn't bespelled to turn her skin green or give her digestive issues.

"Yes, *Brighid*, I was just joking!" Ribbon cursed and stubbornly stamped her foot.

Maeven was satisfied it wouldn't cause more distress to her system and allowed the cream on her lower back and tailbone. It gave immediate relief and comfort to her body which screamed in agony. The inability to control her *intent* was vastly unfamiliar to her. She was safe with her magic, and didn't try to fly because past attempts always ended in *falling*.

"I have called you here for my granddaughter. When will her body be returned to me?" Mama Elva banged her crozier cane on the wood floor, her voice boomed at the two women on the couch. Maeven closed her eyes when the anger rolled over them, stifling the light momentarily and causing the candles to flicker around the room.

"Her body is with the acolytes." Maeven replied instantaneously. The time for games was over and Mama's patience was wearing thin.

"Damn stargazers," the matriarch muttered.

"We can release the body in a week," Maeven said without knowing if that were true. She'd find out from Beck later if she was even supposed to give a timeframe.

"Two days,"

"Five,"

"Three,"

"Agreed." Maeven nodded to seal the agreement. Before she could stop herself, she asked the next question, quietly, aimed at the ground. She wanted to be sure it wasn't directed at either of the Impians in the room. "Do you know of anyone who might have wanted to harm her?"

The tension thickened, the atmosphere in the room stilling like silence. The only sound came from the crackle and pop of the fire which roared higher and more fiercely. The two Rhosewood women exchanged a glance.

"We don't," Ribbon answered sharply. She moved away from Maeven and walked across the room to grab a towel and wipe the leftover cream off her hands.

The air felt stale, and Maeven sent a small wisp of *intent* into the room to stir a breeze. It rounded once and died of humidity.

"But you suspect?" Maeven gently urged.

"Tempest was the best of us," Ribbon gave a sigh and tossed down the towel with a nod of her head. Her mouth formed a snarl as she sucked a breath in through her teeth. Ribbon folded her arms over her chest and her fingers balled into fists. A gasp from Mama drew Maeven's attention. The matriarch clutched a fist to her mouth, biting into it, tears streaming down her cheeks.

"She really was—" Ribbon's voice choked as her tears fell freely. She swiped them from her face and turned away from the fire. "She was going to get off-island." Ribbon's voice sounded muted and strained. She cleared it several times as she spoke. "She got a scholarship to the University on the fourth island; early acceptance this spring for *hospitality and tourism*, of all the subjects to study." She barked a laugh. With the industry the Rhosewoods were known for, renting short-term campsites and entertaining adventurers as a circus act, it *was* kind of a shock. Tempest wanted to become a delegate like Maeven?

"When was the last time you saw her?" Maeven realized her remaining time was limited; the air became staler with the burning fire.

"Before winter set in, right after Yule." Ribbon nodded and moved about the room away from the heat. Perhaps she could sense the tension too. "She was going to look at apartments on the fourth island, with him."

"Him?"

"Emrys,"

"Her boyfriend?"

"He was supposed to move there with her," Ribbon confirmed, and Maeven wondered why he left that piece of detail out of his initial interview. She's memorized every detail, what little there was, of Beck's reports. Emry's story always seemed odd to her, she just couldn't quite put her finger on it.

"But?"

"But he delayed the trip for months, polo practice or a shift at the inn. He needed another few days, another week—

finally, Tempest confronted him and said they needed to go before the frost hit. I saw her on the beach during the Yule bonfire after she had a fight with him. I'd just finished the grand finale at the Big Top and met up with her there, but we parted later. I came home and she stayed to find Emrys." Ribbon turned toward Maeven who shifted her eyes again.

"And you, Mama?" Maeven asked the elder.

"That day as well," she spoke softly into the fireplace. "She asked me for the family blessing."

The woman paused, her eyes lost in the fire, farther into space than Maeven could see. Mama was in the past, thinking of her last words, her last movements with her granddaughter. Wondering what she could have said or done differently to change the outcome.

"I denied her, of course." Mama waved away the comment, confirmation that she'd cursed her granddaughter. "It isn't our place to leave the island. To think we can make something of ourselves." Mama Elva coughed a few times and straightened her posture from its slumped position. She cleared her throat and spat into a gold and gem-studded urn that looked to be made of a single piece of sardonyx, priceless in Maeven's eyes.

"Tempest could have made a name for herself," Ribbon hissed toward her grandmother. Maeven suddenly wished she were anywhere on the island except that wondrous library. The air felt steamy, and the room hummed, the books quietly vibrating on their shelves.

"She would have *disgraced* our name." Mama retorted, slamming her cane on the carpet—the Eastern pixie made carpet—and *the Lismore Crozier!* —Maeven finally placed the intricate satyr carvings of the cane head.

"She would have made us great!" spat Ribbon in response. "And you *hate* that she would have made us greater than *you* ever could." With her final word, Ribbon spun on her heel and disappeared through an arch with nothing but blackness beyond. Maeven assumed this was the entrance and exit as there wasn't another door in sight.

"That girl is a menace." The matriarch muttered with a shake of her head. Mama Elva smiled, though, as she rested her chin upon her hands, a sigh escaping her lips as her gaze returned to the fire, "Just like I was."

It appeared as if Mama Elva forgot Maeven was there. The elder became lost in her thoughts and Maeven shifted uneasily. She pulled at her blouse and arranged her skirt, crossed and uncrossed her ankles—all the while waiting.

"Maeven?" a small voice asked, appearing suddenly beside the Overseer. Clutching her chest in fright, Maeven decided she needed to do a much better job of being aware of her surroundings.

"I am Council represent—"

"Shh, just come with me," the girl interrupted before Maeven could finish her introduction. The imp couldn't have been older than eight, yet rolled her eyes and huffed at Maeven's expression.

Honestly, Maeven was shocked at herself for *still* being shocked by what she encountered on the island—even more so with believing that the imps would treat Tempests disappearance and possible murder with more respect.

Maeven stood and took a long look around the room as she slowly followed the little girl through the archway. She wanted to soak in every object with the acute knowledge that she may likely never see this room again.

"You will return," Mama Elva spoke from the fireplace with no other movement.

Maeven blinked and looked over. She was ignored, but still gave a nod of acknowledgment, perfectly aware Mama saw it. Maeven couldn't help but smile as she turned and walked through the archway, back up through the tunnel with no light, and out into the meadow with Beck.

Chapter 16

Hike across the seven Islands of the Council with a chartered ferry,
personalized itinerary and private Guard to accompany you.
Completing the hike typically takes 2-4 weeks but can be accomplished
in a shorter time frame with alternate routes.
**Additional fees may apply.*

"We need to find Tempests' boyfriend, this Emrys kid." Maeven nodded and started down the path where Caius waited. She was disoriented from being inside the mounds and her stomach flipped in circles trying to find North.

"Emrys? He's either at the Dew Drop or the Academy," Beck followed and held out a canteen of water which she tried to grab. Her arm drifted left of its own accord, and she missed. Beck chuckled, reaching out to direct her arm then pressing the canteen into her hands and guiding it to her mouth.

"Find Emrys—story doesn't add up—speak to him—anyone who last saw—with Tempest," she explained in between deep pulls of water. Her eyes felt dry from leaving the heat of the library and re-emerging into the cool Spring air. Tears rolled easily down her cheeks which she swiped away with the back of her hand.

"What is happening to me?" she asked through the liquid.

"It's the effects of the mounds; it will wear off in a couple hours," Beck explained and helped steady her whenever she veered off at a diagonal angle without realizing it. He managed to get her back to the gig with only a few scrapes—she fell into two bushes on separate occasions and watched a tree branch so intently that she forgot to duck and smacked directly into it.

Once in the gig he strapped the seatbelt tightly across her lap.

"I'm not going to fall out," Maeven bemoaned and tucked the blanket back around her legs which helped prevent them from lurching out of the carriage with every turn.

"Your bones may have lost some density while underground." He explained and grabbed the canteen seconds before her fingers lost their grip and it dropped. "They're just a bit weaker and will revert back with rest."

"Damn the rest, Beck, we need to hightail it to the Dew Drop! Do you hear that, Caius!" she insisted toward the poor moose who docked its ears backwards.

"You don't need to shout; your senses are a bit off. Just sit there and don't move." Beck laughed and jogged to the driver's seat. He lightly swiped the reins, and Caius started his slow jaunt back to town.

"We're going to the Dew Drop, correct?" Maeven turned her body—more dramatically than planned as her arm swung wildly—toward Beck and grabbed onto him.

"Stop moving, yes, I'll take you to the Dew Drop." Beck brushed off her arm and she fell back into the side of the carriage, unable to straighten her back. She remained quiet so she wouldn't distract Beck from taking her to the inn but eventually her body started to slide off the seat and she called for help.

Beck sighed and dropped the reins to help resettle her again.

The Dew Drop Inn came into view and Maeven narrowed her eyes when she remembered the dilapidated state. There was a gaggle of teenage merrows standing on the sidewalk beside the beach, Bennie at the head—her hands raised toward them like a preacher except she looked to be calming them down.

The teenagers pointed exaggeratedly toward the ocean. Looking out across the waves, her eyes squinted against the glare of the blue waves. There didn't appear to be anything amiss on the surface though she had no idea if something was going on underneath.

"I'll check the Dew Drop, if you want to wait here," Beck pulled the gig close to the Inn, enough distance away that Maeven couldn't hear what Bennie was saying. Beck dropped the reins and checked that Caius was settled before heading inside. Maeven did her best to ignore the fountain that had started shouting poetry again while the naiads groaned and opened their umbrellas.

Maeven sent a whisper-wind over to get her friends' attention. Bennie turned and spotted her in the gig. The merrow raised an arm in greeting.

"Apologies, I just came from the imp mounds and can't walk straight yet," Maeven joked as Bennie headed in her direction, followed by the teenagers.

"My condolences to the family," Benthesikyme nodded her head. Today her hair was in braids that hung down her back with a thin crown made of sea stars and shells atop her brow. Her dress was caramel colored, intricately stitched hanging loose around the floor. Her body draped in the same thin gold chains as before, hanging from her neck and wrists, and connecting to the golden waist beads hugging her hips. She was the daughter of a sea king and always looked the part.

"I'll pass them along," Maeven nodded as the group of teenagers joined them, "What seems to be the problem?"

"Ah, you've come at the perfect time," Bennie turned toward the group. They were the new lifeguards. Each merrow wore a matching white-and-green striped band around their upper forearm to signify 'in-training'. When two years of successful training were completed, they would then be given a probationary band with thicker green lines. After five years, they would be full-fledged Lifeguards, responsible for keeping the beaches and waters safe. "We've run into some problems with the G.I.N. coins."

"Ah, yes, I spoke with Marisol yesterday and brought up the concern from the meeting." Maeven murmured as she pulled her office bag onto her lap and began to rummage inside for a pad and pen. "What are they exactly?"

"G.I.N.—like G I N—Giant Island Neighbors," a bright red mohawk merrow spoke up from the circle. Maeven wrote furiously on her pad as the voices chimed in around her.

"It's a coalition of the giants spread out across the islands," Bennie explained as others interjected to add information.

"It started a few years ago,"

"—nah, nah, nah my father said it was *way* back in the day—"

"Ahh, it may have been an underground movement at first—"

"—they get such a bad rep—"

"—the giants or the Adventurers—"

"—there aren't as many bridges as possible nowadays,"

"—right, gold coins, all over the different islands—"

Bennie's smooth voice floated amongst the youth, and they fell into a hush, "Thank you all for your voices." She turned to speak directly to Maeven, "The giants ask us to hide gold coins in the waters, so the visitors have something fun to find while swimming. The Adventurers can spend them like real money at the village carnival."

"They can also collect all seven and trade a giant for a wish,"

"Beg pardon?" Maeven glanced up at that comment from a teen. It would be highly negligent of the previous Overseer, Marisol, to allow giants to trade wishes for gold coins. Maeven obviously misheard that.

"No Adventurer has ever been successful in finding a troll under a bridge," Bennie laughed off the comment and shook her head, "The coins are becoming quite the nuisance this year,"

"There aren't enough for the summer?" Maeven was still trying to understand how these coins had slipped past the Council for so many years. How had she never noticed them before?

You don't exactly stay long when you visit. And you never go swimming in the winter.

"—they're everywhere—"

"—hundreds of gold coins—"

"—filling up the beaches—"

Bennie calmed the group again with a wave and shooed them off to complete their training. "The opposite, actually," Bennie continued, her voice moving with the cadence and rhythm of slow rolling waves. "Marisol is refusing to allow them in the rivers and washes them downstream to the bay."

"She failed to mention that to me yesterday." Maeven tried to keep her own voice steady and not let her irritation or confusion sneak out. Why hadn't Marisol mentioned this fact when Maeven gave her the file?

Why did you give her the file?

Well, you thought you could trust her...

"There are too many coins?" Maeven clarified bringing her attention back to her friend then continued.

"Perhaps collect them in a basket and we'll have them delivered to the Forum. We can hand them out as a prize for completing the *Historical Tour*. I wanted to find something to entice more viewers." Thinking quickly, fixing two problems at once.

The *Historical Tour* was set up in the auditorium of the Forum around the main level floor. It was a chronological timeline of the island's history. Pictures and paragraphs showed the conception of the island, its first year's opening and subsequent improvements and upgrades. The various celebrations over the years and special Holiday openings. A lot of Adventurers would spend their days reading through the history and Maeven thought a coin would be a great prize.

She would have to speak with Marisol again. This would add another referral against the Naiad coalition. Maeven wasn't quite sure what category this violation fell under but made a mental note to speak with Beck about it when he came out of the Dew Drop.

"Perhaps you could speak with Marisol and remind her that *all* waters of the island are sacred?" Bennie asked with her eyebrows raised.

Maeven agreed to discuss the matter with Marisol—the second she saw her again—and jotted the task down on her list.

"Would you have a moment to discuss the water activities schedule?" Maeven flipped a few pages on her pad.

"Of course! You will come to dinner, since you missed last night." Bennie climbed into the gig and sat beside Maeven. She wrapped her arm around Maeven's shoulder and pressed their cheeks together, giving her a big hug before pulling back with a smile. "In a few days, yes?"

"Oh, well—yes, that sounds lovely—but this really won't take that long, and I'd love to knock it out if possible—"

"Yes, but come to dinner, meet my family first." Bennie continued to nod her head along with Maeven who could tell the two women were not agreeing to the same thing.

"I'd love to meet your family, properly," Maeven reassured her while finding the correct page and running her eyes over the list to see what might be most important to bring up at that moment. "But about the fanfare schedule, I really need to know what times the performances will be so I can make sure the *Unicorn Petting & Picture* is appropriately spaced out with the *Mead Making Class* and the *Bubble and Brew Princess Tea Party*—"

"Yes, yes, I will get all of that to you when you come to dinner. I have it in my house." Bennie said reminding Maeven that she lived on a houseboat, docked at the marina—Maeven made a note to add the marina to her list of locations she needed to double check for structure damage. The last thing they needed was a gangway breaking or a pier going out of service. That would make boarding and disembarking from the ferries a nightmare and throw the entire schedule off balance.

"Tell me about your life," Benthesikyme looped her arm through Maeven's and patted her hand, looking out across the bay. Maeven looked up from her notes, a glance at

Bennie's arm which she wasn't accustomed to and followed her glance.

Maeven hadn't realized how late the day had gotten—how long she had spent underground—and saw the sun dip against the surface of the water. She watched the waves gently lap against the shore. What could she say about her life? What would Bennie need to know that was better than the view they currently shared?

Her life was boring compared to the beauty of the island.

Her life consisted of schedules and meetings; appointments with people she didn't know and didn't like all too well. She missed event after event with the people she *did* know—and *somewhat* liked—to keep grinding away as a junior delegate. There was nothing to share that Maeven was proud of, so she kept her mouth shut.

Small heads began to bob along the surface of the water as the sun swept low. They grew larger as the merrow emerged from the water, their tails melting away into two legs as they transfigured. It was always an impressive bit of magic to watch—though it was strictly disallowed once the Adventurers got on-island to keep the magic of the merrow alive. The merrow headed over to the Lifeguard Hut starting the night shift as the group of teenagers ambled to clock out.

"Are the patrols already on duty?" Maeven wondered why they would need to guard the beaches at night if there weren't any Adventurers on-island yet.

"Oh no, just training new security for when the season opens." Bennie reassured her with a few strokes on the back of her hand.

Maeven that was silly!

Of course they needed to train for the night shift!

Like the lifeguards who watched over the adventurers is the wading section or amongst the coral reefs; security patrolled the wider banks where fewer tourists typically went—but was still open to them if they so wanted—however the wild creatures, most importantly the kelpie—ghouls who like to take the form of a horse and prey on villagers and Adventurers alike—would emerge.

Beck walked out of the Dew Drop, laughing with Aldrick. The two certainly looked chummy. Bennie stepped out of the gig as the men reached their side.

"I'll see you all tomorrow, then," Bennie waved and began to walk back toward the beach. "Dinner, day after tomorrow, yes?"

Maeven found herself agreeing to dinner at Bennies, provided they went over the list of questions she had about the water activities, schedule of fanfare performances, and the status of the various aquatic equipment—kayaks, canoes, paddle boats in the shape of a dragon—that were accessible to visitors.

"Settling in okay, sea legs?" Aldrick teased—Beck apparently told him about the imp mounds.

"Aldrick." Maeven gave a tight smile, an uneasy, greasy, scent coming from him. He had on a chef's apron that was stained and disgusting.

"I'd still like to talk to you about including my cups in the tourist packages—" Aldrick began as Beck walked around and unhitched Caius.

"I'll make sure Beck gets you the correct forms to fill out." Maeven interrupted before he could continue. She really didn't want to hear about his money-making scheme, and she was tired. Her *brain* was tired from thinking. She needed to go over the interviews again and see what clues she could find.

"No Emrys?" She asked Beck as he stepped back into the gig.

Beck waved goodbye to Aldrick before he answered. "He doesn't work today; we can find him tomorrow."

"Why not tonight?" Maeven asked as Beck aimed Caius away from the Inn and back to Eliza's cabin.

"It's getting late, you need to get home, eat something and rest. The imp mounds can do a number on you the first time you enter." Beck explained and handed her the bag he'd been carrying. She felt the outline of a food container, probably something Aldrick cooked.

"I shut the kitchen down until water was restored, why is Aldrick cooking?" Maeven asked with her eyebrows raised.

"I'll take care of the sheep tonight," Beck ignored her question which only irritated her further. She wanted to be angrier, but she was also hungry.

"Are you sure you don't want to ask Siofra?" Maeven muttered under her breath.

"Still mad?" He snorted in reply

"Still married?" She snapped.

"Still engaged?" He nudged her with his elbow. "Don't be such a child."

"You are *entirely*, a child."

Chapter 17

Report Prepared: 1 Junius
Reported By: Maeven Mathers

Summary:

[1] FarrowHaven AdventureLand is 23% completed in preparation tasks for the upcoming Summer Season. Multiple residencies are without water which, at present may, temporarily, delay the opening of Adventurer dwellings due to sanitary concerns.

[2] Welcoming Port repairs are underway with druids working daily to fix objectives assigned.

[3] The unearthing of a missing villager was recently discovered along Kelpie Beach. The Island Overseer and Protector are working together alongside the Guard to learn cause of death. The autopsy report will follow.

[4] Market Day schedule has been set for the season to begin the second week of Julius.

Objective/Achievement:

Our objective is to raise completion to 67% by week two
We hope to achieve 96% completion of remaining tasks by week three

Tasks and Assignments

The following tasks are assigned as listed below...

Maeven rubbed her dry eyes vigorously with her fists, feeling the itchiness inside. She'd been staring at Tempest's file all night, going over the scraps of information Beckwell gathered this past winter. Reviewing the previous interviews, retracing the steps Tempest took the day she disappeared according to what the witnesses described them.

"Let's review again," Maeven announced to Rickashay who was curled up by the fireplace. The dragonling was pretending to sleep but Maeven heard her huff since they'd reviewed about thirteen times already.

"Emrys said he was the dishwasher at the Dew Drop the night of Tempests disappearance. It was the same night as the Yule bonfire, special occasion for the Adventurers before the hard freeze," Maeven stood and refilled her hot tea while talking out loud.

"He finished his shift and went home for the evening." Something about Emry's timeline didn't add up but she couldn't put her finger on it.

"Aldrick and the other staff said that Emrys was there the entire night because they were busy. He left with both cooks, Rand and Aldrick, around eleven fifteen and they confirmed he went straight home."

"Ribbon, was on shift at the Big Top Tent, completing the nine o'clock performance for the Adventurers. When finished, she met up with her sister and several faeries at the Yule bonfire on Kelpie Beach. Tempest was crying and said she had a fight with Emrys earlier."

That seemed perfectly plausible. Ribbon was one of the main performances in the aerial acrobatics show and would have been on stage for the Grand Finale, around nine forty-five. Afterwards she would have been at the beach by ten or ten-fifteen. If Tempest and Emrys had fought that evening it would have been earlier than ten, but Emrys was working during that time?

A loud barking from Roscoe outside pulled Maeven from her thoughts which in turn caused the washrag drying dishes, the broom sweeping the floor, and the laundry being folded to stop abruptly. She focused better when she distracted herself with mind-numbing housework.

Rickashay hissed when the broom handle slapped her head, startling from slumber and alarming her enough to send an honest-to-Brighid stream of fire at the ceiling. The candles upon the banister and upper chandelier flared in warning that the house was upset. Maeven calmed them by billowing the ashes in the furnace and sending a blast of warmth around the dragonling.

She extinguished the remaining flames from the kitchen table and opened the door to see Beck being devoured in slobbery kisses by Roscoe.

"Good morn," he smiled widely toward Maeven as he stroked Roscoe's fur.

"Morn," she mumbled under her breath and drew her sweater around her torso, folding her arms as she leaned against the porch railing. Beck muttered gooey words toward Roscoe, saying he was a "good boy" and "the best."

Beck could communicate with all creatures, one of the many reasons he was such a good Protector. He could see the tiny changes in the earth and trees that wild griffins or an Ursidae bear made. Could feel the footsteps of a unicorn miles away and sense the slightest sounds of giant-winged predators hunting their prey.

Beck's intuitions were astounding thanks to his ancestors. If only his fight or flight instincts didn't harken toward the *flight* side.

"Why are you here, exactly?" Maeven glanced around to see if anyone was with him. She hadn't expected him to contact her so early; she hadn't even realized how early it was now that she was beginning to gain her bearings and adjust to the sun. She stepped off the porch and let her toes sink into the earth to regain some grounding. Raising her hands above her head, she took a few deep breaths—*two, three, four*—with a slow release of each one. Mornings were the absolute *worst* sometimes.

"I thought I'd check on the animals and offer you a ride into town, in case your body was still all wibbly-wobbly." He scratched intently at Roscoe's ears and avoided looking at Maeven.

"I can take care of the sheep, Beck. You don't need to feel obligated to do it for me now that I'm back." She began to move slowly through basic yoga poses—she only knew a few moves and wasn't *that* flexible, but she could do a decent warrior, mountain, downward dog, routine.

"I'd be concerned about Samson's wellness if left to your devices." He chuckled in response.

"My devices are perfectly capable of cutting off his horns,"

"Hence my concern."

"Be on your way then, feed the animals; collect the eggs as well, please! I'll get changed and meet you at Caius— is he hitched at the first circle?" she walked inside without waiting to hear his reply.

Half an hour later they met at the gig which was hitched beside the mock *Witches House*. The drive back to town consisted of Maeven and Beck bickering back and forth with each other about what important task they should tackle first that day. Maeven was perfectly fine picking separate tasks, but Beckwell insisted on working them together.

Beckwell steered Caius down the one-way back alley that ran behind the village stores. It was mostly used by the inhabitants for cutting through the mess of tourists in the main square and avoiding the trouble of navigating the fountain. The gig rounded the back of the Dew Drop and Beck pulled Caius to a stop by the kitchen door. Emrys' file said he worked as a dishwasher there.

Not many dishes to wash without water.

The Dew Drop was shaped like a U with an old stable courtyard in the center where deliveries would drop off. It was accessible by the back kitchen door or by walking around from the front porch. Either way, there wasn't much back there except a picnic table and wooden boxes used for storage. A gas lamp towered with a single candle that was usually forgotten about and therefore never lit at night.

Maeven had spent her seventeenth summer living and working at the Dew Drop when her mother's house became infested because of a backfiring spell on Maeven's part to clean the tree. Eliza didn't believe in chemicals, so they'd evacuated for several weeks while she naturally rid the bark of bugs.

Carmichael, the aging faun who owned and operated the Inn, was happy to hire Maeven on as a waitress and rent them one of the staff rooms on the fourth floor. Carmichael usually only showed up once a week to cook his famous ribs that were known island wide. Chester's cows were immortal but *did* breed quite prolifically so it was a win-win for everyone involved.

The kitchen of the Dew Drop looked the same as it had when she was a teen. The staff stairs, hidden from the Adventurers, were to her left, while the rest of the kitchen spanned out to her right.

The noise that filled the kitchen stopped when they entered. The Dew Drop transitioned between three servers each shift: one for each dining room and a third to help run food between them or take over the deck if it became too busy. A single bartender and two cooks were also on rotation. During the summer, various teenagers were hired for the more unwelcome jobs: bussing tables, cleaning dishes, etc.

"Good morn, Beck," Aldrick called out from where he stood chopping carrots. Maeven saw not one, but two, cooks standing in the kitchen preparing food and a third druid—a teenager with straight, mousy, black hair—leaning against the counter looking bored. She wondered how they were managing without water.

"Morn Al," Beck greeted and snagged a few pieces of bacon off the warming tray.

"Hello Aldrick," Maeven greeted with a wide smile. She hoped her eyes would bore into him and project the irritation she felt toward the druid.

"Good morning, Maeven," Aldrick responded just as sarcastically. The way he said her name caused her eyebrows to furrow and her lips to snarl.

She could hardly contain the disgust that washed over her face.

"This is Rand," Aldrick pointed toward the other cook who was cutting celery stalks "—and that's Olfra," the girl looked up from her place by the sink and popped a bubble of gum in her mouth. Maeven wasn't keen to speak to any of them, she was looking for Emrys, but knew they would have to interview the staff at some point.

"Nice to meet you," Maeven nodded toward Olfra who gave her a slow glance up and down. She adjusted her pants suit under the teens stare then turned away. Maeven pulled out her pad and pen from her bag to take proper notes while they talked.

"What brings you here?" Aldrick asked without looking up from his work. Maeven didn't like how he ignored them. Aldrick might be old friends with Beck, but something tingled uneasily in the back of her neck.

"We spoke with the Rhosewoods earlier," Beck explained.

"Sad news," Aldrick shook his head, his lips forming a frown—but it felt fake and forced. Maeven watched him more intently then, standing straighter to observe his reactions.

"Sad indeed—"

"Did you know her?" Maeven interrupted with her eyebrows raised. She stepped near Aldrick and watched as he slowly glanced up and gave her a quizzical smile.

"Didn't everyone know Tempest?" his smile grew, and a shudder ran down her spine.

"I thought you might have a hard time remembering, since you seem to forget that I shut the kitchen down until water could be restored." Maven let her bag fall onto the serving counter and dramatically flipped it open to pull out the Dew Drop file.

"We still have a season to prepare for, don't we?"

"It's not safe to prepare food without water."

"What does water have to do with cutting vegetables?" Aldrick responded, which made Maeven wonder about the sanitary conditions of the kitchen.

"Okay you two, give it a rest." Beck interrupted before Maeven could unleash the tirade of remarks she'd built on the tip of her tongue. Something about Aldrick stirred the fight in her and urged her to lash out. "We're looking for Emrys."

"Haven't seen him," Aldrick snapped.

"You told us last night he would be working today." Maeven could feel her customer service smile falling and her jaw tensing even more. She hated having her time wasted.

"He works *later*." Aldrick shrugged and shook his head like he didn't care that he had purposely misled them.

"You might check the school." Olfra spoke from her place.

Maeven turned. "Why the school?"

"He has practice this morning." The teen shrugged and went back to picking her nails.

"Don't you know, Mathers?" Aldrick used her last name, which she *also* didn't like being called. "Rainmeadow is going to take us to the Championship this year!"

Aldrick dropped the knife he was holding and backed up, mimicking winding his arm back for a big, low, swing with the perfect form of a polo player. Aldrick and Beckwell had been teammates in school until the accident.

Aldrick, arrogant as ever, caught a gorgeous black kelpie from the waves during the summer spawn one season. He drove the beast too much in training and practice and it fell during a game, breaking its ankle. In the fall, it threw Aldrick over its head, and he landed on his knee. He was out for the season, and the rest of their Academy years, with a torn ligament. That was also the last time kelpies were allowed in the games and the Council switched to unicorns for player safety.

"Oh, this is a games thing?" Maeven's eyebrows rose in confusion about why that mattered.

"A game thing? Maeven, it's polo!" Beck said as if that were an obvious answer.

"Can you confirm Emrys was working the night Tempest died?" Maeven changed the subject since the men were distracted by polo.

"What night was that?" A single eyebrow rose on Aldrick's face and Maven found it unnerving.

"We don't know that she *died* that night, we only know when she disappeared." Beck explained over Maeven and Aldrick's stare off.

"Her family confirmed it was the evening of Yule," Maeven refused to back down from Aldrick. She was descended from a great family of witches; her lineage gave her seniority over druids because her powers could be traced back through centuries of matriarchs. Aldrick, however, was from a simple family of mixed bloodlines with no direct hereditary power.

It made him chaotic and unstable.

"Who was on shift?" she repeated with clear diction.

"Rand and I, for sure—Olfra was off; Emrys worked dishes. Shoney and Deidre in the dining rooms and Leif at the bar." Aldrick rattled off. Maeven's eyes narrowed suspiciously. He either knew the information and kept it to himself or had practiced that sentence until it came easily— too easily.

"How late were you here? Did anyone take a break during the night?" Maeven pushed.

"Who has time for this?" Aldrick shook his head irritatingly but continued to answer when Beck didn't say anything. "We were slammed from the festival and understaffed. You do the math, Mathers." Aldrick shrugged and chopped the carrots into larger chunks of uneven thickness and odd angles, not the symmetrical shapes he'd been cutting when they arrived.

"Do it with me, run me through the evening." Maeven persisted and took a wide stance with her legs. She leaned back against the counter, arms crossed, making herself comfortable and as intimidating as *some* men tried to make her feel.

"Are you serious? The kitchen closes around ten; how long did it take to clean up that night?" Aldrick turned toward the satyr Rand, but only received a grunt in response.

Satyrs were similar in size and leanness to fauns, but their horns were like mountain goats that curled in on themselves and needed routine trimming. Rand's horns looked like they'd been roughly shaved down years before and never touched or polished again. He leaned back on his tail, as thick as a kangaroo, and sucked on a half-smoked cigarette hanging out of his mouth; the ashes clinging to the end for dear like.

Maeven made a mental note to avoid eating there during the summer and to also put a larger fine on the Inn.

"Sounds right, it took us an hour to get everything cleaned the way Carmichael likes, so eleven—eleven-thirty. Emrys took the trash out, Rand did a last sweep, and we locked up and left by midnight." He slammed a lid down on the jar of carrots he'd prepared and swept the extra pieces into a compost container.

"And Emrys didn't leave at any earlier point in the night?" Maeven confirmed again just to see if she could pester Aldrick.

"We were *slammed*. There wasn't an opportunity for a break, and I wouldn't have noticed if he *did* have one."

"Not even for the dishwasher?" she wasn't going to point out that dishes could be cleaned in bulk with the foot-pedal machine Carmichael installed. He could easily have gotten ahead in dishes and taken a break in-between service that night.

The inn was stationed along the beach, and it would have been easy for Emrys to slip out the kitchen door, run down to the community bonfire, fight with Tempest—either there or at the Inn; maybe they walked together and *then* fought—the interviews weren't clear—before he returned to complete his shift.

That would explain the fight Ribbon witnessed on the beach.

It wouldn't explain Aldrick lying.

"Thanks Al, we'll head out to find Emrys—" Beck gently grabbed Maeven's arm and began to lead her out the kitchen, through the front of the Dew Drop.

"But since we're here—" Maeven interjected and pulled her arm from his grasp. "When was the last time *you* saw Tempest?" she turned toward Olfra. The faerie was startled, her eyes darting back and forth between Maeven and Beck and began to pop her gum faster, her jaw working overtime.

"Uh, the night of the bonfire, for sure." Olfra nodded her head and snapped another bubble.

"Hmm, what did you do that night?" Maeven's eyes glinted toward the teen, hoping for more details and ignoring Aldrick's dramatic sigh.

"I was with my friends, Ribbon, actually." Olfra explained and pointed out her connection to the deceased sister.

"Then you saw Tempest, on the beach?"

"I don't remember a lot about the beach..." Olfra's voice softened, and her eyes dropped, her words becoming slightly slurred and mumbled.

"What was that?" Maeven clarified.

"The bonfire is mostly for Adventurers," Olfra shrugged, "we bailed after the ritual sacrifice and headed back to the mounds."

"What did you do at the mounds?"

Please don't be what I assume it is

"Faerie-dust?" Olfra made it sound like a question. Was she asking Maeven or telling her?

Brighid.

"Well, drugs—especially faerie-dust, are incredibly bad for your mental health so please wait until all your brain cells have developed before you begin to kill them off—"

"Rich," Aldrick muttered with a scoff that interrupted Maeven's speech. She was *not* going to address that comment.

"Secondly, no one here saw Tempest? She didn't come here to see Emrys?" Maeven turned back to the others with a finger out as she ran through the mental list in her head.

"Like we said, Mathers," Aldrick stuck the knife in the cutting board and leaned into it. He moved around the counter and advanced toward her, closing the distance so she had to look up to see his eyes. Maeven ground her back teeth together to keep a smile on her face. She hated the way her name sounded in his mouth, like he was degrading her family, "No one saw Tempest. She wasn't here."

"Did anyone—?"

"Beck, what is this?" Aldrick turned toward Beck with a chuckle and returned around the counter to pick up his knife. "You still Protector or has Maeven Mathers waltzed into town after ten years and taken back over?"

He gave her a look that dared her to refute his words. She could feel the change in the atmosphere. What was slightly carefree before was suddenly tense and uncomfortable.

"Alright, give it a rest." Beck interrupted before either could continue, again.

He said goodbye and turned Maeven around directing her out of the kitchen. Maeven could walk perfectly fine and hated that Beck bossed her around when his friends were present.

"Let's double check the dining rooms and bar," Maeven whispered as they walked through the tight hallway. It was squat and narrowed because they exited under the grand staircase in the front foyer.

Walking into the foyer was like a jump back in time. Nothing changed about the décor, still thick fabrics in red and gold with tapestries and rug carpets. The grand staircase leading to the second floor spanned a majority of the wall opposite the entrance doors.

Maeven scoffed when Beck pushed past her because dead center stood the stuffed wyvern, he'd killed.

"Hello old pal!" Beck greeted and stroked the nose of the wyvern.

"Would you like a room?" Maeven fluttered her eyes flirtatiously toward the two of them. She waved vaguely at the large book that held reservations. It sat on the built-in host counter attached off the staircase and held an ornate vintage brass cash register. The buttons were polished, and the drawer made a satisfying *ding!* when the lever was pulled. It was Maeven's favorite part about working there.

Maeven and Beck previously spent a good chunk of time making out behind that counter when he did his stint as a line cook in the kitchens.

"Uh, don't give me that look, Mae." Beck responded with a large grin. "You would have been terrified of Archie if you'd been there,"

Maeven heard the story so many times that summer she practically witnessed it herself. The wyvern attacked out of nowhere, flying down onto a field of senior level physicality students during their track and field practice with their griffins. Beck had gallantly grabbed a sword, flown his griffin after the wyvern and defeated it before anyone was fatally wounded; a few faeries were scratched when they scrambled to get off the bleachers. Beck had been glorified as a hero and the village insisted on preserving the beast as a statue. The wyvern now lived permanently at the Dew Drop and had always unnerved her. The damn things eyes followed you wherever you walked.

"Archie?" Maeven observed the dining room to the left of the stairs which held about twenty tables for casual dining and bar seating at the long wooden bar. Maeven used to spend nights there with Beck, throwing back cider shots and spilling themselves all over each other.

"He has always been named Archie; you know that." Beck responded as they headed into the dining room.

"Aldrick is ridiculously suspicious." Maeven commented.

"He has a wife and two kids, why would he be suspicious?"

"Because he answers every question I ask with a question of his own." Maeven wondered if Beck even noticed that Aldrick spoke in riddles that way.

"That's just the way Aldrick talks, he's protective of his family and friends in that way." Beck cut her off and she glared toward him.

"Protective? That was more *defensive* than protective. He was practically accusing me of taking over!"

"You *are* taking over." Beck cut her off and she met the pointed glare he aimed at her with one of her own.

"Yes, I am." Maeven agreed.

"What?"

"I'm going to take over this investigation. We can't let this go unsolved and if I don't start getting to the bottom of it, the Council will be unhappy, and then they might replace me and—" Maeven could have gone on if Beckwell hadn't interrupted her.

"Okay, I get it, solve the case if you want." He gave up without waiting to hear the rest of her reasoning.

"You don't understand, Beckwell."

"What do I not understand?" he mockingly repeated back at her.

"I'm here as a representative of the Council—"

"Oh, stop with the Council crap, Maeven, please!" he wailed as they both walked up to the bar where Leif was drying off glasses. He had two buckets in front of him, one with soapy water and the other clean. Leif chuckled while over-hearing their spat.

"I will not!" Maeven spoke over Beck.

"If I have to listen to you say, one more time, that you're from the Council—" Beck continued.

"—it is important that you take your job seriously and follow proper procedures, Beck. Look what has happened!"

"—I hope you're not insinuating that the lack of paperwork is the reason Tempest died."

"—You know perfectly well that's not what I'm talking about; how dare you say such a thing—"

"—Well sometimes I have to clarify with you because you don't always—"

"—I don't always what?"

"—don't always let me finish what I'm saying before interrupting me!" he completed as she proved his point in the process.

Maeven crossed her arms aghast.

"Ouch, that's got to sting," Leif joked.

They spoke with the bartender briefly, but he didn't have any information to offer than what they already knew. The bar preoccupied his attention all evening and he didn't notice anything until the crowd slowed down around two in the morning.

"The kitchen usually closes around ten, but the bar stays open until the last customer leaves."

Shoney and Deidre showed up for their shift, though Maeven didn't know what they'd do without water, and answered a few questions. Their stories were similar—too busy with Adventurers and no time to breathe, but Shoney had left early because her son became ill. The bar had served its last call around 4am, a round of vodka and tomato juice to a group of merrows.

Maeven watched Shoney as they answered questions and talked to Beck. She was from the third island and had married Aldrick right out of university. Maeven always wondered how he'd snagged the fiery red-haired druid since the two seemed like complete opposites. She was bubbly and sweet, her words moving quickly from her mouth in excitement to get out.

"Ah, the boys are at the shore." Shoney explained, mentioning the two children she shared with Aldrick. "The tree was cleaned up and the scene all blocked off but their huntin' for clues about what might've happened to the poor girl." She tugged at the long sleeves of her shirt. Aldrick had probably smooth-talked Shoney into overlooking his faults, including his crabby personality.

"Those acolytes spook me enough to keep me from looking," Deidre continued with a shake of her head and body for emphasis. Maeven rolled her eyes and scoffed.

"Couldn't agree more!" Shoney nodded and the two went off to see what they could help with. Maeven changed her opinion; maybe Shoney and Aldrick were perfect for each other. There were old prejudices against the centaur acolytes that a few druids still harbored. Maeven found it ridiculous and petty simply because they looked different.

Leif placed two tall glasses filled with sparkling red liquid in front of Beck and Maeven and pushed them toward the two. "It's a new concoction I'm calling, *Lovers Tryst* inspired by the constant tension between our dear Council Representatives. Let the suppressed feelings fly!"

Leif threw his hand in the air and released a flurry of his electromancer *intent*. Glitter rained around them, each spark vanishing into the wood it touched.

Chapter 18

The gig drove up to the Academy and Maeven wrinkled her face. She never got the chance to attend high school on-island but did spend many summers attempting to participate in the production, polo games, and griffin jousting, that the students performed for the Adventurers. Unfortunately, she was not very good.

Maybe the interview with Emrys would go smoothly and she could do a quick review of the Academy grounds. That would be beneficial so she wouldn't have to make a return trip.

The Academy was tucked into the North-Western side of the island. Adventurers had to walk about twenty minutes before the tips of the highest tower flag began to appear in the distance.

The main castle building and surrounding activity fields hadn't been updated since its conception centuries before. The classrooms were designed to look like familial homes or medieval rooms used for practicing magic, agility, or physical training. They used torches instead of gas lamps to keep an old-fashioned feel which barely gave off any light when the flames bounced off the stone. Lots of heavy rugs and tapestries added a bit of warmth into the halls.

The Academy castle sat atop a small hill, looking down upon the outdoor arena with raised stadium seating. During the season, the students would serve as squires to professional trainers. The trainers would joust griffins and show off the mythical beasts that lived on-island—a dragonling, phoenix, and unicorn—among the most popular. They held unicorn races around the track, and polo games in the center that doubled as field competitions in late summer. The students would train year-round to be chosen as a beast wrangler or to compete in the games. The menagerie barn and training gym were behind the arena, hidden by the castle hill where most Adventurers preferred to spend their time exploring the perfectly curated antique items.

Every day during the Adventurer season at high noon, a parade, showcasing the various creatures that lived on-island started in the center of town square and slowly paraded to the arena, gathering a crowd of watchers. There, an Adventurer would be randomly selected and crowned King or Queen for the day then get to hand out awards after the jousting, races and games.

Just beside the academy grounds, the Council constructed eatery stalls and a few rides for enjoyment: a Ferris wheel, flying swings, and a carousel that only spun in a slow circle and never moved up and down. They also set up unicorn rides and a petting arena. Students at the academy could earn extra credit by volunteering to help during the summer.

Beside the fairgrounds was the Big Top Tent where the imps performed their acrobatic and circus routines. They shared the menagerie with the Academy and many of the animancer druids helped to participate in the performances with the animals. Ribbon performed there, and Maeven wondered if they needed to stop in and check on her after her abrupt departure the day before.

Instead, Maeven and Beck walked the wooded path between the arena and climbed the steps leading to the castle doors. The path curved around the hill bottom of the hill where they came upon the menagerie, a regular-enough looking wooden building with open windows at the top. The menagerie was three times the size of the castle and boasted a glass dome that opened and closed during the seasons to keep the weather warm inside. It had individual stalls and family units —griffins preferred to stay with their young for two years before they left the nest—and the animancer druids trained and cared for them inside.

They bypassed the building and headed toward the gym right behind it. During the summer season, the Academy transformed into a zoo where Adventurers could observe the rare animals that didn't exist in the other worlds. It easily became crowded and crushed with bodies, so the gym was used for private training.

The building looked the same as she remembered. A large dirt-pack floor with carved track outlined the circumference. Various stations were set up in the center: jumping, hurdling, disc throwing, archery, fencing, and gymnastics.

Maeven spotted Emrys in a group of friends at the far end of the gym. They stretched their limbs and swung their arms with wide circles around their bodies, warming up to hurl discs and rocks for practice.

Emrys was a geomancer druid and produced a large ball of stone and earth with *intent* which he threw across the gym. The rock soared for a few seconds before losing momentum and tumbling into the sand pit, the second farthest distance of his group.

"Excuse me!" Beck yelled toward the group of teens as he and Maeven walked closer. "Emrys, we need to speak to you for a few minutes." Beckwell beckoned with his finger toward the dark-skinned druid like a disappointed dad. Maeven saw the heads of the group shoot up; their movements stopping and turning to watch.

Something felt off. Maeven slowed and paused to watch as Beckwell continued forward.

She saw the panic flash across Emrys' face. Jaw dropped, eyes darting wildly around the building for the exit. Emrys stomped on the ground and caused a crack to open in the floor. It rippled toward the two adults and would have split them off from the youngsters. Maeven threw her *intent* toward it and managed to push the crack off-course. It turned left and ran *between* Maeven and Beck. He opened a chasm, separating Maeven alone on one side and Beckwell on the other with the teens.

Emrys then threw out *intent* directly at the adults causing them to dive aside just as the clumps of earth crashed over their heads to slam into the wall. Emrys looked shocked but wasted no time sprinting out the nearest emergency door.

"Are you running?" Maeven shrieked after Beck who took off after Emrys.

"Why aren't you?" Beckwell yelled back from where he sprinted, gaining lost seconds with each long stride of his legs. Maeven had to shake her head from staring but scoffed at the thought of running. She'd already ruined two pairs of flats; she wasn't going to ruin her last decent pair by jogging after a geomancer.

"You are all to report to the Forum immediately, with or without your parents, for interviews." Maeven chided the remaining teens who watched silently.

She nodded once then turned on her heel and walked back out the main gymnasium door. The door of the gymnasium shut behind her just in time for her to see Emrys come darting around the left side of the building, Beck on his heels. Beck gained a last ounce of speed and closed the distance with a giant leap forward. He tackled Emrys and wrestled him to the ground on the front lawn.

Maeven sent a blast of *intent* separating the two as they rolled on the ground with each other. Weaving her *intent* into a fist, she used it to grab the front of Emrys' shirt and lift him from the ground and hold him steady.

"I didn't do anything! I never hurt Tempie!" Emrys exclaimed, still struggling against the fist holding him in midair.

"Why would you run?" Beck leaned over, his hands resting on his knees to steady his breathing, then coughed a few times and took a deep, gasping breath.

"Will you survive?" Maeven teased as they waited for Beck to regain his composure. Surely, he couldn't be *that* out of shape though he did seem to exert a lot of energy when running.

"I don't run as often as I should." Beck responded before he straightened and stood beside Maeven to address Emrys.

"Why would you *run* if you didn't do anything wrong?" Beck gave a disappointed look, hands on his hips and seconds away from shaking his pointer finger.

"How did you even know we were here to ask about Tempest?" Maeven said at the same time.

"I have the right to Council representation." Emrys demanded. It always shocked Maeven when the villager's showed knowledge of the Council rules.

"As a representative of the Council, I hereby invoke—" she began.

"Not here," Beck interrupted and nodded at her *intent* which still clutched Emrys in a fist, his feet dangling off the ground. "Let's take him to the Forum."

Maeven agreed and released her *intent* on Emrys. He fell to the ground, rightfully deserved, and Beck kept a firm grasp on his upper arm as he stood. The trio walked back to the gig where Caius waited. Maeven took her seat and Beck squeezed Emrys into the small space between them.

The ride back to town was quiet and uncomfortable. Maeven mulled over the situation presented to them.

Emrys previously claimed he didn't know anything about Tempest's disappearance. If he was sticking to the same story, that he had been at work all night and didn't remember seeing Tempest, why would he run just now?

Why would Ribbon say they were fighting if Emrys claimed he never left?

When they reached the town, Caius pulled in front of the Forum and Beck tied off the gig. Maeven waited at the entrance for him to retrieve Emrys and followed them inside. Beck led the way downstairs to the various offices and interview rooms. They didn't have many problems as there was usually a tonic that the bartenders would administer to the Adventurers to calm down or sober up quickly to avoid being held in the labyrinth long.

"Through here," Beck held his arm out and indicated one of the first doors. She followed the geomancer into the room, sparsely decorated with wooden furniture, a square table, four chairs and a desk shoved in the corner that was overloaded with unorganized files. Maeven's eyes narrowed on the pile, and she made a mental note to grab the entire stack before she left.

"Do you need anything to drink before we begin?" Beck seated Emrys at the table and brought out a fresh file with empty forms to fill out. Maeven guessed it was a new incident report and wanted to be sure the correct notes were taken this time.

"I'll write," Maeven indicated the empty file. Beck glanced down and back at her.

"Sure," he mumbled and slid the paper across to her.

Maeven smiled and clicked the pen as she straightened the form and looked at Emrys. She laid her left-hand palm up on the table and nodded at Emrys to place his own upon hers. He did so, and she covered it with her right hand before she spoke. "As representative of the Council, I hereby invoke the protection of the Island over the words you speak today."

She and Emrys both bowed their heads and released their hands. He sat back in his chair, relaxed, and waited. "What do you want to know?"

"When was the last time you spoke with Tempest?" Maeven asked before Beck could begin.

"I told Mr. Cromwell before, the last time I saw Tempie was the night of Yule." Emrys took a deep breath then launched into his story. "We'd been fighting a lot about her scholarship to the University on-island four, I wasn't so sure I wanted to move, and I thought she might be messing around behind my back."

"Messing around?" Maeven perked up as this was new information. "Why did you think that about Tempest?"

"I didn't," Emrys shook his head and swallowed, "some of the guys said they saw her at the Dew Drop when I wasn't there. When I asked Tempie, she freaked out on me and started accusing *me* of trying to break up with her so I wouldn't have to move off-island."

"Did you want to move off-island?" Beck questioned.

"Of course I did, I loved Tempie." Emrys quickly responded with a shake of his head.

"Loved?" Beck noted.

"Love. I love her, I always will." Emrys enunciated each word and made a pained look toward Maeven.

Something still felt off, though she couldn't quite pinpoint *what*. She knew Emrys was telling the truth. When she offered him protection, it allowed a small, white, tendril of *intent* to reach between the two that only she saw. Technically, Emrys *could* see it, but he didn't have the training to hone his senses for clarity. It gave Maeven the ability to tell when he was lying, though the sensation was more like playing a game of hot-and-cold than receiving specific answers. It was left up to her own interpretation and decision—which could sometimes lead to bias against Council members.

Naturally, Maeven took her job and responsibility with the utmost seriousness. She focused on Emrys' words and tone to make sure she understood his reasoning in the way he meant whenever her wrist grew warm, cold or somewhere in between.

"When you say you 'love' her, can you be more specific?" Maeven tried to get a read on whether his response was leaning more cold than hot.

"Huh?"

"Tell me more about the arguments you were having," Beck interrupted before Maeven could ask another clarifying question.

"Like I said, my friends saw her with someone at the Dew Drop and when I asked Tempie about it, she bugged out on me and started yelling. I yelled back, and the next thing I knew, we'd broken up so then I left." He shrugged like he wasn't that upset by the news.

"Left where?"

"The Dew Drop," he shrugged again, "that's where we were when we fought."

"You're sure?"

"Yeah, I'd just gotten off my shift for the night and we were out back, you know that place behind the kitchen?" Emrys pointed in the general direction of the Dew Drop Inn and its facilities. Maeven and Beck both nodded that they knew the place. "We fought out back and I left to enjoy the rest of the festival."

Emrys dropped his head between his hands and hung his head, looking tired and defeated. "I should've stayed to make sure she got home."

"What time did this argument happen?" Maeven spoke before Beck could escort Emrys from the room. A thousand more questions were going through her mind, but the two others appeared to be wrapping up the interview.

"We were slammed until ten, so it was just a little after that." Emrys shrugged a third time and Maeven wondered if it was a tick or a new gesture that the youth thought was a good form of communication.

"Why did Ribbon say you fought at the bonfire?" she pushed.

"The bonfire?"

"Yes,"

"Oh, no, no, that was during my break, earlier in the evening." Emrys confirmed nodding his head.

"Your break?" Interesting.

"Yeah, even when we're slammed, Carmichael makes sure we get a quick break to throw our sacrifice in the bonfire." Emrys nodded his head and waved his hands while talking to emphasize his words. "I ran down to the beach, threw my dried satchel in the fire and had to turn right back around because of the rush."

"What time was that?" Maeven pulled her notes from Ribbon and those at the Dew Drop out and scanned the times indicated.

"Right after the bonfire was lit. I offered my ransom and then ran into Tempie who wanted to fight but I didn't have time. I told her to find me later."

"Later at the Dew Drop?"

"Yeah, we had that fight out back and that was the last time I saw her."

"You didn't seek her out the rest of the night? Did you go to the mounds at all?" Beck leaned forward picking up on Maeven's unease about the situation. There was still something that didn't make sense and was tickling the back of her brain.

"Not with the rush and no extra hires from Carmichael," Emrys rolled his eyes. Maeven did agree that the old faun was getting stingier with extra hiring around the inn. The outside certainly looked like it could use a group of druids to fix up the appearance.

"Been a bit stingy with the budget lately?" Beck joked.

"He said the Dew Drop couldn't afford to house and feed the extra staff and needed to rent out the rooms to Adventurers instead." Maeven's eyes narrowed at that news. It wasn't a problem briefed by the Council and she certainly hadn't been aware that Carmichael might be in financial trouble with the Dew Drop.

"It's a shame what the tours have done to the island," Beck muttered so low under his breath Maeven almost imagined it. She pretended to be preoccupied with her notes so he wouldn't know she overheard.

"Did anyone else have a break that night?" Maeven needed to connect a few more dots.

"Uh, I really don't remember" shrug "I wasn't paying close attention."

"What about in the kitchen, Rand or Aldrick?" she pressed.

"No, they didn't have time. Rand is a beast during rush time and Aldrick never stops screaming; Shoney left early that's about it."

"Shoney left early?" her pen flew across her pad; grateful she learned dictation at the University. She remembered it had briefly been mentioned but no one had enumerated.

"One of their boys got sick, off fluff-mellow at the booths. She and Aldrick fought about it in the kitchen, then Carmichael told her to go take care of it. Shoney left to pick up the kid and take him home."

"What time did she leave around?"

"Eight-thirty or nine?" Emrys nodded and watched her jot that down on the notes. She met his glance and gave a reassuring smile.

Alarm bells were going off all around her brain as she tried to connect the missing piece of the puzzle. The tendril still wavered in a lukewarm temperature so she couldn't tell if Emrys was lying, telling the truth, bending the truth, omitting it or a combination. *Something* still didn't feel right. Emrys had yet to tell a clear lie, but his answers were...off.

"Alright, you took a break earlier in the evening, you don't remember when, but we could assume it was seven, seven-thirty since that is when the sun would have set, and the bonfire lit—" Maeven rehashed to make sure she kept up. "So, you ran down to the beach just as the bonfire was lit, threw in your sacrifice—good on you—got in a small disagreement with Tempest, and jogged back to the Dew Drop to finish the evening. Shoney left around nine, what time did you leave for the evening again?"

"Uh, eleven?" Emrys leaned back and ran his hands over his short, coiled hair with a relieved sigh. Maeven sat up straighter though, because his answer was different this time.

"Eleven?"

"Yeah," Emrys' hands fidgeted but he took a deep breath and kept talking, "We had to wait for the late-comers and stragglers to finish eating. The bar was going strong, but the kitchen closed so we could clean up. I took the first load of trash out and that was when I saw Tempie and we broke up. I had to finish the rest of the dishes and when I took the next load of trash out, she was gone.

"So, you didn't take off after you fought with her?" Beck interrupted and clarified Emrys' earlier statement before Maeven could.

"I guess not, it was a long night and six months ago, I can't remember all the details. But I know I got the dishes done around eleven, Aldrick took the last trash out while Rand swept, and we all left soon after."

"Aldrick took the trash out?" Maeven paused her pen against the paper.

"Yeah, there was a lot that night, everyone was helping. Aldrick took the last load out for me and when he came back in, we all left."

"Out the back door?" Maeven tapped her pen against the paper and mulled over the timeline.

"No, the front doors." another shrug which Maeven was starting to detest. It felt rather nonchalant while discussing such a serious manner. "Aldrick treated Rand and I to a round at the bar and I couldn't pass that up."

"How nice of him." Maeven muttered with a forced smile.

Usually, Carmichael allowed a complimentary drink after each shift. Maeven imagined a second free drink would be heartedly accepted on the night of Yule.

"That changes your story a bit, Emrys," Maeven said and tried to keep her voice light and calm, soothing. "You said that you left from the Dew Drop to enjoy the festivities of the festival."

"I did, after I had a couple drinks at the bar, Lief can tell you he saw me there." Emrys held his hand up in protest.

"No one faults you for having a few drinks," Beck calmly calmed the kid down. "We just need to make sure your story matches and you're not misremembering."

"Or lying," Maeven smiled at the two as they turned toward her. Emrys' face was one of shock and surprise and Beck one of annoyance.

"Was that needed?" Beck asked.

"Was it not?" Maeven responded looking between the two. She knew that Emrys wasn't lying, but he wasn't honest either. "Alight Emrys, so you stayed and had a few drinks—what did you do after that?"

"I went to the bonfire." He responded.

"Did you *actually* go to the bonfire or was there another detour?" Maeven's eyebrows rose as she waited for the teen to be honest with her.

"I went to the bonfire and spent the rest of the night with my teammates," Emrys nodded, and Maeven could sense he was being distinctly truthful. It irritated her for no reason.

"Well, I think that wraps things up." Beck interrupted before Maeven could respond. "Cut the bond Maeven, if we have more questions, Emrys, we'll come speak to you at your house. Let your parents know they can contact me with any questions."

Beck escorted Emrys out of the office after Maeven cupped the teens hands in her own and whispered the reversal words to cut the bond. She picked up the stack of files once the two had left and walked them back to the main office that she decided to take over and quasi-share with Beck.

The office was centrally located—the first room she'd found him in—easy to find. It was big enough for her to move two of the desks into an L-shape, a total of eight drawers, so she could spread out with extra space. She also moved a large rectangular table into the middle of the office which she spread the new files over to sort and stack.

She moved Beck's desk to the other side of the table, with only two drawers, and began assigning him files to work through when he returned. She made a note to plan on spending a day in the office doing housekeeping and sorting.

Everything was a discombobulated mess, and it drove her crazy to look at.

Maeven found herself mulling over the information that was still missing from Emrys' answers. The reports didn't quite match up. Emrys claimed he couldn't remember the last time he'd seen Tempest—whether it was the bonfire or at the Dew Drop—and even though he hadn't been lying outright, he was obviously keeping secrets from them.

The fact that Aldrick lied wasn't surprising to her. Aldrick said earlier that Emrys had taken the trash out, but Emrys just confirmed that Aldrick had *actually* taken the last load out—could he have seen Tempest after her fight with Emrys?

Aldrick also claimed that no one took a break that night—except Emrys went to the bonfire and fought with Tempest—according to other witnesses. Aldrick also failed to mention that his son was sick and his wife, Shoney, had to leave early to pick him up instead of taking one on the chin and leaving the kitchen with one cook instead of two for the evening.

Who was he protecting? Or was he protecting himself? Maeven didn't *want* to admit she could see Aldrick doing something so horrible, but the possibility wasn't far from her mind.

Chapter 19

Faerie & Friends Bakery offers a variety of delicious
breakfast & bakery items spanning all your dietary needs.
Hours of Operation are from Sunrise–Mid Afternoon.

"Emrys is innocent," she said as soon as Beck returned to the offices.

"Why is that?"

"His story has an immense number of holes in it—"

"Immense?" Beck teased while nodding along, his curls bouncing with each bob of his head.

"—but I didn't get any sense of ill will or outward deception from him." Maeven continued and ignored him. "His answers were lacking but he was mostly telling the truth. Whatever he drank or smoked that night is likely at fault for his lapse in memory."

"Or it could be the six months that passed." Beck responded.

"I don't see why you're being so casual about this."

"Not casual, more like reserved. I'm not accusing every villager who was within proximity of Tempest that night."

"Perhaps you should be," she gave him a pointed look, still angry over his own lies. She turned to the large table and began sorting the new files, her arms hovering over the table as she worked with her *intent* to move the papers into proper piles. Some of the files needed to be re-copied or needed new folders so she set those aside to work on later. "You need to bring Aldrick in for questioning."

"Why should I do that?" Beck asked, then paused and looked at her with a chuckle. "You can't be serious about shutting down the Dew Drop; they *have* to get ready for the Adventurer season. They're understaffed as it is and—"

"It's not about the Dew Drop—although I will have to fill out *another* referral for the direct disobedience related to that matter, but that is another subject—this is about his lie this morning."

"What lie?"

"He lied about seeing Tempest that night. There's no way he didn't know Emrys went on break, and he didn't mention Shoney leaving early."

"That doesn't mean he saw Tempest," Beck shook his head and crossed his arms over his chest. Maeven was distracted by the cut of the muscles in his forearms, his button-down shirt rolled at the sleeves to the elbow. She glanced back at her work and focused.

"It absolutely does, it places Tempest at the Dew Drop the night she disappeared."

"That doesn't prove Aldrick saw her or was any way involved."

"Aldrick is a naturamancer." Maeven pointed out.

"There are twenty of them on-island, at least," Beck countered.

"He's the best with wood,"

"Don't let him hear you say that his ego is big enough."

"Did you see how smooth the inside of the tree was? It could only have been made by a naturamancer with talent." Maeven paused in her organizing to rummage in her bag for the piece of bark she'd kept from the beach.

"Again, that doesn't mean it was—"

"How many druids, living on-island since last Yule and stayed on-island during the freeze," she pointed out as a fact since most of the inhabitants went off-island for the winter freeze. The temperatures dropped so low the entire bay froze over and it was five miserable months without any off-island travel until the spring thaw. "Who can mold wood in that way, who saw—or at least *heard* if they fought outside the kitchen—Tempest the night she disappeared?" Maeven ticked the items off her fingers and held her hand up for Beck to see.

He high-fived it and she rolled her eyes.

"Look at the signs, Beckwell."

"The acolytes will tell us how she died."

"Didn't Epona drop off the report? Where did it end up?" she started to look around the office since Beck had been the one to receive the report.

"I don't remember where it ended up," Beck muttered and casually looked around without a real worry.

"Did you even look at the crime scene? There were signs of asphyxiation around her neck." Maeven continued and indicated her own neck to emphasize where the marks had been.

"That's a big word for you Mae," he rolled his eyes and then rubbed them slowly. "But why kill Tempest?" Beck asked, moving in the opposite direction of where she thought he was headed.

"Emrys said his friends caught her with *someone* at the Dew Drop. If she was messing around with Aldrick, maybe she broke up with him to leave for university?" The explanation was the best she could come up with at the time.

"His solution was to *kill her*? I think his wife and kids would argue against such an extreme measure." Beck countered.

"Well, if they'd been fighting that night in the kitchen, it wouldn't be surprising he would lose it again later when Tempest broke up with him."

"I don't see Aldrick doing this; he and Shoney have always had their fights; it was a busy night and they were both exhausted."

Maeven's fingers flashed *intent* toward the cup on his desk and flung it toward his head. Beck's reflexes caught it a moment before it smashed into his face. He looked at her in shock before his hands traced the cup. The mug was one that Aldrick sold at the Dew Drop Gift Shop and asked to be sent home with each Adventurer. Beck had several lying around the office, half filled with whatever concoction he'd been drinking at the time.

Beck studied the cup, and she could see the cogs working together in his mind; teeth turning slowly as the gears warmed up.

The cup was identical in color to the tree Tempest was entombed inside.

The cup had a smooth, polished inner which held liquids in the same fashion the tree was like a coffin.

"The cup could be tested against the pieces gathered on the beach." Maeven whispered, aware of the delicacy of the situation.

"I, uh—I'll talk to—" Beck cleared his throat and shifted uncomfortably. "I'll have the acolytes do the test, let's wait for the results.

Maeven stopped by the Tavern on her way home, deciding that a hot meal from Carwyn was better than whatever snacks she could scrounge up. Thankfully the next day would be market day, when she could stock up on food for the cabin. She wanted to avoid the bakery, mostly Siofra, the head baker, as long as possible.

"Good eve, Meadhbh," Nore greeted as she entered, the bell above the door signaling her arrival.

"Hello, Nore, all well?" she asked, taking a seat at the counter and dropping her office bag on the floor with a loud thud. She'd spent the last few hours organizing the forgotten stack of files and packed up the smallest pile to tackle at her mother's house.

"Indubitably," he responded with a chuckle. Nore loved to pick a different word every day and see how many times he could use it in a sentence.

"That's good to hear," she sighed with a smile. Her brain hurt after the long events of the day, and she was ready to fall into bed that evening. Carwyn appeared from the back kitchen, a line of dishes along his left arm. Chester emerged from behind him looking visibly agitated. Shaking his head, the animacer quickly left the Tavern.

Carwyn swept around the dining room, dropping off plates and bowls and picking up dirty dishes. He refilled drinks and made a table of faun children erupt in laughter. Lastly he returned to the counter, dunked the dirty dishes in a bucket of water before passing it off to Nore who disappeared into the back. Carwyn picked up an empty teacup and set it in front of Maeven to end his dance.

"Any news from the Council?" Carwyn asked by way of greeting while pouring the tea.

"No updates to report," she smiled and gladly accepted the cup; cream and one dab of honey.

"Do you prefer savory or salty this evening?" he asked, and she mulled over the choices.

"Savory," Maeven concluded with a nod of her head and Carwyn retreated to the back kitchen to prepare her dish.

Maeven considered the events of the day, running back the conversation at the Dew Drop and separate one at the Forum. There was still a missing piece that bothered her mind, like a burning itch she couldn't reach and scratch. Lost in her thoughts, she didn't hear when the door opened again, the bell ringing lightly, until it slammed shut.

Turning to see who had entered, Maeven met the narrowed eyesight of a small faerie-faun. She supposed that was her lineage: half stag goddess, half faerie. Her features were eerily like her father's; a mob of similarly colored curls around two knubby antlers that emerged from beneath—she wouldn't grow a proper set until her teen years—tan ears that flicked back and forth, and a pointed, delicate face. Her eyes were wide and bright, darting from side to side, appraising the dining room before locking back on Maeven.

She stepped forward timidly then gained confidence and closed the distance between them to sit on the stool beside Maeven. Her hands barely cleared the counter, and her feet dangled off the ground, but she sat facing Maeven, who glanced at her nervously while clutching her tea.

"Who are you?" the girl aimed toward Maeven with fierce curiosity. Maeven felt like she was being pressed against a fence by the weight of the *intent* behind her words. Beckwell's daughter might be more powerful than Maeven assumed—not that she had thought very long about it so far, she hadn't had the extra time with the island's conditions, the death of Tempest, and limited time before the Adventureland opened.

"Who—I, um—I'm an old, your dad and I were—I spent summers here, as a kid—you're a kid, when I was a kid—like you," Maeven stammered as she drew upon her own *intent* to wave away any residual leftover from what the girl threw. Maeven was lucky she was still a child which meant weaker magic easily dispelled. But Maeven's stammering was proof enough that she was momentarily compelled by the little one.

"Who are *you*?" Maeven finally managed a full sentence though it wasn't exactly what she'd hoped for. Her own eyes narrowed toward the little girl as if *she* were the one to be cautious about.

Brighid above what has gotten into you, Maeven?

"Faris Pompeia Etiennette Danu-Cromwell." The girl confidently announced, chin held high.

"And you?" Faris held her gaze and spoke with more ease than Maeven could muster.

"Don't you be interrupting our Overseer, now, little Faris." Carwyn chided as he emerged from the kitchen again, this time carrying a plate filled for Maeven. He set it down in front of her and her mouth watered at the potato hash with gravy that was before her.

"I'm not bothering her!" Faris responded loudly, in protest. Carwyn chuckled and ruffled her hair with his hand.

"Surely with all that hollering you are!"

"I won't keep hollering," Faris giggled.

"I'll bring you something sweet, my little faun." He replied, pouring a glass of milk and setting it down in front of Faris. The milk reminded Maeven of Chester's hasty exit.

"Is everything alright with Chester? He looked agitated," Maeven tried to sound nonchalant about it.

"When?" Carwyn replied, also trying to sound nonchalant.

"Just now, he left as I arrived." She took a bite of the buttered roll smeared in gravy.

"Ah, old Chester is always grumpy about something, he'd complain about a clear day." Carwyn brushed the question off and retreated into the kitchen again to make something for Faris.

"Why is my ma mad?" Faris set her milk down, a line of liquid still above her upper lip, and turned to Maeven the second Carwyn was gone.

"I don't know your ma," Maeven shook her head and turned away. She wanted to make space between herself and the child, she really didn't want to talk to anyone associated with this girl's life—neither Beck, nor Siofra, were on Maeven's current list of villagers to seek out in conversation.

"Me ma is Siofra Danu, you know her well enough, so I hear." Faris retorted with a shake of her head.

Danu.

Maeven forgot about the Danu line. She hadn't realized that Siofra descended from them, the oldest line of faerie lineage on-island. Danu was the Goddess of nature and fertility, and her descendants were the faerie folk that lived throughout the Seven-Isles. Combined with Beckwell's own parentage, it was not surprising that the child could compel an adult, even for mere seconds.

Maeven was cornered but she wasn't bested yet and shoveled another mouthful of food before she replied. "I don't remember the name; I'll have to look at the ledgers when I return home."

"And my dad, you know him, he showed me where you live." Faris continued then drank another slurping sip of her milk.

"I don't know who your da is either," Maeven almost hissed the words through her teeth but remembered that Faris had nothing to do with her father's past and there was no reason for Maeven's rudeness. Lying wasn't exactly being rude, was it? Because Maeven didn't feel like she was technically lying. She knew Beck, of course, but she didn't know *da* Beck.

"Well, my ma says you're going to ruin everything." Faris shrugged just as Carwyn returned with something sweet for Faris.

"I'm not—ruin what?" Maeven's head turned suddenly at those words, but Carwyn gave a roaring chuckle to intervene.

"There's no one going to be ruining this season. It's all going to go according to plan." Carwyn continued.

"Plan? What plan?" Maeven asked, did she miss something?

"Your plan, the Council's plan—for the season, of course." He continued to reassure her that she hadn't, in fact, missed something important.

"Oh, yes—well it would be easier if Marisol would return so I could ask her some more questions." Maeven complained since the thought of wasting another day hiking out to the waterfalls was angering.

"She *is* back!" Faris spoke up loudly and Maeven eyed her with curious optimism.

"How do you know that?" Carwyn asked.

"Because she's at the waterfall, I saw her there." Faris nodded and continued to dig into her porridge with cinnamon and berries.

"I saw here there recently." Maeven so Faris wouldn't feel alone in her correctness. Faris turned to her with a smile.

"See! Told you!" Faris responded to Carwyn and dug a spoon deep into her oatmeal.

"Ah, I supposed you *did* know that." Carwyn wiped down the counter with another chuckle and wink at the exchange.

Chapter 20

Rickashay accompanied her to the village the next day. Puddles from overnight rain caused Maeven to crookedly walk down the lane and avoid the mud. She was finally going to check off an item from her list she had been avoiding.

The Faerie & Friends Bakery.

Maeven rounded the corner of the Tavern when she reached the village and reminded herself that she was now Overseer of the island and had a job to do. The questions would be short, straight forward, and not time consuming.

You can do this even though she scares you.

She found herself walking toward the bakery, its front bay window extended over the street and showed off three shelves of goods baked that morning. Delicious donuts dunked in icing, bagels smeared in cheese, pastries with fruit centers and chocolate.

So much chocolate.

The bell above the door announced her arrival, the inside of the store a bright pink color with lots of upper windows giving an open, airy feeling. An L-shaped counter opposite the door had a glass counter covering every baked good imaginable.

Soda bread, scones, crumbles, cakes, and mincemeat bars. A fruit pavlova, miniature bread pudding and trifles. The confections would be offered to the Adventurers once the park opened. The smell was overwhelming. She sighed and felt instantly at peace.

"Be right there!" called a voice from the back of the store. Maeven had tried to plan it so only Lux would be working and no one else.

"Oh," Maeven muttered when Siofra popped her head out from the back. The faerie walked forward and carried a tray of fresh strawberry pastries, twisted into braids and filled with cream.

"Good morn, Maeven." Siofra welcomed cheerfully without missing a beat.

"Good morning, Siofra." Maeven squared her shoulders and lifted her chin confidently.

"Can I offer you anything?" Siofra swept her hand around the shelves, indicating the array of items.

"A loaf of sourdough, and two of those cherry pastries, please." Maeven ordered as Siofra nodded. Maeven glanced around the shop, looking for anything that might be out of code. It all appeared normal and put together. The walls and floors were cleaned. The shelves were neat, and the counters wiped of any mess or residue.

"How has your time been on-island?" Siofra asked while pulling the pastries from the glass case. Maeven's mouth watered at the smell. She forgot how much she missed the food on-island.

"It's, uh—" Maeven fought for a diplomatic response. Siofra's smile was easy going and felt genuine. Maeven found herself softening, an urge to tell the faerie about all the problems she was juggling. "It's been busy." Maeven smiled and nodded her head a few times as if this was something she and Siofra agreed upon.

"I supposed it would be with the death of that poor girl," Siofra commented and wrapped up Maeven's order. She waved her hand, and the items flew into a pastry box that closed and tied with ribbon. Both the pastry box and bread went into a cloth sack that floated toward Maeven then hovered in midair.

"It's definitely been a lot, with the islands other issues as well." Maeven decided to keep it simple.

"I can hardly imagine what the Rhosewoods are going through." Siofra shook her head. "We all assumed she was already at the University,"

"That's what I heard." Maeven nodded and wondered if Siofra would say more but she only smiled and waited.

"I wanted to do a quick inventory of the bakery stock, if you don't mind." Maeven rushed before she lost her courage. She pointed to the back of the bakery for permission to look behind.

Siofra didn't seem fazed at all and only smiled quizzingly. "Beck said he took care of our review." She held up a finger, signaling for Maeven to wait a moment, then walked to the back room while calling. "He did a sweep of the store and said everything was set. He even gave me the certificate to hang up in the back."

She walked out front again and handed the certificate of approval to Maeven. Sure enough, the bottom showed a large green APPROVED stamp that signaled the bakery passed all regulations for the new season. Strange that Beck hadn't mentioned this to her.

"Oh, oh yes! He did mention something about this!" Maeven responded instead even though Beckwell had *not* done anything of the sort. She handed the certificate back then grabbed the pastry bag gently so the items wouldn't tilt over. Maeven mumbled a rushed goodbye and fled the bakery before Siofra could say anything more.

Rickashay cawed at her when she rejoined the dragonling outside. The bag clutched in her hand and her cheeks seething with anger at Beck. She had brought up her concerns to him the first night when he showed her the import balances for flour and how much product the bakery seemed to be losing. How could he go around her and approve the opening without showing her the paperwork?

Maeven hid herself around the side of the building and stamped her feet. She released a few blasts of angry *intent* into the ground then composed herself with several deep breaths. She still needed to go back out to the town square and check over market day.

It was a weekly tradition for the villagers to set up their individual booths around the town square to hock or trade their wares. Some brought vegetables and fruit from off-island, others traded necessities, while more would sell homemade potions or medicinal concoctions from herbal family recipes.

Her favorite was during the winter market when foreigners would bring in exotic items. Lipstick that doubled as a love spell when used, gems imbued with good luck or necklaces that gave you translation abilities. Carpets that flew on their own and wardrobes that picked out your outfits. Clocks that spoke to you and planned each day, feathers that could turn into pens to write a single letter or rare plants that could eat pesky Clurichaun—Maeven was always on the hunt for those.

You could usually find items needed on market day, or someone who could produce them within a few weeks. Maeven checked the booths and introduced herself to the villagers while she shopped for items. She selected vegetables and fruits from the gnomes, then got some meat and fresh cheese from Chester to go along with her bread. He agreed to start a weekly milk delivery at Eliza's cabin and sent her off with her first quart. She bought honey and spices from the pixies and picked up the newspaper from the fauns.

Beck and Lux stood outside the bakery stall laughing together and selling Siofra's baked goods. Maeven could see the bouncing head of Faris behind the table as she skipped behind her father. Seeing him beside the little girl, they looked like spitting images of each other. A shiver ran down Maeven's spine at the realization that Beckwell was *actually* a father.

The entire while Maeven took diligent notes and listened to the villagers' complaints. Several were concerned about the amount of damage the Adventurers were causing the coral reef. One merrow, selling fresh oysters eaten straight from the shell, had an idea to give a presentation to the Adventurers that swam in the bay before allowing them access. Maeven thought it was a good idea and asked the merrow to write a proposal that she would take to the Council.

Another faun complained that there wasn't proper rest time in between performances along the marina road. Heels and hooves were cracking from dryness in all equine creatures. Maeven agreed to discuss the Councils financial backing of a new ointment that several elderly fauns had developed. The trial runs had proven successful including unicorn and satyr hooves.

She also met with the pixies and promised to order more fabric from off-island to offset the lack of blooms that year. Maeven hoped that Marisol was correct, and this year was a typical period of rest for the tree. She didn't know how financially stable the island could be long-term if they had to import the silk.

The fountain continued to be a nuisance. Dr. Naidu had taken the time to talk with each naiad chained around the base, attempting to hypnotize them into remembering the curse. So far, progress had been slow and unsuccessful. Dr. Naidu delegated several students from the University, who weren't too happy being demoted, to umbrella holder/water guard protecting the doctor whenever the fountain retaliated.

Maeven stopped by briefly to get an update, but the unicorn responded by starting a particularly long Ovid about the first centaur to drop from the sky. Dr. Naidu decided to call a lunch break as they had already heard the tale three times previously.

Maeven spent the rest of Market Day completing paperwork at the Forum and answering questions for the villagers who stopped in to visit. Merchants started to seek her out with problems. It turned out, she was more *efficient* than Beck and made sure tasks were completed to everyone's satisfaction, meaning they would last more than one season.

She special ordered wisteria thread for the pixies from the Eastern islands and had it put on rush delivery. They thanked her for that, then returned an hour later to hand over a rather extensive list of organic ingredients they needed to fertilize the wisteria trees. She didn't know where she was going to find the guano of a ram-horned snake, but she would talk to Bennie and Beck about it.

She then made a round to Chesters's farm to see what she could do to help with his herd. It turns out they were producing less milk because he kept the calves with their mothers longer than regulated. Maeven spent a long day talking to him about the benefits and drawbacks of weaning the youngsters early to allow proper milk delivery around the island. He agreed to *consider* the idea.

Finally, she and Ty monitored the shipments of tools and supplies scheduled for transfer to the Welcoming Port. A team of druids had been selected and would begin rebuilding and repainting the current storefronts. They also needed to make sure the cooling systems were in working order. Crowds were always busy in the beginning and would tetter out during the heat of Augustius—they *had* to get the cooling system up to code before Helios settled above the island. The heat would become unbearable without proper precautions.

Maeven found her chance to investigate behind the Dew Drop the next day when Beck finally arranged to travel up the mountain and complete the task of speaking with the giants. She decided it was the perfect time to do some of the snooping he had dissuaded her from earlier. The first of which was checking out the area behind the Dew Drop.

Maeven left the Tavern after breakfast and took the back alley that Beck had driven down previously. Her plan was to sneak around the porch and look at—what she believed— to be the scene of the crime. It made the most sense based on the ramshackle timeline of Tempest's whereabouts the night she disappeared. Piecing together information from the interviews was unreliable for finding out the truth. With her little knowledge, she assumed Tempest fought with Emrys at the bonfire, then showed up later in the evening to confront Aldrick, which happened when he brought the trash out back—

"What are you doing?"

Maeven shrieked and jumped from her position, crouching in the back alley, across the street from the Dew Drop. Maeven had gotten swept up in her thoughts while sneaking through the alleyway and didn't realize she had caught the attention of a child.

"Go away," Maeven softly whispered to Faris who had appeared over her shoulder without warning. Maeven *really* needed to become better at noticing her surroundings.

"Why?" the girl responded and gave her a weird look. "Who are you looking for?"

"I'm not looking for anyone."

"Okay, what are you looking at?"

"I'm looking at the lamppost to make sure they're not running out of magic." Maeven made something up off the top of her head.

"The lamp posts have candles; they don't run on magic."

"How do you know?" Maeven raised her eyebrows, unsure why she was pretending to argue with a child.

"Really?" Faris questioned and tilted her head confused but also wanting to believe what she said.

"Absolutely, you should check each one in the village and let me know if any are low. Go, shoo." Maeven responded and directed the little girl in the opposite direction. Faris left, giving her a confused smile as she disappeared just as quickly as she appeared.

Maeven didn't wait any longer but tried to nonchalantly dash across the street without being seen and headed to the back of the Inn. She stepped off the porch and surveyed the twelve-by-twelve-foot space, barely big enough for the picnic table and lamp that was back there. The bottom of the walls were gray stone, quarried from the mountains. Maeven ran her hands along them to check for any nicks or missing pieces. She didn't see anything and followed the wall along all three sides until she came to the lamppost.

She paused and looked at its dull black color. The shine had long left the lamp, and it was usually left unlight—because no one remembered it was back there. She ran her hands along the spine, feeling for any denigration points where a bit of residual *intent* might have ended up.

Maeven was about to give up when her hands felt a small lump along the bottom of the lamp post. She felt it again, dark and crusty on the outside but squishy when she touched it, like a blob of paint that hadn't dried in the center. She lifted her finger and felt the wetness on the other side. Opening her fingers, she saw the black crust had a hint of rusty red. It could be blood but was too old to be positive.

The backdoor of the Dew Drop Inn opened with a loud creak. "Hello!?" a cheery voice called out in surprise. Maeven stood and jumped back, her bottom and hands hitting the picnic table which she instinctively gripped. She rubbed her finger along the underside of the picnic table to get rid of the evidence.

Chapter 21

"Everything alright, you look frightened?" Shoney asked as she stepped down from the back steps in Maeven's direction. The woman reached forward and ran her hand along Maeven's arm while searching her face.

"Yes, yes, I'm terribly sorry, you surprised me." Maeven shook her head and pantomimed being scared by the door. Shoney grinned but asked again.

"Are you sure you're, okay? I'm headed home and can make you a cup of tea if you'd like?" Shoney graciously offered. Maeven perked up at that suggestion.

"Yes, that would actually be lovely." Maeven accepted with a sigh and a smile as she fell into a step beside the red head. She could use this opportunity to ask Shoney questions about Aldrick and find out about his behavior in the months leading to Tempest's disappearance.

"How has your time on-island been?" Shoney asked. Maeven found it funny that Siofra had phrased it the exact same way. It must be taught in the staff manual under *Conversation Starters with Adventurers.*

"It's been busy." Maeven responded and the two chatted casually as they walked.

Shoney's home was just off town square. It was...modern and looked like a town home Maeven might see back in the city. Unlike the others on-island, made from natural materials: stone, wood, or clay, the three-story home was wrapped in deep blue siding brought over from the mainland. Black metal iron trimmed the corners as accents.

Maeven remembered reading over the files from when the home's approval had been granted. It didn't fit with the style of the island and therefore had to have special acceptance at the time. The house wasn't one she imagined Aldrick, a sylvamancer with a proficiency for wood, would enjoy living in, but she could see how Shoney's thermomancer *intent* would prefer this style.

The front door was large and appeared heavy. Tall black windows encased the door, and Maeven saw bare white walls stretching three stories high when Shoney opened it. The house felt cold inside, more dark metal ran along the rafters in the open room. A large, black stone counter spanned the kitchen walls with a center island made similarly. The chairs were iron, made with intricately long strips entwined to form a backrest. Maeven spotted a few of Aldrick's wooden dishes spread out, half filled with a drink or leftover food.

The most intriguing part of the house were the lightbulbs on iron chairs or molded into metal pieces throughout. Hung like art around the ceilings and upper walls. There wasn't a lot of furniture, a single black couch and chairs; it was very clean and very...sparse. Any trinket or item of value was probably tucked behind one of the metal cupboards or hiding in the alabaster trunk that doubled as a coffee table—she wasn't sure if it was used or looked at.

Maeven shivered at the thought of living in a place so devoid of life.

She smiled at Shoney, though, and saw a small yellow trail of the woman's *intent* emerge while settling into her own home.

Odd.

Shoney was a thermomancer, usually with silver or gray *intent* because they used heat to mold the materials they worked with. Yellow was typically a mancer that worked with electricity—which didn't work on-island.

"Why so many lights?" she couldn't help but ask.

"Watch this," Shoney smiled and reached out to a panel with four switches mounted on the wall. She flipped the first and the light illuminated the room, heat pressing down in a suffocating manner, the humidity rising instantly and choking her. Maeven gasped at the oppression, her eyes in a trance as she squinted at the blindingly bright light. Seconds were all she could manage before she shut her eyes.

"Oh goodness, sorry!" Shoney's voice giggled and flipped a second switch.

The pressure left and Maeven was able to reopen her eyes. A softer glow spread out, more like a sunrise than the high noon. Shoney's face was turned upwards towards it, eyes closed, alight with pleasure. She was soaking in the artificial light. Maeven knew her *intent* could mold or melt metals at a high degree so the radiating heat must have felt comforting to the pale woman.

Shoney's eyes reopened and she sparkled toward Maeven. "I'm so glad you came over, come and sit." Maeven followed Shoney to the couch, the sound of the woman's bare feet slapping against the stone floor, echoing throughout the high-ceiling room. Shoney left her on the couch and walked over to her stove, adding logs to the fire and grabbing her tea kettle. She poured water from her well-bucket and set it back on the stovetop to boil.

Shoney then joined Maeven on the other end of the couch. She curled into the corner, tucking her legs underneath her body until she was comfortable and smiled at Maeven as if they were two friends about to share gossip.

"How's your son?" Maeven pressed her bag against her chest and sat at the other end of the couch, wondering what to say.

"Me bairn?" Shoney's accent trilled her *r's* and dropped the *t* on nearly all her words. As much as Maeven studied linguistics in school and could understand the language easily enough, heavy accents like Shoney's were harder for her to understand.

"I heard your son was sick recently..." Maeven knew she was stretching the truth a bit...possibly too much since she doubted Shoney would remember if her son was sick at Yule or what it had to do with the current day. But she wanted to test a theory about Aldrick.

"Ach, *Brighid* above, did they let one of the kids eat too much sugar again?" Shoney took a deep sigh of frustration. "The boys have been staying with my family during the separation, but I suppose I'll have to discuss what they're feeding them over there."

"Separation? I didn't realize," Maeven wondered if Beckwell was aware that Aldrick and Shoney were separated.

"Ach aye, we don't speak about it much since Al's mom would have a heart attack." Shoney's accent became thicker the faster she spoke, comfortable in her own home as opposed to the Dew Drop where she had to enunciate. Maeven smiled and nodded along, catching every third word. "Not that it'd be a horrible thing if the old bat finally died, it would give me an easier time through the whole divorce thing, if you catch my drift."

"That sounds like a lot to handle," Maeven's brain was ticking with possibilities. She might be on the right track in thinking Aldrick began an affair with Tempest, either before his separation and coming divorce from Shoney or after. "How long have you been separated?"

"Ach, eight, nine months or so? We were fighting *all* the time, every other day he was starting another argument over something ridiculous." Shoney stood as the tea began to whistle and prepared a tray with cups and saucers to bring over. "He'd stay late at the Dew Drop and wouldn't come home until early in the morning. Even when we had the same shifts, he'd have an excuse to remain behind. I was tired of having the kids to myself, working on trinkets for the Adventurers, do you know—" she paused as she set the tray down on the coffee table, it *was* used, and served Maeven her cup. "—do you know, those new trailing systems the Council wants us to outfit all the Adventurers with? It's been bollocks to figure out the mechanics and the wiring needed to make them work on-island!"

Maeven was only half-updated on the trailing system Shoney referenced. In the past years, the number of Adventurers lost on the Seven-Isle Hike had steadily increased, even with the help of private tour guides or extra Guards who patrolled the mountains and forests. The Council decided on a trailing system each Adventurer would wear to geo-locate exact position on any of the seven islands in case rescue teams needed to deploy.

Maeven found the latest update on the creation of these devices buried in the stack of files she'd stolen from the office. Unfortunately, she didn't fully comprehend everything she read; what metals or wires or other intricacies involved, but she was dedicating some time to learn.

Shoney continued to talk about her upcoming divorce, her mother-in-law that irritated her, Aldrick staying at the Dew Drop while they separated, the boys at her parents and her job at the Dew Drop. Maeven partially listened while the other part of her brain tried to connect the dots to catch Aldrick in his lie.

Shoney mentioned that Aldrick had been alone at the Dew Drop the night of the Yule bonfire. Perhaps Tempest threatened to tell Shoney about the affair, and he retaliated to try and salvage his remaining marriage...but the separation was proof enough that they would have divorced with or without Tempest involvement.

Unless there was another affair!

Now you're just being ridiculous. She reminded herself and focused on the facts. Unless the *affair* is what caused the marriage to break apart. Which brought Maeven back to the point of why would Aldrick harm Tempest if he and his wife were going to separate?

Unless he *wasn't* going to leave his wife?

Maybe he wanted *both* women!

Maeven, you need to calm down.

"Something on your mind?" Shoney's eyes shone warmly. She gently tapped her foot against Maeven's knee causing a small jolt of static electricity.

Maeven winced rubbed the spot as she responded, "Nothing in particular, I wasn't aware of what you and Aldrick were going through."

"Ach, I'm not the first nor won't be the last lass to divorce a man who doesn't deserve her." Shoney replied and waved off her ex like a bad haircut and not someone she had been married to for over a decade, had children with. "But I don't suppose Aldrick would have told Beck or that the men would tell you; they're so secretive with their personal business and with you reporting back to the Council and what all."

Maeven knew Shoney was repeating facts, but it still made her embarrassed to know that the villagers talked about the reports she flew back to the Council every few days. The deadline was weekly, but she wanted to be prudent about her reports and make sure she was doing everything according to the handbook. It was important she did well at her job. To show the Council, Urian, and everybody that she was capable.

"I only report on the items that need fixing on-island." Maeven murmured low, attempting to make a joke.

"The Council business is none of mine," Shoney raised her hands in defense with a large smile to help lighten the mood.

"I do have a question, actually, as I'm trying to piece together reports I've gotten back from the Council—" she wondered how she might ask Shoney if her husband had been in a relationship with the dishwasher's girlfriend? "Did Tempest ever visit the Dew Drop?"

"Well sure, she was there all the time," Shoney leaned back against the couch though Maeven didn't know how she could feel relaxed against the cold leather. "Always skipping around the kitchen and twirling her hair."

"Did you know her?" Maeven casually continued with a dry cough and a sip of her tea—the temperature in the room had risen a degree or two hotter and the air was becoming thick.

"Not personally, I couldn't stand the way she spoke— she was very childish, very whiny," Shoney nodded toward Maeven like they agreed, "You know how *imps* can be."

"Did you see her the night of the bonfire?"

"What bonfire?" Shoney replied with a shake of her head. "We have a bonfire for practically every celebration here."

That was indeed a good point, "The Yule bonfire,"

"Yule? Well, that was so long ago, I can hardly remember what I fed the kids last week!" Shoney joked but Maeven noted that the kids were with their grand-parents. Shoney had already said she didn't know what they were eating.

"It was the last night Tempest was seen, if you can remember anything at all." Maeven took another sip of her tea, minty, and set her saucer back on the tray.

"I'm pretty sure I left early that night," Shoney nodded and gave a single shoulder shrug. She folded her arms around her knees and leaned toward Maeven on the couch, "Was that what you meant when you asked about my son? One of them got sick, threw up all over the concession stands and was laid up in bed the rest of the night."

Shoney then leaned forward and dropped her voice low while staring intently into Maeven's eyes. "Do you think someone at the Dew Drop harmed Tempie?"

The air grew hotter, the stale air palpable. Maeven shook her head and cleared her throat, then wiped her upper brow where a few beads of sweat bubbled. She knew she let her tongue slip *again* and wanted to curse herself.

"I didn't—I don't think, I just needed—" Maeven took a deep breath and steadied herself. She needed to collect her thoughts before she answered. There might not be any harm in letting Shoney know her theory. "Apologies, I didn't mean to insinuate that anyone harmed her. I merely thought, I have a theory—that is—in which she and Aldrick, with your separation now and the tension between you and Aldrick, I assumed he might have been the person she was seeing, at the time, romantically, of course, at the time of her death because we have information that there might have been an affair—"

"An affair?" Shoney stopped her and blinked her eyes once. Maeven felt her stomach sink and her heart started to gallop. Did she just drop the news that Shoney's soon-to-be-ex-husband *might* have had an affair with a now deceased, teenage imp?

"I don't have that confirmed." Maeven explained with the realization

"Tempest was two-timing with Aldrick?"

"I'm so sorry, I assumed you knew since you're getting a divorce—" Maeven responded, trying to backtrack from her words.

"Do you think *I* would hurt Tempie?" The couch shifted as Shoney sat up, quick as lightning. Maeven hadn't meant to suggest Shoney, she'd meant Aldrick.

"*Would* you harm Tempest?" Maeven asked slowly since they had already breached the subject. She thought the druid was in shock. Shoney sat still and stared over Maeven's shoulder. A blank look on her face until a smile stretched across her lips and she laughed.

A bright, hearty laugh that filled her lungs and came out high pitched and free. Shoney threw her head back and laughed until tears ran down her cheeks, clutching her side. She even snorted a few times and slapped her knee while giggling.

At one point, Maeven thought she had calmed down because she buried her head in her hands and sighed but then her laugh turned into a small cry, and after the cry, back to laughing.

"Should I fetch an acolyte?" Maeven asked and wondered if this was a normal reaction to finding out you had been cheated on.

"Ach, no, don't, those star-gazers," Shoney gasped as her laughter evaded into short, hiccupped, chuckles.

"I fail to see how this could be funny,"

Shoney waved away Maeven's concern, "I'm just—I can't believe I didn't see the signs earlier." She shook her head, the tears turning to actual sadness. Streaming down her face, Shoney sighed and sniffed, wiping her face and turning away.

Maeven froze.

She wasn't good at comforting others. She hardly knew how to deal with her own emotions and usually preferred to be alone—not with a stranger watching awkwardly.

"I should go," Maeven murmured slowly and waited to see if she should stand up and leave or not.

"Forgive me," Shoney leaned forward and grabbed Maeven's hands again which forced her to pause. "I don't mean to slobber on, I just—I wish Marisol had listened to me when I told her he was acting weird."

"You spoke with Marisol?" This was newer information since Marisol hadn't brought up any conversation with Shoney nor did Maeven see a note about it anywhere in the files. Unless there were more files she hadn't seen?

"I went to her concerned, Aldrick had been acting so strange, not just staying out late, but selling items around the house, items he made—"

"His cups?"

"Yes, he's obsessed with his cups!" Shoney sighed and pressed her hands into Maeven's, giving it a squeeze in mutual understanding. The only thing Maeven understood is that the village was in a *lot* more trouble than she thought. Why hadn't Marisol mentioned a conversation with Shoney? "And I told Marisol, something didn't feel right."

"What did she say in return?"

"She told me it was just a phase we were going through. That we had been together for so long it was normal to fall out at times." Shoney covered her face with her hands again.

Maeven tried to keep her face neutral. That didn't sound anything like Marisol.

"You know when you're young—" Shoney began, seeming to talk to herself more than Maeven. "—and you think 'He's it. He's the one I'll spend my life with' you know? And then you find out he's been dishonest—it's just, so hard to believe that he would kill Tempie—" she stopped talking with a gasp at her own words.

The two women locked eyes, both stunned at what Shoney had—and hadn't—said out loud. Maeven watched as the lightbulbs lit, the realization that, yes, her *husband* might be responsible for Tempest's death.

"Shoney," Maeven kept her voice steady and eyes on the druid. "Do you know where Aldrick is staying?"

Shoney shook her head and hiccupped as her crying calmed down. "It's not his fault."

"Do you know where he is living?"

"He has a room at the Dew Drop, rents the attic from Carmichael for cheap, eats from the kitchen." Shoney muttered short sentences, zoning out for several seconds, before she took a deep breath and stood with Maeven. With a nod, she shook out her limbs and disposed of her additional *intent* into the ground. The floor absorbed her magic with yellow sparks that were quickly soaked up.

Maeven was then escorted out of the house without a word. The heavy door slammed shut behind her with a *boom*, leaving her with more questions than answers and wondering again why a thermomancer would have yellow *intent*.

Chapter 22

Imps like to play tricks on Adventurers with improper behavior.
Modern day imps like to perform despicable stunts
across the islands and have been known to pickpocket.
Please inform a FarrowHaven Guard or Villager if you have concerns!

The funeral pyre was built on the beach.

Tempests' family demanded an immediate ceremony once her body was released from the acolytes so her soul could be at rest. The villagers worked tirelessly. By the end of the second week, they'd cut and stripped the twenty-seven hawthorn logs used to build the pyre. The wood was stacked six feet high and six feet deep. The merrow kept watch as the body was laid on top, wrapped in a white linen cloth, spread with rosemary, lavender, sage and mint herbs. A crown of flowers adorned her head, and coins lay over her eyes as payment to the underworld.

The villagers were one week from the first V.I.P. Adventurers stepping on-island. Maeven needed to keep her mind busy and prevent herself from thinking about Beck or Urian or a possible murderer walking around.

The wind was sharp and cold that evening as the villagers gathered to pay their respects. Tempest's family stood at the front, closest to the pyre. Mama Elva clutched the hand of her eldest granddaughter, Sebille, with Ribbon holding onto her other arm; face pinched with silent tears.

Sebille's three daughters stood with them and the rest of their clan spread out behind.

"Can you do something about the wind?" Beck's voice sent a shiver down Maeven's spine as he leaned to whisper in her ear. He pressed a hand against the small of her back, a spot of warmth, as she nodded in return.

Eyes closed, Maeven took a deep breath and focused on the wind whipping around her. Her *intent* crept slowly out and began to intertwine with the flow, feeling it a little bit at a time. The wind jumped and lashed past as she caught a tendril at a time until her *intent* grabbed on completely. Momentarily lost in the rush and thrill of its speed and fierceness, she forgot herself.

Beck pressed his hand firmer against her back, pulling her senses back into her body. With another deep inhale, she coaxed the wind to ease. Around her, the villagers visibly relaxed. Their shoulders sinking and knees bending out the stiffness. She noticed the merrow looked much more comfortable as they crowded the beach on lookout for kelpie.

Beck nodded his thanks and stepped away from her, the warmth of his body leaving with him. Maeven stood with Bennie and her family. Her friend had given her a hard time after missing the agreed upon dinner and Maeven had promised to make it up to her as soon as possible.

"I hope her soul finds what she was longing for," Ty murmured as he appeared beside Maeven, breaking her from her grocery list.

Sebille began the keening rights. Her wail soared amongst the mourners and was caught by the wind. It sailed over the waves and was taken by the sea. More women took up laments. Sebille would recite the poem of the dead to ask for safe passage of Tempest's soul. The ancient rites would be for her reincarnation, if not in this lifetime, then the next.

Maeven glanced around at the mourners in attendance. Ty on her left, his posture relaxed as he listened. Beyond him were a larger group of merrows, some who knew the family and some who only knew Tempest. Bennie and her family were on Maeven's right, and behind them spread the villagers.

Aldrick stood with his wife, along with Olfra and Rand, whose heads were bowed. For a moment, she could have sworn he wiped a tear away—no, not a hallucination; he did wipe tears from his face. But why would he be crying over Tempest if he claimed to hardly know her?

Maeven's eyes continued to scan the beach. Emrys stood with his parents intertwined with other villagers. He was trying to be stoic, hands held in front of him, shoulders squared, but she saw the tears slip down his cheeks and knew he wasn't going to make the entire ceremony.

She watched Beck with his family, and Lux, who was dressed in her best funeral attire complete with a large floppy black hat on her dark, wavy hair. Siofra and Lux held hands beside Beck who leaned gently against his wife. His daughter hung on his arms and the two swayed side to side.

Maeven wondered, for a moment, what it would have looked like if she were in Siofra's shoes. Would she have a herd of kids with Beck? She never really wanted them, never considered children part of her future, although her grandmother protested. The Morrigan line needed to be preserved after all.

Beck wanted them, children. He dreamt up their lives after graduation: moving to the island, a cottage, marriage, kids, the whole process. She let him dream and pretended his stories and imaginations were part of her future. They sounded so spectacular. A life she could never grow bored with, and yet...

Maeven was focused on work. She liked the thrill of files and forms and the smell of a new pen or pad of paper. She liked the challenges which trusted in her knowledge and skills. Every time she solved one problem, she was praised and recognized for her accomplishment. Then promoted with more responsibilities and given another task, another test for her mind to work through. The more she was praised, and she hated to admit that she liked the praise, the more she sought those experiences out, leading her to the Council.

Suddenly, Beck's dreams hadn't sat well in her gut. They were a scenario that never felt *real*, never quite *right*. Perhaps that was what broke them in the end.

As soon as the lamentations were completed, the villagers broke their silence and began home. Maeven caught sight of Lux, whispering fiercely with Hadid.

Odd.

When did Lux, a baker, ever need anything from the mushroom hunter, Hadid? Maeven absolutely would have noted if there was an item on the bakery menu that had mushrooms.

Maeven watched from a distance as Aldrick leaned down toward Shoney; they whispered hurriedly to each other. Shoney held onto the sleeve of Aldrick's shirt, and he pointed a finger at her chest. The two exchanged angry glances before they moved apart, in opposite directions, Shoney and the children leaving the beach as Aldrick joined Beck.

Bastard.

She wasn't about to walk up to Aldrick now that he stood beside Beck and Siofra. Especially not when Lux rejoined them and linked her arm through Siofra like a dragonling ready to bite anyone who harmed her friend. The redeeming part of Lux was the annoying and obviously disgusted facial expression she aimed at Aldrick.

Maeven accepted that as a small consolation.

She turned instead to head toward the Forum, but ran straight into the acolyte, Epona.

"My apologies," Maeven gasped and took a step backward, releasing the burst of surprise *intent* from her hands into the ground. The sand erupted with a small *poof* then settled back down.

"We wanted to extend our gratitude for thinking of inviting us to such an occasion." Epona responded with a bow of her head toward Maeven. The witch was confused then quickly remembered the invitation she had extended to the acolytes to attend the funeral. It was customary of the Council to invite the entire village when there was a death and public pyre. Maeven had just been following procedure.

"Of course," Maeven replied earnestly. "We're happy to see you here,"

"Did the Council find our report satisfactory?" Epona asked, "We thought, perhaps, we might hear from you regarding more questions."

It was then that Maeven remembered the report Epona had given to Beck several days before. She hadn't found it amongst her stack and wondered where it had ended up.

"Actually, I'm having a hard time understanding the terminology, would you refresh my memory about the cause of death?" Maeven tried to sound casual, like she *had* read the file and had an idea about what was decided. Epona hesitated, looking out over the horizon as the pyre burned the wood, its flame growing high against the setting sun.

"Contusion, on the back of her head, likely caused by falling backwards and landing on something hard." Epona spoke slowly, keeping her intense stare on Maeven.

"Right, and the marks around her neck," Maeven indicated her own collarbone with her finger as she asked. The information she was getting from Epona was new, not what she had expected.

"We believe the marks appeared postmortem, perhaps an after effect of whatever made her fall."

"You don't think they were the cause of her death?"

"It's possible however the most likely conclusion is that she fell and hit something hard. Anything that happened after the body was moved can't be said for certain."

"Why do you say the body was moved?" Maeven found that curious. No one could account for when the trunk appeared on the beach. Its possible Tempest was killed in another location and placed in her position.

"There were no traces of a crime happening within proximity of where she was found." Epona explained.

"Dr Naidu is here, visiting with the naiads at the fountain. Perhaps she could lend her *intent* to help recreate scenarios."

"Perhaps, but we have no idea who might have been involved."

Maeven was trying to think of any clue that would point them in the right direction. "Was anything found on her? Any hairs or residue that doesn't fit?"

"She had several burn marks on her skin. We believe they were made when she was entombed."

Too many mancers left burn marks when they used their *intent*. Half the druids used various heat sources to bend and manipulate materials. Even Maeven could receive a heat burn from the wind if she used it fast enough. That didn't narrow their list of suspects very much.

Maeven's mind raced with the new information. Everything appeared to point Aldrick's direction.

The more she learned, the more it became apparent that Aldrick and Tempest had a lover's tryst. The most plausible place would be behind the Dew Drop, when he took the trash out. While her death may have been an accident if she suffocated inside of the tree, his cover up will be what earns him confinement in the labyrinth beneath the Capital.

Chapter 23

26 Maius
3 Forum, FarrowHaven Island

Meadhbh Mathers,

You are receiving this: __**First Warning Notice**__
as a result of the issue(s) listed:
- <u>Poor Work Performance</u>
- <u>Safety Violation</u>
- <u>Property Damage</u>—Forum Ceiling due to uncontrollable aeromatic force.

Please be aware that this is the first step in a progressive discipline process and begins a probationary period of **60 days**

We trust that you will correct this matter by improving job performance and/or refraining from continued behavior.

A **Secondary Overseer** was approved by the Council board-members. Expect arrival by 12 Junius.

Have an Adventurous Season!

District Council of Terradium--
Please keep in mind, you are a representative of the Council and must maintain alignment and consistency of Council Brand Messaging.

The Forum ceiling made good progress in its repairs. The tornado on her first night back had made a clean line down the center which allowed the druids to easily place each piece back into position. It would take another few days to complete since most of the druids were focused on the Welcoming Port. Maeven examined the columns which didn't look horribly cracked as she entered the Forum and headed downstairs.

There, she made her way to her shared office and stacked the files from her bag into the piles spread out across the central table. She began to stamp completed ones and separate them from those that needed more attention. Her second round was to separate the pile of attention-needing files into ones of immediate need versus what could wait for later in the season. As time grew shorter, she needed to accept that the islanders would continue repairs into the season's opening. Perhaps they could offer more discounts, or coupons for food, or a free unicorn ride to appease the Adventurers.

Maeven sat down behind her desk to write an updated report for the Council. Instead, she found a box full of mail from the mainland, addressed to the Overseer. It was stupid of her not to keep up with the mail, especially a box that Beck obviously forgot.

Do not make excuses for him like you always do.

With a groan, she sifted through the letters, finding several with Beck's name scrawled across. At the very bottom of the pile, a red envelope caught her eye, and she dove for it. Red was *not* a good color and indicated bad news.

She slit the envelope open, her eyes scanning the passage once, twice, a third time before she let the paper float back to the desk in shock. Her first warning notice! She was charged with poor work performance, a safety violation and property damage—most likely from the tornado damage to the forum.

Maeven screamed.

A raw, guttural scream. It came from the very pit of her stomach, and she could feel it in her bones. The rage built up in her veins burst. Her *intent* gathered wildly around her, and she continued to release her voice in a howl.

It sent the files on her desk to fly against the walls. That felt good.

She did it again.

She flung her arm out and let the papers slam into the concrete. She was done with this island. She was done with these files. These stupid, stupid files that were trash to begin with because Beckwell didn't care to keep actual notes!

Before she knew it, she was ripping the papers and files apart. Like the strips of iron that made up the chairs in Shoney's house or the rooted floors of Eliza's home, she pulled the papers into pieces.

She tore and pulled and screamed and growled. And she continued to use her *intent*, shredding the files with razor sharp precision of air. The papers fell into a clean circle surrounding her which expanded when she collapsed onto her knees in the center; confetti bursting upwards in a shower.

Energy spent; she melted further onto the floor in a puddle of tears. Maeven wanted her mother, and she was angry. Her mother was never there when needed. Eliza was off-island; gone on another grand adventure without Maeven, and she was here, stuck in FarrowHaven, of all places. The *one* spot she'd always wanted to be as a child, and now that she was here, hated it.

She hated the mess that her mother left, that Marisol left, that Beck was *still* leaving in his wake. A mess she couldn't seem to untangle. Every door she opened just welcomed more chaos and she was tired.

The realization hit her like a minotaur.

She was so, very, tired; exhausted. She'd worked late hours every night, pouring herself over paperwork and possible counter-curses for the drought; a desperate attempt to find a solution to the water problem. She got very little sleep and had eaten her meals quickly and without thought to what she was scarfing down. She certainly hadn't kept herself hydrated since the waterways didn't work and every time, she needed to refill her pitcher she had to traipse back to the Tavern then return to the Forum.

"Mae?" Beck crouched down in front of her, his face pulled her awareness back to the office, where she sat amongst the shredded papers on the floor. His voice snapped something inside of her.

She turned toward him, her hands prepared with a ball of *intent*, whatever strength she had left. Containing her anger was no longer an option. All she wanted was to do her job and do it correctly.

And *he* wouldn't let her.

Beck—Beck lied to her—he *still* lied to her about everything that happened on the island, and she had to continue working with *him.*

He didn't keep accurate files, he made excuses for his friends, he hid the report from the acolytes, he didn't even *think* of taking Tempest's disappearance seriously, not to mention his *wife* and *child* which he clearly did not tell her about all the while *flirting* with Maeven. She was exhausted trying to keep his story straight! She wasn't even sure she could trust anything he said or his motives.

"Maeven?" Beck held his hands up and backed away from her circle of confetti. She stood and followed him, throwing her *intent*.

He ducked and it missed but a chunk of plaster fell from the hallway behind him. It left the imprint of a circle, the size of a tennis ball.

He was the reason she struggled every step.

Another blast and Beck yelled as she followed him deeper into the labyrinth.

Let him run away like he always did. Running back to the island because he was uncomfortable in the city. Running away from their relationship because she didn't want to quit her job. Running away to have children instead of...well, no, that reason she thought was very valid and justifiable and it was not her place to keep him from having children.

But it still hurt!

Another tennis ball.

She didn't care anymore. She was done sitting by the sidelines.

"Mae!"

"Stop calling me that name!" She released the *intent* from her hands, her aim getting better but Beck's reflexes keeping up. She barely had the strength for a few more passes. "I hate that name! Stop calling me Mae, I prefer MAEVEN!"

"Alright, I'll call you MAEVEN," Beck yelled back from behind the door of an empty office. "Will you calm down now!"

Calm down? The warning was sharp, demanding, and it sparked another rage.

More orders? Who was *he* to give *her* orders? What did *he* know of running this island? He was the reason she looked like a failure! He was the reason they were sending *another* Overseer to oversee her while she oversaw the island! It made her brain hurt!

The demeaning tone of his voice was enough for Maeven to release the last of her *intent*. It barely scratched the surface of the door and Beck cracked it open. She sank to the floor, against the opposite wall, her knees scrunched in front where she lay her head atop.

"What are you even doing here?" she whined in question since he was *supposed* to be at the Giants camp.

"I just got back," Beck explained, reminding her that he could be an extra fast runner when he needed to be. "The Giants agreed that we can hand the coins out at a prize for completing the Forum Tour and said they'd consider a name change."

"Why won't they change it!" she moaned into her legs and shook her head, which caused her entire body to move with it. She felt Beck sink to the floor beside her, his arm wrapped around her shoulder then pulled her body against him. Her head rolled onto his shoulder, and she sobbed; deep cries that longed for someone to embrace her.

Instead, there was Beck.

Siofra's Beck.

She pushed away from him and ran her hands up her face to wipe the tears and snot. "Stop, you're married."

"I'm not—" Beck sighed then crossed his legs and turned to face Maeven. "Siofra and I are only married by name."

Maeven snorted and laughed at the insanity of his excuse, "You have a daughter."

"Yes, we do, and I love my daughter." Beck nodded and continued. "I co-parent with Siofra and Lux."

"What?" she shook her head, squinting at him, and her brain stopped working. He co-parented—Siofra and Lux?

Maeven thought back to every time she'd seen Lux in the village. She was always either with Siofra, or Faris, or Siofra *and* Faris. Beck was there, Maeven supposed, but usually in the background, or on the sidelines, and always with his daughter.

She thought back to the town meeting, the first night in the Forum; Siofra and Lux sitting beside each other, arms entwined, faces dipped and whispers spoken.

The shop they ran together: Siofra baked, and Lux worked in front, with Faris always at their heels.

Maeven was oblivious to it all!

"Why?"

"To be fair, I never thought I'd see you again." Beck responded, which she fully agreed was fair and understood, because she never thought she'd ever see him again either—especially if she'd gotten assigned to another island which was always a possibility, but that didn't make her feel any better at the moment.

"Siofra, of all faeries, *Siofra Danu?*"

"Our families made the arrangements soon after I returned to the island. The bloodlines need to continue, you know how it can be—" he waved his hands up in the air and Maeven felt the cool metal of the ring on her own finger. Her grandmother was thrilled over Urian. He came from a grand line of warlock ancestry.

"Did you know?"

"No, we—wait, yes, I *knew* of course. Siofra has been coupled with Lux for decades. We all agreed that it would be, I guess, a marriage of convenience?" Beck did his best to explain. Maeven's eyebrows rose and she looked over at him, stunned but listening. It wasn't the most unusual thing she'd heard; she was just processing it as Beck.

"Once Faris was born, we agreed on co-parenting schedules though she lives full time with both of her mothers."

"Lux was fine with the arrangement?"

"Well, that's something you should ask Lux, but I don't remember the last time two females were able to spontaneously create a child, do you?" he gave her a blank stare and blinked several times to show his annoyance.

Maeven would *not* be asking that to Lux and she didn't appreciate the sardonic tone Beck used toward her. She didn't need to be mocked for processing a situation that was completely new to her.

"Are *you* okay with it?" Maeven asked him instead.

"I wouldn't have agreed to it if I wasn't comfortable with it." He shrugged. "Like I said, I love my daughter and both Siofra and Lux are great moms, so I consider Faris the lucky one."

"Why didn't you tell me this before,"

"It's not something we hide, it's pretty common knowledge, and I guess—I assumed, you read about it in some file or already knew, I have no idea what knowledge the Council gave you." He shrugged, still as nonchalant about serious subjects as he was in his teens and early twenties.

"I just can't believe you didn't tell me," Maeven continued, still wrapping her mind around the next *thing* with Beck.

"Get over it, we dated ten years ago!"

"Dated?" Maeven hissed, her eyes widening at his audacity, "We were engaged, Beckwell. You left me, in the middle of the night, with no explanation and never returned. All *she* got was a lousy, *I'm sorry* and now *Get over it*?"

"You know why I had to leave."

"And why you married Siofra?"

"Did you really expect me to *wait* for you? Like you were suddenly going to choose the island over your precious, pretty, position on the Council?"

"Apparently I shouldn't have expected *anything* from you."

"I have duties to my family, to continue my lineage."

"What was so wrong with me?" Maeven asked that question for many lonely nights before she was matched with Urian through mutual friends.

"Nothing is *wrong* with you, but you didn't want kids, and you made that abundantly clear every time someone announced a pregnancy or Brighid-forbid invited us to a baby shower or child's birthday party, you scoffed and rolled your eyes every time you saw a kid." He responded and she didn't realize he remembered those things.

She had spent a lot of time talking about her ambitions. Talking about her next project, next promotion and how much she *didn't* want children, not yet. That was always the excuse, *not yet.*

"Kids weren't in my plans," Maeven muttered, wanting to kick herself, not for her decision to stay child-free but for realizing she could have been less vocal about it, especially knowing it was something Beck *did* want. But that didn't mean it hurt any less to find out he'd married Siofra and had a child less than a year after leaving her and returning to the island.

"I know; *I* was never part of your plans, Maeven. I was your tag along." Beck ran his hands up the back of his hair and scratched the top of his head with a sigh.

"I'm sorry," Maeven said, knowing she would have acted differently if she had the chance.

"Thank you." He responded with a nod.

"We don't have time for this Beck," Maeven shook her head and forced it to wipe away any emotions or thoughts of what *could have been*. She could unpack those feelings another time when she was back home.

Eliza's home.

"We've got so much work to do before the season starts and someone killed Tempest and you're not going to like it, but you need to look at all the facts and consider Aldrick." She turned to him and pleaded for his trust.

"Okay, show me." Beck stood and gave a pointed look to the confetti mess that had trailed behind them through the labyrinth halls.

"At least it will be easy to find our way back."

Chapter 24

Maeven followed Beck back through the labyrinth hallways to their shared office and tried not to stomp the entire time. She was still furious at him for keeping so much information from her and simply wanted her questions answered to find the best solution for, not only the island but, getting along with Beck while they worked together.

"He couldn't have done it!" Beck claimed as they entered the office. He walked directly to his desk and began to pick up and move files onto the center table which Maeven picked up one at a time and began to sort.

"I'm telling you; it was Aldrick. I know it!" she responded and continued to flip through page after page of Beckwell's handwriting, what few files had survived the massacre.

"You simply want it to be him because you never liked him." Beck dropped another stack of files onto the table and his voice continued to rise. Maeven hated it when he got loud, as if that was going to make his point more correct than hers.

"I'm able to keep my personal feelings separate in this matter. We are talking about a murderer here." Maeven corrected while pointing a single finger at him.

"We're talking about a guy we've both known our entire life. He wouldn't do something like this." Beck shook his head.

"You don't know everything, Beck."

"I know this."

Maeven had to admit it didn't make any sense. Aldrick had been with Rand all afternoon and evening while on shift. Emrys left first; Aldrick and Rand at the same time a short while later, and everyone claimed nothing unusual happened.

"Let's go back over all the facts. Where is the report on Tempest body from Epona?" Maeven asked and wiped confetti off the table to make new stacks.

Beck fished it out and handed it to her, thankful that all the important documents had been protected during her tirade. Maeven glanced through the report but there wasn't anything new to learn. Epona had already told her how Tempest died, and the report didn't find anything unusual.

"What about Aldrick's lies? He had the timeline from that night completely different from Emrys,"

"I spoke with Aldrick about that, he said he must have gotten his nights mixed up and most likely *did* take the trash out." Beck crossed his arms and leaned back against the desk, waiting for her to continue with her next point.

"Most likely?" her eyebrows rose. That was the vaguest answer she's ever heard.

"Be realistic, the end of the season is crowded with Adventurers and every day there are lots of different faces moving through. Everyone wants to be fed, everyone wants to be entertained, not one of them *really* cares about the happiness of the villagers who make their dreams happen day after day. It's completely plausible that Aldrick got his nights mixed up." Beck counted off the reasons on his hand and she had to give that one to him.

"Did you ever receive anything back from the druids who evaluated the cup?"

"When was I supposed to do that?" he muttered in response and leafed through the pile of papers. Maeven closed her eyes and clenched her jaw, how long had he avoided reporting the cup? He had asked her to wait until the report came in from the acolytes and she assumed he would get the cup evaluated at the same time.

"I asked you to do it about a week ago, I assumed it would be ready by now." Maeven responded. She realized the naturamancer's and sylvamancers were busy with repairing the Welcoming Port but surely someone could be spared to look at the cup and compare tree rings.

"You asked me to go to the giants a week ago as well!" he barked and shook his head. For a moment she saw what a future married to Beck would have been like and she wondered if the reason Siofra preferred Lux was because of his unhelpful responses.

"Is it too hard to ask you to do your job?" Maeven crossed her arms over her chest. She'd often had to work with difficult men in the city. When she first arrived, Maeven assumed it would take Beckwell a few days to settle into the idea that they were partners on-island. It was their responsibility, *together*, to make sure the Adventurer season was a success.

But the more she worked with him, the more she wondered if he was increasingly annoyed and irritated by her directions and being difficult in spite of them. She almost believed he was jealous that she did the job *better* than him or maybe he was upset that she, technically, out ranked him.

"Brighid, help me against the wails of you women, that report is here somewhere! I sent it in after you nagged me about it." Beck growled gesturing to his stack. Maeven took a deep breath and held her hand out, waiting. She was *not* going to repeat herself.

Beck rolled his eyes at her, clearly, he thought she would use her *intent* to sort the papers faster. She wasn't going to help him when he was making the investigation difficult. When he located the file, he handed it over and Maeven snatched it from his hand. She was reaching the end of her limit with him and his lies, or omission of truth, whichever you wanted to call it.

The cups were *identical* to the tree trunk.

The cups that *Alderick* made with his druid *intent* were identical to the tree. It was confirmed in bright red paper which meant Beck already knew that Aldrick was guilty.

"Were you going to hide this from me too?" She held up the red report, waiting for him to deny it.

"He wouldn't do it." Beck shook his head against the bright paper and denied it stubbornly.

"He did, Beck." She urged him to look at the facts and see for himself.

"Aldrick doesn't have that kind of power," Beck played the advocate of his friend and argued with Maeven.

"He obviously does," she held up the form, knowing how wild her eyes probably looked as she stared intently at him—disbelief that he could continue to deny what the facts showed.

"I'm telling you; the guy does *not* have the power to do this. Not when he puts so much strength into making the cups."

"How many of these cups does he carve a year?"

"We sent one home with every tourist last year,"

"Every tourist? Beck, we had seventy-thousand tourists that visited last year! How does he have the strength to make one for every single Adventurer if he doesn't have the capabilities?"

"He makes them over Winter."

"So, in four, *five* months he made *thousands* of hand carved wooden cups? Beck, none of the druids can do that. They would be exhausted producing only a *few* every day, which would take much longer. The math isn't mathing! Aldrick is stronger than he looks."

"The magic on the island is waning, there isn't enough for someone to have made a tomb out of wood—"

"When are you going to stop protecting him?"

"Aldrick is my friend!"

"And I'm not?" but once she shouted the words, she realized it was true. "I'm not." She said it again with a forceful nod.

Maeven had been a fool to think they could be friends all this time. To think that they could set aside the feelings they kept buried within themselves and denied each other. They had too much unsettled, unsolved, history to even be cordial during an important conversation about murder.

It wasn't all his fault either. She'd been too stubborn to face him after he left. She'd returned to the island a few times to see her mother and made it known that she had no desire to see or speak to him and would refuse to have any conversation that brought up his name. She stayed as little time as she could get away with, her record being only three hours, and never gave herself the opportunity to even *think* about Beckwell Cromwell.

After ten years of doing that, it became a habit to avoid all those *emotions*.

"He did it," Maeven said with finality and dropped the file on the table. "Whether or not you want to see it, he killed her."

She left to continue doing her damn job.

Chapter 25

The rain fell in soft patters, lightly tapping against the window. Maeven lay in bed, clutching the pillow around her head and staring at the early glow of the rising sun. She decided not to get up that morning and allowed Rickashay to curl up beside her on the comforter. Her hand fell to the dragonlings head, and she stroked the scales, contemplating if she would go into town today or stay home.

The quilted bedspread she lay under was handmade, embroidered by the pixies. Their small hands were able to weave intricate details in the patterns. Maeven could feel the power cascade like a sand leaking through her fingers, tucked neatly into the stitches but crinkling. It was ironic they could knit protection, love, or healing charms in each stitch, but can't add a heating option!

A desk and chair took up the space at the end of the bed and her mother's former armoire was now stuffed with Maeven's clothing.

The wooden, four-poster bed had sheer white curtains that lifted against a breeze entering from the small round window above the headboard. It brought the scent of rain and calmed her racing thoughts. Her mind was exhausted from shuffling paperwork and reading files. The island was weeks, if not months behind schedule, yet still had to open in less than six days.

None of the occupants seemed bothered by this fact and simply shrugged going about their day. They disregarded the fact that the village was nowhere near ready for the foot traffic expected.

Maeven tried to talk to many of them when she'd left the Forum yesterday, tired of listening to Beckwell's enablement of Aldrick's behavior. She still had a few residences and businesses to check off her list, so she made her rounds to get an idea of their needs.

It had taken two long hours of interviewing the fauns at the Three-Horned Newspaper and Novelty Bookstore, the faeries at the Bubble N' Brew Tea Shop and the gnomes at the Wild Buds Flower Shop but she added three problems to her list instead of marking any off.

First, the three stores were located on the opposite side of the town square with walkways that were crumbling from old age. She would need to pull druids from the Welcoming Port to begin work on the street so the Adventurers would not be turned off.

Second, seasonal changes were causing allergies among the rare books at the Three-Horned Shop which resulted in having to air them out in the main lobby. Unfortunately, the curse that was thrown at the fountain also bounced off the bookstore and the books were now flying in midair, flapping their pages and cover like wings. If a patron tried to sit down in a chair to read, the books would swoop and shred themselves on top of the perpetrator.

Thrice, the faeries said their tea had molded from a leak in the roof. Maeven didn't know tea *could* mold but believed them and promised to have the roof looked at as soon as she had a free druid. The faeries had the tea shop steaming with heat to dry fresh herbs faster for new tea bags. Maeven made a note to order more supply from the mainland to tide them over.

Lastly, the gnomes had complications with the privately paid gnomes who worked for the Bloodstone Mansion and accused them of robbing irises from the town flower beds. Maeven assumed the Bloodstone Mansion could afford its own flowers, but she added it to her list.

She'd spent another hour compiling the complaints into reports and by the time she'd realized the time it was so late she hardly got any sleep.

Her pulse quickened and she started to feel sick. Her hand went to her chest where she felt it beating wildly, even though she lay down, and she found herself gripping Rickashay a little too tightly.

The dragonling screeched and puffed a cloud of smoke at her face. It caused her to cough, burning her lungs from the inhalation, and seek out a cup of water. The overwhelming fear of failure left her, though, and she threw off the comforter to bounce toward the edge of the bed. Rickashay roared and flapped underneath the blanket.

Maeven shivered against the cold morning and wrapped her sweater around her torso, crossing her arms as she jogged down the stairs. Rickashay flew over the banister, her gliding form distracting Maeven who tripped on the last step. She caught the banister and wrapped her arms and body around it as she fell, socks sliding forward to catch herself on the floor. Her missing *intent* was probably coming back to bite her. Growling, she straightened and plodded toward the fireplace. It was, indeed, down to its cold, white, ashes.

"Rickashay!" she called toward the dragonling and her fire-spitting puffs. She flew haphazardly toward Maeven and landed on her head, talons digging into her skull and pulling at her frizzing hair.

"Oh, for *Brighid's* sake, get off me!" the dragonling spouted tiny blasts of fire from its mouth as it screeched back at her. She threw several logs into the hearth and pointed toward it with a look at Rickashay. "Light it, please."

Except the dragonling had already taken flight again and hovered near the front door, scratching at its bark to be let out. The house hummed its disappointment at that, and Maeven knew she had better let her outside before the house got upset. She stomped across the room, clutching her sweater to herself and promising to unpack her luggage that day.

"Brighid burn!" Maeven cursed as Beck gave a dramatic high-pitched squeal in surprise. He jumped away from the door as Rickashay erupted in his face. The two swatted and shrieked at each other on the porch before they were able to break apart. Beck dove inside the house and slammed the door with a loud bang. It rattled the walls and caused the floors to creak, a single ripple running through the roots beneath them and a loud, upset, groan emanating from the roof. The house swayed once.

"Apologize to the house, Beck!" Maeven hissed; eyes wide. He shouldn't have slammed the door and might as well listen to her for once.

Beck's knees were bent from holding his balance, but he straightened, hesitantly, and placed his hands on either side of his waist then bowed, "I do apologize for the improper treatment that I bestowed upon you. I shall take great care in the future to remember the momentous structure I tread upon and treat it with the highest degree of reverence."

Maeven blinked, impressed, but waited to see how the house spirit felt about it. It could see through the flattery of men and sometimes didn't care to accept any. The traitor sighed and let out another groan, this time higher in tone and slowly drawn out—before it shed flowers from the ceiling.

Petals of purple, cream and light pink with a particular scent.

Foxglove.

Fitting.

She looked over and met Beck's eyesight. He smiled and tilted his head toward her as he spread his arms wide amongst the falling flowers. "You have to admit, this is pretty enchanting."

"You'll be cleaning this up, Beckwell." She pointed to the raining flowers. "It would be enchanting if you didn't upset the house in the first place—why are you here? I said I could take care of the sheep."

She turned back to the desk in the middle of the living area and started to sweep petals off the top, even as more filled their space from above. The house was still raining petals and Maeven wondered when it would stop.

Beck gave a forced cough. He scratched at his head, a tight strained look on his face but he remained silent.

"Is everything alright?" she asked, wondering why he wasn't spitting it out. Beck had never been shy about speaking around her. Her mind started to make a quick list of the remaining tasks on the island while she waited for him to find his tongue.

They had a week left and could now do a proper cleaning of the hotel rooms and make sure the kitchens of all the businesses were up to speed.

"I took another look at the evidence you showed me, concerning Aldrick." Beck looked anywhere but at Maeven as he rocked on the balls of his feet, a nervous habit. "I'm going to bring him in for questioning this morning, you should be there to observe."

"Of course," Maeven nodded immediately but wiped the smile from her face. She knew this was a difficult task for Beck, she would support him in his decision—and wholeheartedly agreed to be a witness for him. Inside, she was bursting with happiness that he listened to her.

"I'm going to stop and water the sheep, check on the new lambs, and then I'll meet you at the Forum." Beck nodded once, looked up at the ceiling and saluted, then left without another word.

Maeven remained, a rain of petals falling around her. A small tightness in the pit of her stomach. A gut feeling that it still wasn't *quite* right.

Chapter 26

"Beck, I can explain the cups." Aldrick began.

"What happened, Aldrick? I need the full story." Beck gently coaxed. The white tendril of Council protection hummed between their wrists. They'd reconvened at the Forum after finishing their tasks for the morning. Aldrick wanted to give his confession to Beck, and Beck alone, but Maeven watched through the interrogation window, a one-way mirror facing Aldrick, and heard every word.

"It was a fight. She fell back and hit her head on the lamppost. It wasn't supposed to happen, and I panicked. All I could think about was Shoney and the boys, so I hid the body in the wood and moved it to the beach. I wasn't thinking straight." Aldrick quickly confessed without being provoked.

Maeven crossed her arms over her chest and tilted her head to the side.

Huh.

It was the confession she had been waiting to hear and yet it didn't seem to stick properly. Quite the clean-cut story. But she still had the nagging itch at the back of her head that something was unsolved. A puzzle piece was still missing yet she couldn't put a name to it.

"Why?"

"She was moving off-island," Aldrick shrugged like that explained everything.

"Is that why you fought?"

"She was going to move off-island," Aldrick repeated.

"You mentioned that. Did *she* start the fight or did you?" Beck continued and Maeven was rather impressed by his line of questioning. Aldrick's answers were vague and avoided specifics.

"Look, Shoney and I were going through a rough patch, she kicked me out and I was staying at the Dew Drop—it was a moment of weakness, just a one-time thing, but she became obsessed!" Aldrick started to explain in more detail.

"How so?"

"She wanted me to go off-island with her. Wanted me to move but I told her I couldn't, my kids are here, so I don't know---I guess, she just fell!"

"Where did all of this happen?"

"The Dew Drop,"

"Where exactly, inside, outside?"

"Outside the kitchen, the night of Yule."

"When you took the trash out?"

"Yeah, she was there waiting for me."

"Did Emrys know?"

"Emrys? Know what?" Aldrick asked as if the kid hadn't crossed his mind. Maeven found that odd since Emrys had been his dishwasher last year and was in the kitchen with him almost every day. He'd also be very aware that Emrys and

Tempest were dating if it was true what Shoney said about Tempest liking to skip through the kitchen.

Aldrick's story seemed entirely feasible. Maeven's arms were crossed, and she chewed on her nails. Her skin itched and the sickening feeling that this whole situation was wrong. Everything was out of order and incomplete. There was *something* missing and she couldn't put her finger on it!

"Oh, Emrys, the kid, no, he had no idea." Aldrick shook his head, his knees bounced nervously underneath the table, hands clutched on top as the tendril leading to Beck sprang from the vibrations.

"Is there anything else you'd like to get down in your statement?" Beck sighed and pursed his lips together, buckets of patience that swelled with anger.

"I'm really, terribly, sorry this happened." Aldrick stared at the table intently, tears slipping out the corner of his eye which he angrily swiped away. Beck coughed and cleared his throat as he stood.

"Okay, right, stay put."

He released their bond and set a binding between Aldrick and the table.

"He's telling the truth," Beck nodded once he rejoined her in the separate room.

"Something feels off," Maeven muttered, chewing on her thumbnail and staring at Aldrick. The druid had confessed to everything. He was at the same place, same time as Tempest. His *intent* matched the tomb of wood. He gave a realistic explanation as to how it happened and yet...ugh, it irritated her!

"I sent a letter earlier this morning, the Council will be expecting me on the last ferry." Beck explained to Maeven.

She was surprised he had jumped the broom and done so but realized this wasn't the time or place.

"Do you want me to take him?" She thought about her dinner with Bennie that evening and knew her friend would understand, as apologetic as she would be to cancel *again*.

"No, I'll do it." Beck shook his head toward her then took a deep breath. "The role of the Protector is to keep the islanders safe. This is my job."

Chapter 27

"Hey little Maevie," Ribbon greeted throwing herself into the iron chair across from Maeven.

She was sitting in the town square, watching the naiads and fountain, while killing the last few hours before she went to dinner at Bennies. Maeven was still trying to figure out a possible counter-curse while Dr. Naidu and her delegates frantically worked through spell after spell.

There was a stack of used books with spells that weren't useful piling up beside the fountain. The Three-Horned Bookstore was having issues accommodating the works that Dr. Naidu needed, and many of her students were creating their own spells and aiming whatever they wanted at the fountain. It was causing quite a stir with the symbiotes who shouted poetry at them in response.

"Hello Ribbon," Maeven greeted quietly and sat straighter in her chair. She closed the files related to Tempests death and slowly tucked them at the bottom of the stack.

"Tea?" Ribbon asked holding out the extra mug she held in her hands. Ribbon smiled pointedly at Maeven, her eyes twinkling with suspicion.

"No thank you," Maeven responded since she wasn't in the imp mounds and it wasn't rude for her to refuse.

"Suit yourself," Ribbon replied then took a sip from the mug she just offered.

Maeven rolled her eyes but cleared her throat, which could use some tea, before asking, "How can I help you?"

"Hmm, don't you mean: *Is there anything I can do to assure you have an Adventurous season?*" Ribbon mocked. The phrase was another example from the staff manual.

"Is there?" Maeven was beginning to hate speaking with the villagers and their ring-around-the-Maypole conversations.

"What about an update on my sister's death?" Ribbon turned her head. Her dreaded hair and clinking jewelry fell to the side. Her snake shifted along her skin and raised its head from her shoulder.

"I can't talk to you about an open investigation—"

"But you haven't opened an investigation, have you?" Ribbon stopped her before she continued. Maeven closed her mouth because she was afraid Ribbon might be right. "You've written a somewhat vague letter to the Council outlining the scenario, but you haven't *officially* opened a case, correct?"

Had Ribbon been reading Maeven's outgoing mail? How would she have known that Maeven was jotting those notes down to Urian? How did she know what information Maeven had sent to the Council and that the investigation hadn't been made official yet.

"Are you reading official Council mail?" Maeven questioned.

"Is that what's important right now?" Ribbon retorted. "I'll owe you one."

"What would you like to know?" Maeven immediately agreed but shifted in her seat. While she was happy to give *limited* details knowing Ribbon will owe her a favor in the future, the town square wasn't the most private spot to have such a personal conversation.

"Whatever *you* know." Ribbon shrugged.

Maeven, obviously, wasn't going to tell Ribbon everything she knew. She'd be surprised if that didn't start a rebellion from the imps against the druids, and she needed the Welcoming Port to be completed without delay.

"Your sister fell and hit her head." Maeven did her best to keep her words political and keep to the Council rules. Ribbon waited, a tight smile on her face. Maeven wondered which one of them might be more stubborn. "The acolytes believe it was a contusion on the back of her head that killed her."

"Tempest fell and hit her head." Ribbon repeated before rotating her hand toward Maeven as a signal to continue. "Where did she fall?"

"She was at the Dew Drop. We think she went back to wait for Emrys to get off his shift."

"Did Emrys kill my sister?" Ribbon asked more calmly than Maeven would have in her position. Maeven would have been ranting and raving up and down the Forum until the creature responsible for her sister's death was found. If she had a sister, that is.

Ribbon seemed calm and...normal. She acted like this was another Adventurer lost in the woods who was written off as a sacrifice to the island every tax season.

"Your sister had an argument, with a yet to be confirmed suspect." Maeven was treading in shallow naiad springs and needed to be careful with the information she gave the imp.

"Did someone hurt my sister or was this an accident?" Ribbon's question was pointed enough but Maeven chewed on the inside of her cheek before answering.

"The Council can neither confirm nor deny—"

"Stop with the Council crap," Ribbon hissed, her snakes tail rattling against her collar bone its body shifting under her skin.

"We don't know if someone harmed her or if she fell on her own."

"How did she end up in a tree on the beach?"

"She was placed there." Maeven shook her head knowing she already said too much. "We're still confirming with witnesses—"

Maeven stopped talking because Beck and Aldrick emerged from the Forum. Beck had handcuffs wrapped *intently* around Aldrick's wrists as he and a few merrow Guard escorted him to the marina.

"I guess that answers my question." Ribbon hissed and leapt from the table.

Maeven stood abruptly, afraid that Ribbon was going to retaliate against Aldrick, but the imp only stormed off in the opposite direction of the marina.

Chapter 28

*Get an in-depth view of life underwater with a
private submarine ride to the underwater Kingdom of the Merfolk.
You and your group (max 6) will get a 2-hour ride to see coral, fish and
merrow up close and listen to an in-depth history of the civilization*

The sun sank over the western mountains, the pink and orange melting into darker red and purple. Maeven loved to watch the sunsets on-island as the sky changed into a borealis of colors. She gripped the file in her hand and watched Beck walk Aldrick up the gangplank of the ferry. Ty was at the wheel, preparing to take them back to the Welcoming Port.

Maeven eyed the marina, searching for anything that needed upkeep.

"Good Eve!" Benthesikyme greeted by opening the door and waving. "Checking that she's up to code?"

Maeven blushed at her friends teasing since that was exactly what she was doing. The boathouse floated in the marina, a green two-story home made to weather the salty water and hot sun.

Bennie waved her friend onto the ship and Maeven stepped off the pier to join her. She followed up the walkway and embraced her merrow friend in a big hug.

"I'm so glad to see you," Bennie smiled and danced between her feet, causing the two women to laugh and sway together. Maeven could feel Bennie's excitement radiating.

Bennie wrapped her arms through Maeven's and led her down the walkway, the two bumping into the sides as they crossed their legs over the other with each step. They giggled like schoolchildren, though much older, uncoordinated, with wider hips that couldn't quite make the dance work. They laughed and emerged onto the forward deck, hanging lights strung around, a table and chairs set for the dinner Maeven finally attended.

The table was spread with prepared dishes, awaiting her arrival: rice, scallops, shrimp, and steamed mussels, alongside buttered corn, and potatoes.

Maeven's mouth watered.

"Brarios is an amazing cook!" Bennie beamed at her husband who joined them from the kitchen inside, carrying another bowl with a sweet creamy fruit salad.

"Come, sit, sit," Brarios motioned to the table and served an appetizer of calamari for the women to enjoy. "Fifteen minutes, I promise!" he called, and Bennie rolled her eyes. He poured two glasses of wine, and his wife graciously took hers with a kiss. Maeven thanked him with a nod of her head as he returned into the house.

"He always says fifteen more minutes when he really means thirty." Bennie murmured and sipped her drink.

Maeven grinned and helped herself, she hadn't eaten a full meal in a while.

"Tell me, what have you and Beck found out?" Bennie asked, "Who was on the ferry just now?" she indicated her head toward the ferry that had just taken off from the marina.

"Aldrick Barringham,"

"Ach, no!" Bennie gasped and swiped at Maeven's hand. Maeven nodded and quieted as the boys ran outside.

"No, no, no, your father said fifteen more minutes!" they were shooed back inside, and Maeven continued once they left.

"He said he was having an affair with her; apparently they got into a fight because she wanted him to move to island four; during the fight she fell and hit her head." Maeven wasn't sure if she should be spilling the entire cauldron, but they'd already caught Aldrick, there couldn't be any harm done now.

"She fell? Did he push her?" Bennie asked the same question Maeven had been wondering. It seemed implausible that she merely fell backwards and hit her head hard enough to do permanent damage.

"He wasn't clear about that, but his *intent* was a match for the tree. He said he placed her there after the bonfire ended."

"I'm surprised he didn't burn her *in* the bonfire." Brarios commented, stepping outside with the final plate, a salmon baked in lemon and maple syrup, then refilling their glasses. Maeven hadn't even considered that option, gruesome as it was.

"Well, it would have been over by the time she died, right?" Maeven ran the timeline through her head. "He said he locked up around eleven-thirty, after he took the trash out."

"The bonfire went well past two, three in the morning." Brarios explained while helping himself to the appetizers he'd made.

"Ah, he wouldn't have been able to bring the tree over to the beach without being seen. The lifeguards were on patrol, there was practically no chance of that happening until the next day." Bennie continued, picking up where her husband stopped.

"Well, whenever it happened, that's his story." Maeven shrugged and chewed on the end of a celery stick, mulling the facts over again.

"But you're not convinced?" Bennie questioned, watching Maeven's face.

"What will his punishment be?" Brarios leaned forward offering a tray of finger foods.

"Confinement, most likely." Maeven bit into the calamari after she dipped it in the buttery sauce that Brarios provided. It melted against her tongue and tasted divine.

"My worst nightmare," Bennie agreed with a shake of her head.

"I feel terrible for those boys, though." Maeven sighed and thought about Shoney being a single mother with two young children.

"Shoney has her family to help." Bennie thought it over, "But what will the boy, Emrys, do now? Wasn't he going to move off-island with her?"

"I'm not sure, he's a decent geomancer so we should probably find him an apprenticeship." Maeven commented and thought about the opportunities the Council could offer to the young druid.

The children returned at that moment and Brarios declared that dinner was ready.

On time even!

The family sat around the table with Maeven, a little bit of everything offered chosen by all the children. They dug into their food and talked loudly with their parents. The boys were boisterous, energetic, and filled with laughter which Maeven loved being around.

"I saw Calum's da' on the ferry with Uncle Ty!" Aodhan announced through his mouthful of food.

"Who is Calum?" Maeven glanced at Bennie confused.

"Aldrick and Shoney's oldest, he's in the same class as Aodhan." Bennie explained as she, too, turned toward her son.

"Are they going to the portals?" Bran asked, ever curious.

"Yes, they are." Bennie looked up and met Maeven's eyes with a wide glance.

"His dad is going to stay at the Capitol for a while." Brarios said as a way of explanation.

"He'll be spending more time with his ma now,"

"Aw, he doesn't like his ma'," Aodhan continued and frowned.

"Really?" Maeven perked up, "Why doesn't he like his ma'?"

"She doesn't play with him. He plays with his dad. His dad takes him to school and picks him up and makes the best dinner. Callum gets to eat at the Dew Drop every night!"

"Doesn't he eat dinner with his mom?"

"No, she's never home, she has a boyfriend."

Chapter 29

*The Council strives for accuracy & clear communication
with all matters related to FarrowHaven Adventure Park.
In the event you are unsatisfied with your adventure,
Please fill out an Adventurer Advice Card!*

"What did you say?" Maeven dropped her fork and turned to Aodhan as the table quieted and all eyes faced the young merrow.

"I didn't mean—Calum swore me to secrecy." Aodhan responded and shook his head.

"You haven't done anything wrong." Bennie reassured her son and reached forward, placing a comforting hand on his forearm. "But we don't keep secrets, only surprises, yeah?"

"Yeah,"

"Come now, tell us what this is all about?" Bennie continued to gently encourage Aodhan.

"Speak, now." Brarios' voice boomed across the deck of the boat and created a ripple across the water.

"Calum's ma' has been seeing someone else." Aodhan immediately responded.

"Who?" Maeven was shocked.

"He works, sometimes, at the same place as her," Aodhan shrugged and put another piece of fish in his mouth.

Bennie's eyes narrowed; lips pursed.

"Do you know his name?" Maeven leaned forward in her seat as she contemplated what Aodhan said.

"Calum doesn't." Aodhan shook his head as the adults narrowed in on him in a bid to get information. "He heard his ma say, she liked to sit and talk on the porch with him—or the picnic table—and she cried about Tempie."

"What porch?" Bennie coaxed but Maeven already knew.

"The Dew Drop." Brarios spoke up as well and the adults stopped.

"Tempie." Maeven muttered and stood up so suddenly her chair fell backwards. She knew what had been bothering her for so long. It was the nickname, Tempie. She'd only heard it from a few people.

"Apologies," mind racing, she left in a hurry.

She knew who *really* killed Tempest.

Chapter 30

In the event of a medical emergency such as unknown rash,
bite, sting or reaction to any food or drink on-island,
Please contact a member of the FarrowHaven Guard or any
FarrowHaven Villager for immediate help!

The fastest way to the Dew Drop Inn from the Pier was by beach or forest line. If she ran along the sand, her calves would burn and give out by the time she reached her destination. If she ran up into the woods, she would risk a twisted ankle—tree roots—or bruised and broken limbs—and would probably break a bone.

She plundered on through the sand and gave herself a boost of *intent* every few hundred yards. This caused her to jump, three times as high and fall forward in a long arch landing further along the shoreline than before.

It was like long jumping with a jetpack. The movement took her several attempts to ease into: using her *intent* sparingly and directing her steps into longer trajectories. She scared a group of seals that were plopped along the coast, their *arf-arfs* following her as she ambled forward in thin bursts and crookedly placed jumps.

She knew the building was near when she reached the town square. The sun had long set; the colors of the sky turned to darkness as the stars appeared like freckles in their place.

The naiads, still chained around the base, were asleep, but the fountain cried out toward her.

"And three times round the fountain go,

She straight forgets her tears and sighs,

Hearken to my tale of woe!"

"Beg pardon, I can't slow down!" she called back as she continued to bounce past them. She wasn't quite in control of her *intent* at the moment. She didn't want to chance a stop until she reached her destination.

"Now round the well her fate she braves,

All, alas! and well-away!

Save us all from Fairy thrall!"

"Please, be quiet!" the merrow moaned and the other statues added their complaints.

"Miss Maeven?" Faris called as she ducked out from underneath one of the umbrellas. Maeven was surprised to see her there.

"Faris? Go home!" Maeven instructed and the little faerie faun's face fell in shock. Faris gasped and ran off, hopefully toward home.

Maeven collapsed in front of the inn, out of breath but full of adrenaline-fueled *intent*. She shook out her hands and crept quietly along the first-floor porch of the Dew Drop. Shuffling around the back of the inn was easier than she expected since the lights were unlit inside.

With Aldrick's arrest, she supposed Carmichael would have to place someone new in charge of the kitchen. She followed the porch by tracing her hand along the railing, stopping at her second left and peeking first around the corner.

Shoney sat on top of the picnic table, the gas lamp lit above her for the first time Maeven could recall. Shoney's head was buried in her hands, loud sobs muffled beneath her shaking body.

"Shoney?" Maeven whispered into a whisper-wind and guided it slowly and gently toward its destination. It flew past the curly redhead, her hair floating momentarily, and would have sounded like a whisper, except Maeven misjudged her *intent* again and it shouted at the poor woman.

Shoney's head shot up and their eyes met. Maeven smiled shyly and stepped forward into the light, as if she just happened to bump into her—alone—in the dark—

Maeven this was a very stupid choice.

"Hello!" Maeven sang-spoke with a slight cheer and walked forward, pretending she was confident in what she was doing. "May I sit?" she smiled and pointed to the empty picnic bench and waited for Shoney to decide.

"Yeah, yes, sure." Shoney nodded. She used her palm to wipe her face, her pale skin was blotched with splotches of red and pink, her eyes bloodshot under the light. "I must look like a mess."

"You look great," Maeven waved the comment away and tried to keep her voice light as she sat sideways, she didn't want her legs trapped underneath the table—just in case. "What brings you here?"

"It's my favorite place," Shoney's voice was strained. She looked around at the back of the inn. Maeven looked as well and tried to see what the older woman might envision. They were in a small courtyard, enclosed on three sides by the inn's walls. The picnic table sat across from the kitchen door, a metal dumpster in the space between. Beside the back door was the lamppost.

When she turned back, Shoney watched her, eyes wild and anxious. "It was an accident," she whispered.

"I—I know," Maeven stammered and nodded her head softly. Her immediate response was to sympathize with Shoney; to make her think they were on the same side; she could be trusted, confided with. She could prove Aldrick's innocence, even though she'd been trying to prove his guilt the last two weeks. Total confinement for a crime he didn't *fully* commit wasn't fair. After all, he did confess to entombing and moving the body.

"I didn't mean to spark her."

"Spark?" Maeven tried to make her voice sound nonchalant. Shoney was a *thermomancer*, her powers were in heat, not...sparks.

Electricity. It flowed now between Shoney's fingers. Small bursts of blue lightning that danced between her knuckles, white as snow.

"Menopause brings on so many changes to a woman's body." Shoney looked at the electricity flashing between the blue and hot white along the tips of her fingers. She seemed entranced by her own power, her own abilities. "It's not just the hot flashes, you know? She kept saying she was going to leave with him."

She smiled but it was twisted, cruel. The tears were dried up and gone.

"Who?" Maeven nodded to be sure that Shoney offered her confession without being led.

"*Tempie*," Shoney spat her words through her teeth, saliva bubbling between her lips. "Tempie, Tempie, Tempie, the little *brat!*"

"You called her that earlier," Maeven nodded and remembered now, how Shoney was the only other druid who used the nickname, beside Emrys.

"Ach, that's what he called her, I supposed I picked it up as well." She rolled her eyes and continued to rant. "Always flitting about the inn, wearing practically nothing—her shorts were smaller than her shirts, what little they covered; my ma—you know, my ma, would have walloped me if I ever were to go out in public wearing such a thing!"

Shoney's voice changed again, and she leaned into Maeven, grabbed her hands across the table, and held them, girlfriends trading secrets. Maeven did her best to play along with Shoney, she needed to wait, to give herself time for someone to come and rescue her from the situation. *Please* let someone come and rescue her.

Does anyone even know you're here?

Maeven wasn't a hero; she didn't want to be a hero. She wanted to live through the moment, and she desperately wanted someone to come and do the saving part instead.

"She rubbed it in my face. *Brighid,* all the time! Whenever she was at the hotel, she would fly to the kitchen and brag about her future off-island, that stupid scholarship she'd gotten and how she was leaving before the winter freeze and taking him with her."

Shoney barked another laugh; her jaw tensed, hands clenched and unclenched fists in her lap, the sparks from her *intent* lighting and disappearing with the movements. Maeven drew *intent* and sent a breeze sweeping across Shoney's back and neck, hoping to cool her down. The druid's neck moved in an irritated angle; she shook it back and forth while scrunching her shoulders as if the feeling were uncomfortable. Shoney's hands grasped at strands of red hair and pulled them down over her eyes.

"I *loathed* her and her pathetic dreams. Flaunting about her future, like the rest of us weren't even there! Like I'm not chained to this island for the rest of my life and then," Shoney's train of thought jumped so quickly Maeven was having a hard time following it. "Then! She was going to take *him* with her."

Each word was pierced as if Shoney believed she had been personally victimized by Tempest and Aldrick. Then again, Maeven would probably feel similar if her husband planned to leave her for someone half her age.

"Aldrick?" Maeven nodded to confirm he was involved before she reminded herself not to ask leading questions. A Council attorney could argue that Maeven coerced Shoney into her answers and that would not look good for a prosecution.

"What?" Shoney paused, her eyes wild and confused as she shook her head, "Aldrick? No, Emrys."

Maeven blinked and her mind blanked.

Brighid.

Chapter 31

Emrys.

Emrys was the same age as Tempest. He was—*he* was seeing someone else! That lying little—Maeven almost laughed at how quickly he'd fooled her, fooled all of them. Of course, she'd automatically assumed Tempest to be the one who'd cheated, she wasn't here to refute the accusation. Emrys could say whatever he wanted, and it was believed.

Ribbon claimed she witnessed a fight between Emrys and Tempest on the beach. Everyone assumed Tempest ran off with another man. Emrys delayed going to island four because *he* and Shoney were having an affair.

And Shoney lived on-island.

"When—" Maeven wasn't even sure where to begin with her questions and reminded herself that she needed Shoney to think she was a friend.

"We met here," Shoney smiled at the memory and looked around the drab back of the Dew Drop as if seeing a different version. She had a dreamy gaze and was lost in her delusion. Maeven could feel the tension of her precocious position. Shoney appeared to trust her, opening up about her story. Maeven needed to thread a thin needle and be cautious.

"We'd both be here, waiting, always waiting. Aldrick worked late hours," Shoney sighed, and her *intent* lessened. She lay her hands on top of the picnic table and let the small sparkles from her fingernails burn into the wood. "I was always with the kids, night after night. I picked up a few shifts just to get out of the house—thank *Brighid* for grans."

Maeven chuckled but wouldn't really know as she didn't have kids and was wanting them less with this conversation.

Shoney stared off into space. "We would talk for hours at this table."

"What did you talk about?" Maeven asked and listened while wondering how she might send another whisper-wind to a rescuer without Shoney noticing.

"Our lives, our hopes, dreams—" Shoney's smile faltered. Wrapping her arms around her chest she curled in on herself. "I had so many dreams when I first got here, I'm from the seventh island." Shoney was back to the friendly, gossipy girl.

Maeven heard life was harsh on island seven. Its landscape boggy; producing little warmth in the sparse swampland. They used peat for fires instead of wood and struggled to grow produce.

"Working for the tours was going to fulfill that for me and the kids, I suppose—" Shoney paused again, and her eyes narrowed, the rage returning. "But that little *imp* kept coming to the Inn. She was always there, always popping—" she stammered over the–*p* as she clenched her jaw. "—up like a bubble of rainbows. Always joyful and smiling and just—so happy, it *killed* me!

Shoney bit her lip, her hands fisted on the table, then relaxed them open, spreading them out. Maeven needed to wrap this up. Shoney was going to lose control if she used her powers. Maeven doubted she would be a good conduit for the extra energy. White and blue flickered between the druids' fingers, sparking without realization.

Maeven wondered how she might use her own *intent* to deflect the flow. She didn't think hanging Shoney in midair with an aeromancer fist would work. Shoney's *intent* was electricity that could spark Maeven without being restrained.

"I didn't even want to hurt her, just talk to her—that's all!" Shoney explained. Maeven nodded along in agreement, whatever she said, her mind raced with various possibilities to de-escalate the situation.

Where were Bennie or Ty with their ability to compel when she needed them?

"Because it was an accident?" Maeven urged since Shoney had already confessed that.

"Yes! You understand." Shoney smiled enthusiastically.

"I do, what I don't know, though, is what happened?" Maeven shrugged and almost rolled her eyes, trying to sound super nonchalant about listening to someone's demise. "Was Aldrick there?"

"Not until after," Shoney stared at a spot by the lamppost. The same spot Maeven had looked at earlier. "I didn't mean to lose control; the shock was an accident." Shoney pointed to the lamppost and wall behind it while describing the scene.

"I needed to work that night, it was the busiest night of the season, and the coin was always good. Emrys was working too; I wanted to see him. Rabbie got sick. I had to go pick the boys up and drop them with gran. When I got back, *she* was here, in our spot, waiting for him too."

"She told me they were leaving. Tempie said she knew about us; told me I was trying to relive my youth with a younger guy." Shoney rolled her eyes at that comment which she turned into a snarl and huffed. "She called me pathetic, the little *witch*."

Maeven chose not to take offense.

"I'd been having hot flashes—lately, and I was *so* angry, I released a few jolts—just a few! I didn't even think it would hurt her; I've always been so weak, you know? My *intent* never really used or stretched except to make the same objects for the Adventurers." Shoney fluttered her hands wildly and Maeven found it hard to follow the sparks

"I just wanted to let off some steam, to scare her a bit—get her to leave without Emrys. She didn't deserve to take him with her! She was already getting off-island, she didn't need him! I needed him here, with me. He was the only good thing I had in my life!"

"But she fell?" Maeven looked toward the lamppost and perked up at the sound of muted whispers from around the porch. Finally, someone was coming her way!

"She just lay there, and I told her to stop playing, to get up from the ground but she didn't move—and then Aldrick was here, with the trash, and he told me everything was going to be okay."

Shoney looked at Maeven, her smile large, as she waved her fingers again to show her *intent*, sparking into a small ball. Light passed between each knob on her hand.

"And he was right," Shoney giggled and shook her head in joy or disbelief. "He was right, everything worked out for me. Tempest is gone. Aldrick is gone. And I have Emrys, all to myself."

"Shoney," Maeven said slowly and softly. She approached her sentences the same way she did when Beckwell was spooked, so she wouldn't frighten her more. "Tempest isn't *gone*, she's dead. And Aldrick—"

Shoney's face fell and she shook her head forcefully. Covering her ears with her hands she repeated 'no' under her breath and rocked against the table.

"Aldrick is going to the Council Forum to be confined for eternity in the labyrinth." The labyrinth of cells, a hundred times more complex than the one on-island, running beneath the Capital city, made her shudder.

"Stop! Stop, stop, stop!" Shoney screamed and pulled out more mats of burgundy hair. She held her fisted hands and stamped her feet. Her fingers released shocks of *intent* into the wood grain and disintegrated the pulled strands.

Maeven jumped off the bench and released a flow of *intent* just in case any lightning jumped out at her. She was aware of how small the area around them seemed as she prepared a weak defense. What could air do against electricity? She could try to reroute the surge but what if it went straight through her *intent*? When has lightning ever bowed to the wind?

Where on the island was her rescue brigade?

"Aldrick was an unreliable husband and deserves every year he gets from the Council!" Shoney shrieked and stood as well, her palms facing forward, toward Maeven. The light that sparked off her nails ran down to the ground.

Scars covered Shoney's forearms. Her skin looked raw, like third degree burns. A white light blinded both women and a fresh scar sizzled into Shoney's skin, the smoke rising as she cried out. Her missing *intent* was burning her back.

Maeven wound a long rectangle of air around her arm like a hose. She hoped it would work as a shield. Layering intent wasn't something she'd tried before, but it could work if she kept her focus on making the forces solid. Shoney's crazed eyes stayed on her.

"Shoney, Emrys wasn't going to leave you." Maeven learned customer confrontation when she went through her former training and kept her composure calm. It was her duty to politely, but firmly, advise Shoney that she was violating the safety rules.

When someone was as unstable as she presented, it didn't benefit anyone to match their energy with a negative one of her own. "I hear in your voice that you were worried and anxious when you thought that."

"Do *not* lie to me!" Shoney screamed.

"I'm not lying, Emrys was going to break up with her. He wasn't going to leave." Maeven responded and saw movement out the corner of her eye.

Shoney's *intent* eased as she looked at Maeven, stunned. "He wasn't going to leave me? But Tempie was moving off-island, she said they were leaving."

Maeven shook her head and continued to keep Shoney's eyes locked so she could work with the *intent* needed to suppress her. "Tempest lied to you. They broke up, Emrys wanted to stay."

Shoney gasped and clutched her chest. Her *intent* building in her hands again. Before Maeven could react, a figure flipped past. Ribbon landed beside Maeven and threw her arm out, her familiar leaving her body, its fangs raised in a hiss that sank into Shoney's cheek. Shoney screamed and grabbed at the snake on her face as she fell backwards and hit the wall.

"Oh, my Brighid." Maeven cursed and held a hand to her mouth in shock. She sincerely underestimated Ribbon's abilities.

"Maeven!" Faris yelled and ran toward her, wrapping her small arms around Maeven's waist and burying her head. Shoney, crying, collapsed on the ground, after Ribbon subdued the druid with a solid forward kick to the chest.

"What are you doing here?" Maeven shrieked and pulled Faris with her back to the front of the Inn. She did not need the little girl to watch whatever might happen next. She did need to make sure Shoney was confined though.

"I found help for you!" Faris called as she flew beside Maeven.

"That was very brave of you, but you should have gone home. Your mothers are going to kill me." Maeven responded trying to keep her composure while panicking that Faris had seen Ribbon's attack.

"My mothers know I'm playing in the fountain." Faris shrugged slumped down in the front porch rocking chair.

"Stay here," Maeven instructed. She was worried Ribbon might be the next person the Council had to arrest if left alone with Shoney too long. Hopefully she wasn't already too late.

Maeven had seen the anger simmering underneath Ribbon's skin each time she spoke to her. Even amongst her crazy shenanigans with the tea, Maeven highly doubted Ribbon wouldn't pass this opportunity to take out her revenge.

Returning, however, she found Shoney knocked out. Ribbon at on her back, legs crossed, hands held in the air in a meditative position.

"Oh, thank *Brighid!*" Maeven gasped trying to catch her breath.

"Wanna call in that favor?" Ribbon asked in response, an eyebrow raised in question.

Epilogue

<u>To Complete:</u>

Objective: ~~Repave & resettle stone structures, including parkway road~~,
Assignment: Geomancer, CP: 97%

Objective: ~~Resettle & sand wood structures, stairway,~~ balcony railing,
Assignment: Sylvamancer, CP: 90%

Objective: ~~Replant flowers~~, vines need to trail along outside of castle,
maybe add trellis – see sylvamancers. ~~Bring trees back to life!~~
Assignment: Naturamancer, CP: 56%

Objective: ~~more iron benches & trash cans, polish lampposts~~, fix stained
glass window
Assignment: Metalmancer, CP: 77%

Objective: ~~Weave new flags/tapestries for hanging in castle foyer~~, new
banners for advertising
Assignment: Pixie, CP 37% –more silk ordered for banners, additional
wisteria flowers ordered from Eastern islands

Objective: ~~Repaint signs for ticket sales~~, double check accounting books!
Assignment: Faun, CP: 75% –speak to Grandover at the Three-Horned
Bookstore.

Objective: Set up "fishing village" scenery at Welcoming Port, ~~sanitize all
cooking items for food preparation & create mock tasting menu~~
Assignment: Merrow, CP: 88% –fishing village still being reconstructed
now that wood has been resettled along docks

"Ribbon reached me before Shoney could strike." Maeven explained to Bennie. They sat on the porch of her houseboat, an untouched deck of cards on the table with an almost empty pitcher of spring wine. Bennie poured the last of the drink evenly between their glasses and they clinked.

The ferry was due back any moment from the mainland. Maeven was impatient to hear what happened with the Council. Bennie said she had a solution to make the time pass quickly. The wine certainly made the time faster, and Maeven was happy, relaxed, and didn't give two hoots about what happened to Shoney or Aldrick or possibly even her job.

That was a lie. She cared deeply about her job.

"How did she know you were at the Dew Drop?" Bennie asked while Maeven sipped her wine.

"Faris, the little sneak!" Maeven gasped in shock at the brave, young girl. "When I bounced past her at the fountain, I told her to go home but she grabbed the first person she found, which happened to be Ribbon."

"Did she really karate chop, Shoney?" Bennie raised her eyebrows in question.

"Who said that?" Maeven giggled.

"That's what Beck told Brarios," Bennie shrugged.

"No, she didn't karate chop him, it was more like a door-busting front kick thing," Maeven unsuccessfully demonstrated from her seat. "I thought she was going to eeek her," she moved her finger across her neck, tongue out at an odd angle.

"I wouldn't put it past Ribbon to avenge her sisters' death." Bennie agreed and took another sip of wine.

"Is she usually so—"

"Insane?"

"Erratic?" Maeven countered trying to pin down Ribbon's reactions which swung between being happy, as if nothing had ever happened, or angry about the outcome.

"I don't think I've known an imp that wasn't a bit like that. Except Mama," Bennie confirmed with a nod.

Maeven thought the same thing and remembered that gorgeous office full of trinkets and books.

"Do you know that Mama has the Spear of Lugh?" Maeven asked, turning to Bennie as if present day gossip.

"It's wonderful the water is back!" Bennie changed the subject and congratulated Maeven.

"Isn't it amazing!" Maeven agreed and sipped more of her wine; her glass never seemed to stay full. "Dr. Naidu is billing the Council for her time. She said the clue was in the fountain, apparently it was spitting some really, *really*, old poetry or something."

"Old poetry?" Bennie giggled, sipping her glass straw and shielding her eyes against the sun. She looked out over the water where her boys splashed and played in the bay. The crystal green of the water reflected the sun-bleached coral underneath.

Was coral supposed to be sun-bleached? Maeven wasn't sure.

"Yes, like Samuel something or another, anyway—the point being, the counter-curse was in the poem. She looked it up in our own village bookstore and reversed it within the hour!"

"Amazing," Bennie agreed and nodded her head. The two made eye contact before they burst into laughter. Something about the entire situation brought tears to Maeven's eyes. The last forty-eight hours had been a whirlwind. Once the water was restored, Maeven had rallied every able-bodied villager to get the island glistening and glowing, sparkling and shining, razzling and dazzling. They helped with minimal complaints. Many of them were thankful for how diligent Maeven had been the past several weeks in completing long-forgotten tasks. Others still complained about lack of preparation time, but still, no corner was left unpainted, unrepaired, or uncleaned under her overview!

The park opened in five days for V.I.P. Adventurers. They had another week after that, before the large crowds started to arrive which was plenty of time to get more areas looking spick and span. The enthusiasm was flowing through the air, and the villagers were getting *excited* for once.

The ferry appeared at that moment. Sailing in from around the forest-line bend. Bennie stood and stretched from her position and Maeven followed, sipping the last of her wine.

The women walked down to the pier, watching as the gangplank was lowered and the few passengers, druids who were working on the Welcoming Port, disembarked. Beckwell followed behind them, his hair a mess from the wind, getting caught in his ears and antlers. Maeven thought he looked rather cute, boyish, as he ambled toward where she and Bennie waited.

"I told you Aldrick was innocent," Beck passed by her grazing her hand, so she turned around to face him. His scent of pine wafted over her senses. Maeven huffed and shook her head.

"He's only partially innocent, he still helped cover it up and hide the body." Maeven responded while crossing her arms over her chest. "What did the Council decide?"

"Two years for Aldrick," Beck nodded as they knew he would be getting a lesser punishment. "Shoney was given twelve."

"Seems reasonable."

"It is," Beck paused, mouth open to say more but remaining silent.

"What is it?" she asked, unable to read if he was happy or uneasy about something.

"Maeven—" his voice cracked, strained. Her eyes widened in laughter and she met Beckwell's green, serious, his lips set in a thin line. Her stomach somersaulted and her hand tightened around her clipboard.

Heavens, Maeven what are you doing? Focus!

Before Beck could say more, another sound broke through the silence.

"Meadhbh!" The familiar voice made her smile drop.

What was *he* doing here?

It was the worst possible time imaginable!

Maeven turned to see him wave at her from the gangplank. He rolled a suitcase in his left hand, holding a garment bag in the other as he jogged toward her. Placing the items on the ground, he swept her into a hug then smashed his lips against her own in a crooked kiss.

Her feet hit the ground with a gasp, and she pushed away from his arms.

"Urian?"

We Hope You'll Join Us for the Summer Season!

Pronunciation Guide

These are purely how I pronounce them in my head.

Aldrick (All-drick): Sylvamancer-Druid
Arron (Ar-ron): Giant

Beckwell (Beck-well): Stag
Benthesikyme (Ben-the-si-kie-me): Merrow
Brarios (Brr-air-os): Merrow

Carwyn (Car-wynne): Minotaur
Chester (Ch-es-ter): Animacer-Druid

Deidra (Deer-drah): Druid

Eanna (Ay-anna): Animacer-Druid
Emrys (Em-riss): Geomancer-Druid
Epona (Ee-poe-nah): Centaur

Jay (J-ay): Naiad

Leif (Leef): Druid
Lux (Lucks): Faerie

Hadid (Ha-deed): Gnome

Kitty Vex (Kit-tee Veh-cks): Pixie

Marisol (Mare-ee-sol): Naiad

Meadhbh (Mee-ve) / Maeven (May-ven): Aeromancer-Witch

Naidu (Nie-doo): Merrow

Nore (Nor): Minotaur

Pacey (Pay-cee): Naiad

Olfra (Ol-fra): Imp

Rand (Rand): Satyr

Ribbon (Rib-bon): Imp

Ryes (Rie-z): Naiad

Shoney (Shaw-nee): Metalmancer-Druid

Siofra (Shee-frə): Faerie

Tempest (Tem-pest): Imp

Tierna (Tear-na): Gnome

Typhoboeu (Tie-foe-be-ah): Merrow

Urian (Ur-i-an): Warlock

Glossary

Loosely based on Celtic Mythology, slightly based on modern day, but mostly based on my imagination.

Centaur: Upper torso of a human, lower body of a horse. Descendants of the Goddess Epona. Centaurs live in the mountainous region of the Avontane Mountains and run the Grannus Wellness Center & Healing Springs. They are prolific astronomers and healers.

Dragonling: Dragonlings are typically twice the size of a housecat. They're oversized lizards with batwings. Some Dragonlings may produce fire but usually only smoke. Dragonlings are hunted for the central horn that grows out of their forehead and sold on the black market.

Druid: Large villager of four to eight feet in height. Descendents of the Dullahan. Druids have human bodies with no special additions. Druids have various *intent —magical—* abilities that generally fall into the following categories:

> *mancer: mancie, mantia - divination by*
>
> Aeromancer: *aero* air
>
> Naturamancer: *natura* nature
>
> Electromancer: *electro* electric
>
> Geomancer: *geo* earth/stone
>
> Metalmancer: *metal* metals/iron
>
> Sylvamancer: *sylva* wood—dead wood/planks
>
> Thermomancer: *therm* temperature/heat
>
> Traighmancer: *traigh* sand

Dwarf: Medium villager of three to five feet with short fingers adept at digging. They work the Tanmear Caverns, digging, tunneling and giving tours on the Northern side of the Avontane Mountains. The caverns are only reachable via the train.

Faerie: Large villager of five to seven feet in height. Descendents of Danu. Faeries have six to ten iridescent wings, depending on body size. Many can have *intent* though some have specialties such as seduction, empathy, telekinesis, and compelling charms.

Faun: Medium villager of two to five feet in height. Body of a man, legs and horns of a goat. Naturally adept at reading, writing, poetry, music and dancing. The fauns run the Three-Horned News & Novelty Bookstore in town. They commonly work as teachers, judges and lawyers around town because of their good judgment, honest integrity, and peaceful nature.

Giant: Extra-Large villager of ten to fifteen feet in height, they're often slow of mind though warm of heart. The giants are promoting their species by hiding G.I.N. coins around the island. Children may exchange coins for prizes at the fairgrounds.

Gnome: Small villager of one to three feet in height. They're naturally adept with nature *intent*. Two groups work on-island, a privately funded group work the grounds at the Bloodstone Mansion, and a second, park funded, group serve as gardeners around the village.

Griffin: A creature with the torso of an eagle and the lower body of a lion, complete with the tail of a scorpion. Griffins are majestic creatures of land and air. Trained at the Worlds Famous Academy Menagerie & Training Center, FarrowHaven Griffins boast extraordinary sire lineage and rave reviews in our jousting show!

Imp: Medium villager of five to seven feet in height. Descendents of the Tuatha de Danaan and the native people of the island. Imps are naturally curious, sneaky, and manipulative in nature. They do not have *intent* but have animal familiars that accompany them through life and possess the skills related to said familiar.

Kelpie: Water horses of the ocean that hunt on land during the evenings, devouring flesh to satisfy their appetite.

Madrai: A giant hound with the ability to walk through walls. Requires very little sleep and sustenance. An endangered creature with less than 100 left in the wild. They are often bred and sold on the black market to collectors.

Merrow: Large villager of four to seven feet in height. Descendents of the Sea God, cousin of the mermaid. Human bodies with legs that transfigure into a singular-long fish tail. They breathe and swim underwater. Merrow possesses compelling charms in their saliva. Many also have animancer *intent* to speak with sea creatures. Most are Lifeguards at Kelpie Beach or part of the Guard spread through the Island shoreline.

Minotaur: Large villager of eight to ten feet in height. Technically Greek/Roman mythology but, again, it's a fantasy book. Minotaur possess the torso and lower body of a man and the head & shoulders of a bull.

Naiad: Large villager of six to eight feet in height. Naiads are spiritually connected to the waters, specifically lakes and rivers of the island.

Pixie: Extra-small villager of four to six inches in height, pixies have 2-4 wings and delicate hands that can weave the flower blooms of wisteria into silk.

Satyr: Medium villager of three to six feet in height. Similar to fauns but with a kangaroo tail and goat horns which circle backwards on the head. Horns need to be routinely cleaned and trimmed for proper hygiene.

Stag: Large villager of six to eight feet in height. Human body with antlers. Abilities include strength, stealth, speed, and skittishness. Cromwell lineage, King of Creatures. Title must be passed down to male heir remaining permanently on FarrowHaven Island.

Unicorn: A horse with one spiraling horn in the center of its forehead. Unicorns serve multiple roles on-island including pulling the carriages, trail rides, and petting zoos.

Witch: Large villager of five to seven feet in height. Descendent of The Morrigan. Witches are rare and only within the Morrigan family, one female in every generation. Magical abilities differ.

Wyvern: Wyverns are the deformed offspring of dragons, usually born without arms. They can grow to be eighteen feet in length and are extremely vicious in the wild. Rarely spotted in the village.

Acknowledgements

My biggest heartfelt thanks and gratitude to my son who has been
with me through every phase of dreaming, noting, outlining,
writing, editing, reading, and publishing this book.
I hope you always remember that you're brave, kind, and smart!
You will achieve amazing dreams of your own one day!

To my sister, Madeline, who has been endlessly supportive the last
thirty-something years. Everytime I got excited to share my writing
you would get excited for me. You listened unconditionally and
encouraged me every step of the way.
I'm so thankful to have a sister like you!

To my other brothers and sisters: Thank you for being in every
wedding, church, or pokemon play that I scripted and forced you to
perform as kids! And thank you for not stealing my floppy discs and
reading the little stories I created as a tween. They were so
embarassing and I would *not* have lived the teasing down.

Arianna, the peaches to my mango, thank you for always, always,
always believing in me! From late nights as teens swapping books—
to our twenties when I would text: *"I have a new novel idea"* then
proceed to give away the twist and you'd respond: *"I'd read that"*
without fail, you have been an amazing cheerleader! I'm so glad you
read my little book and loved it—even though its fantasy, which
isn't your jam, and even though it doesn't have a lot of smut...yet...

To author Kate Minty and my friends in the Ink Meets Paper, IMP
Club: I would never have done this without your guidance and
support! I would have written an outline, maybe a couple of scenes,

and then tossed it on the backburner with the rest of my ideas.
Thank you for being a group of writing obsessed women who just
get it when it comes to talking about imaginary characters.
For encouraging me to finish my book, giving me grace and
allowing the down weeks to happen, always being great ears to
listen when I'm complaining about self-publishing, and lastly for
always reminding me that you won't let me publish a bad book!
I'm eternally grateful for everyone and thrilled for the future!
Rising tides lift all ships!

To my teachers and professors throughout the years. Thank you for
always being the voice of encouragement that I needed to continue
writing, especially thankful to Lisa Malone, Dr. Britton Gildersleeve,
and Dr. Mercer.

Continuous thanks to the female authors I grew up with who wrote
badass female heroines I could look up to and for inspiring me to
keep at it everyday: Diana Wynne Jones, Tamora Pierce.

Lastly I would like to thank myself, because I did the damn thing!
This book may not be a New York Times Bestseller, might be the
worst writing you've ever read, might be an obsession of mine that
makes me act single; but it was completed in spite of a lot of
naysayers. So thank you to myself, my Irish stubbornness, ADHD
enthusiasm, and Capricorn energy, and mantra: *'Whats the worst
that could happen? You write a book and no one reads it?'*

Well, at least you wrote a book.

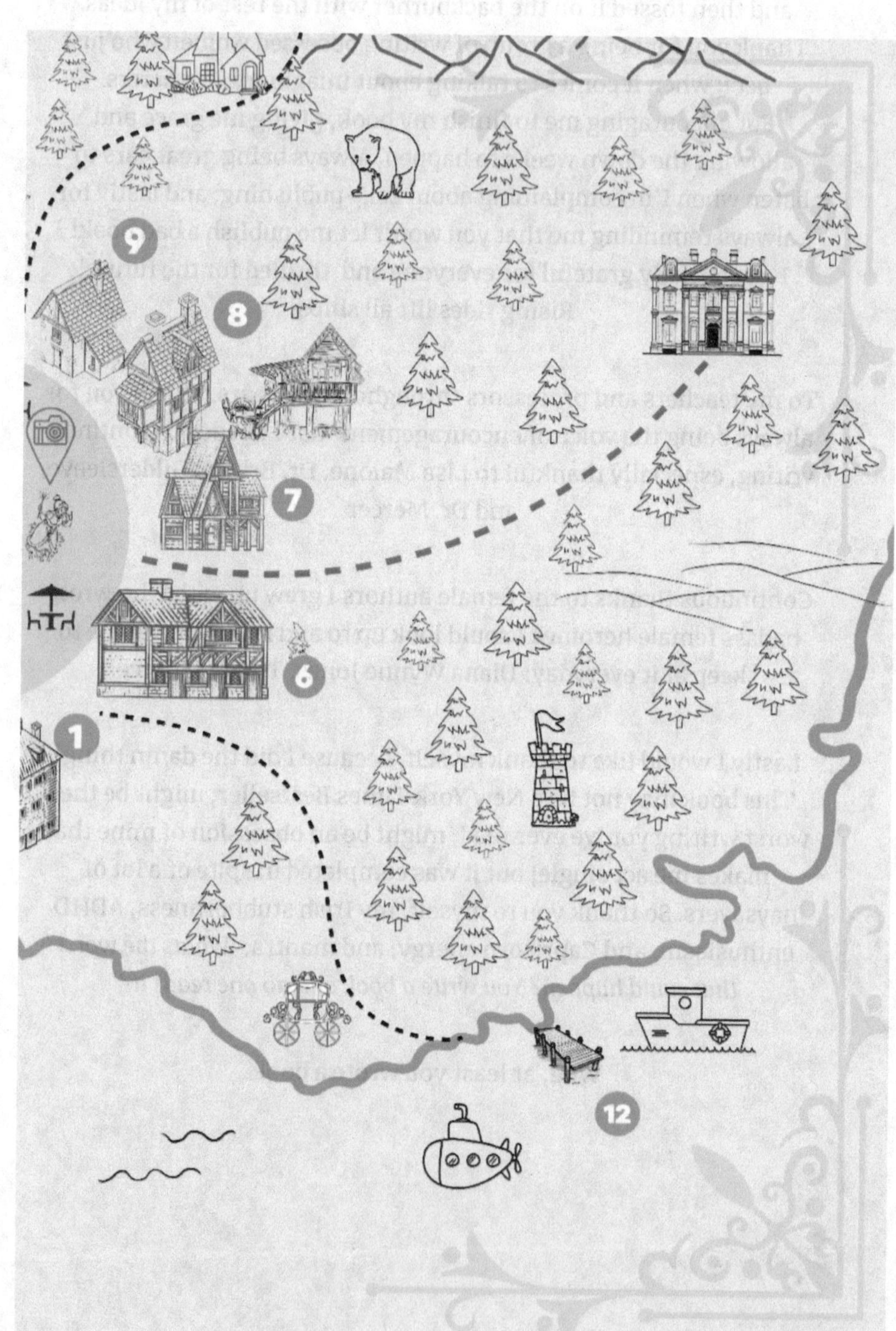

9
8
7
6
1
12

About the Author

Gigi Shoe earned a BS in English Education then achieved her MA in English Literature while 38-weeks pregnant. Since 2011 she's taught middle school English and loves being the Mrs. Frizzle of Writing.

She lives in the Midwest with a rowdy cast of family, friends, and four-legged creatures who can find her reading in the garden and daydreaming of other worlds.